I0667137

A Promise of Tomorrow

Rowan McAllister

Dreamspinner Press

Published by
Dreamspinner Press
4760 Preston Road
Suite 244-149
Frisco, TX 75034
http://www.dreamspinnerpress.com/

This is a work of fiction. Names, characters, places and incidents either are the product of the author's imagination or are used fictitiously, and any resemblance to actual persons, living or dead, business establishments, events or locales is entirely coincidental.

A Promise of Tomorrow
Copyright © 2010 by Rowan McAllister

Cover Art by Paul Richmond http://www.paulrichmondstudio.com

All rights reserved. No part of this book may be reproduced or transmitted in any form or by any means, electronic or mechanical, including photocopying, recording, or by any information storage and retrieval system without the written permission of the Publisher, except where permitted by law. To request permission and all other inquiries, contact Dreamspinner Press, 4760 Preston Road, Suite 244-149, Frisco, TX 75034
http://www.dreamspinnerpress.com/

ISBN: 978-1-61581-596-8

Printed in the United States of America
First Edition
September, 2010

eBook edition available
eBook ISBN: 978-1-61581-597-5

To the love of my life,
without whose encouragement, support, and indulgence
this would not have been possible.

One

London, July 15, 1818

THE sky was leaden and the air heavy and humid as his coach pulled into Eaton Square. It had been threatening to rain all day, but the blessed relief from the summer heat hadn't come. The moment his carriage had reached the crowded streets of London, their pace had slowed to a crawl, robbing him of even the slight breeze flowing in through the windows and leaving him sweltering inside the compartment.

James, Lord James Alfred Warren, Viscount Sudbury, released a heavy sigh and adjusted his cravat as another bead of sweat slid down his neck, though whether the sigh was one of relief that his journey was almost at an end or in dread of what lay before him, he couldn't have said.

And so it begins, he thought morosely as his carriage rumbled to a stop in front of his sister and brother-in-law's brick townhouse.

Today was the start of his annual sojourn in London; four interminable weeks of suffering through the same old round of balls and assemblies, calls and return calls with people he had little to no liking for and even less interest in, weeks of fending off widows and simpering debutantes on the hunt for husbands and weeks of being on his best behavior, lest he slip up with his country manners and embarrass his sister and her family.

Truth be told, he hated London, during the season or no. The press of humanity, the noise, and the smells all combined to foul his usual good humor within moments of entering its streets, and today was no exception.

As a man full-grown, at almost five-and-thirty, London held little of the allure it had for him in his youth. Oh, the plays and lectures could always keep him entertained for an evening or two, and he rather enjoyed a bit of boxing or cards at the clubs, of course. But he couldn't quite say that he wouldn't find just as much pleasure from a ride through his own park or a day of shooting in his reserve, and *there* at least he could rest and relax in his library and find a moment's peace when he wanted one.

He was a man of simple country pleasures and not in the least ashamed to admit it. He was neither fashionable nor elegant. In fact, his sister would often tease him that he had more in common with his farmers than his peers, and she was usually disappointed that he didn't take it as the reproof it was. His farmers were good, hard-working men more worthy of respect, in his opinion, than many of the dandies and fops he was forced to associate with in town.

Yet here I am again trundling down the cobbled streets to waste another few weeks of my life in idle chatter and silly parties.

Using his handkerchief, he wiped his brow and neck before donning his hat and gloves in preparation for stepping out into the street. He took a moment to brush any dust off his coat, then grimaced as he realized he would soon need to make a trip to his tailor to make sure his clothes weren't going to make him an object of ridicule.

Heaven forbid the cut of my coat be even a single season out of date. I'd never hear the end of it from Charlotte. He rolled his eyes.

If he thought his sister would allow it, he'd dress in sackcloth and leave his hair uncombed and his face unshaven for the entirety of his stay in town. Then at least the marriage market might leave him alone and allow him to visit with his family in peace.

He grinned for a moment at the thought of appearing in public looking like a madman and the ladies of the ton scurrying away from him in terror, then sobered when he realized it probably wouldn't make any difference. For a chance at his title, family name, and fortune, he was fairly certain most of them would be willing to overlook anything he might do.

Well, perhaps not anything, he thought with a wry twist to his lips. *It's the rare woman indeed who would happily turn a blind eye to a husband who prefers to share his bed with men and one who would never be able to give her children.*

And even if he could find such a woman, he'd never be able to live out that kind of farce. His honor would not allow it, nor would his patience. As a confirmed bachelor, he fully admitted he was set in his ways, and having another woman, in addition to his sister, meddling in his life and home would be intolerable.

No, the ladies of the ton pursued him in vain, and he would have to spend the next few weeks desperately trying to avoid them without *seeming* to avoid them. As subtlety was not his strongest suit, it was tantamount to torture, but there was no getting out of it.

Years ago, he and his sister had made a bargain, and Charlotte was not a woman to be crossed. If he did not show up at her house in town at least once a year, she'd descend on him at Kentwood Hall, and there would be no peace. She'd force a house party or some other nonsense on him, and *there* he wouldn't be able to escape the people living in his house, eating his food, and demanding to be entertained.

God forbid.

And if she were feeling truly spiteful, she'd invite some marriage-minded young chits, and he'd find himself cornered in his own library or some other private place, desperate to get away before a scandal forced him into matrimony. It had happened once, when Charlotte was still trying to find him a suitable wife to help him run Kentwood, before he'd been old enough to tell her where to put her matchmaking skills. He'd only narrowly escaped, and it was not an experience he intended to repeat.

No, London could be tedious, but he'd take it in a heartbeat if it meant he wouldn't have to suffer through another house party.

James sighed again and looked up at the house. His sister meant well. She worried about him all alone on his estate, attending only the rare party and never hosting unless there was no way to avoid it. Perhaps she was right to worry. He did get lonely and a little melancholy from time to time, but he wasn't the kind of man to stay maudlin for long; he was too practical for that. He'd made his choices long ago, with good reason, and there was no point in mourning them now.

My, aren't we sanguine today. James shook his head at himself.

Adjusting his cravat for the hundredth time that day, he took a deep breath and let it out again in resignation. There was no help for it. He'd have to get out of the carriage sometime, and delaying wouldn't help matters any. At least on the street he could stretch the cramps out of his legs and perhaps the linen of his shirt would come unglued from his back.

When his footman opened the door, James stood up and descended the step to the street. As he turned to give final instructions to his driver, a flash of pale gold caught his attention momentarily, distracting him from his servants. Out of the corner of his eye he spied a young, towheaded carter passing in the street, the defined muscles of his forearms flexing beneath rolled shirtsleeves. The boy looked up, and a pair of sweet brown eyes briefly met his before the young man quickly ducked his head and mumbled "m'lord" as he trundled past.

Raising a single brow but otherwise giving no sign he'd seen the boy, James lowered his head a little and pretended to swipe a bit of dirt from his coat. Watching the boy a few moments longer, he was rewarded with the sight of a firm, high backside flexing beneath coarse linen trousers, and he felt a different kind of heat infuse his body. Brief as it was, the sight reminded him of at least one of London's saving graces: pleasures he could find in town that he could not in the country.

Well, not without running the risk of blackmail or possibly a mob of outraged villagers. He grinned to himself.

After the carter disappeared around the corner and he was able to rein in his wandering thoughts, James exchanged a few words with his servants and headed toward the house with a smile on his lips.

Yes, there were definite advantages to spending a little time in town, pleasures to be indulged in, and it had been far too long since he had done so. His pulse sped and his boots lightened a little in anticipation.

He'd have to pay a visit to Madam Renard's, and soon. If his reaction to the sight of a simple carter going about his work was any indication, his year of celibacy was obviously having an effect on his mind.

He knew of other men, of course, who did not share his scruples, who made little to no effort at discretion, trusting title and wealth to keep them safe from any real scandal, men who were whispered about far and wide, though no one would dare speak against them openly. Long ago, he'd promised himself that he would never be one of them. He had worked too hard for the honor of his family to throw it all away with such foolishness. His sister and her children were the only close family he had left, and their good opinion and reputation meant too much to him to throw it away for lack of a little discretion and restraint.

He mounted the steps to his sister's door and reached for the bell. The first chime had barely sounded before he caught a splash of color out of the corner of his eye and grinned. His niece, Anna, wearing a lovely blue calico, was grinning and waving at him from the front parlor window. He barely had time to wave back before she turned and disappeared from view.

Smiling, he turned back to the door in anticipation. If his niece and nephew couldn't lift his spirits, then nothing would. The twins should be all the proof he needed that any sacrifices he might have made had been worthwhile. Whatever he might have given up had been repaid a hundred times over with the joy of sharing their lives and watching them grow into a fine young lady and worthy young gentleman.

The door opened and Wilton, his sister's butler, bowed, saying, "Good afternoon, my lord. Welcome back."

"Thank you, Wilton, it's a pleasure to be back," he replied, handing over his hat and gloves.

The moment he was free of his belongings, Anna flew into his arms to kiss him hello. He indulged himself in her sweet embrace for a few precious moments before setting her back on her feet and taking a good look at her. She'd grown a little since the last time he'd seen her, but she still looked tiny next to his bulk. At a few inches over six feet, he resembled his farmers in body as well as temperament, and he still needed to bend nearly in half to give his niece a proper embrace.

Of course, he shouldn't have allowed her to embrace him at all. She was nineteen now and a full-grown young lady, but he couldn't help being secretly delighted by her greeting and decided only a gentle rebuke was in order.

"I see your governess still hasn't managed to tame you, my wild little beast," he said, though the corners of his mouth couldn't help but quirk when she snorted in response.

"Oh Uncle, you know it's been ages since I needed Mrs. Holt to watch over me. I've learned my lessons as well as anyone, I assure you. I will comport myself with utmost decorum when we are in company, but when we're alone, I had hoped that my favorite uncle might continue to indulge me for a few more years, at the very least," Anna said, smiling at him coyly through her thick brown lashes.

"Imp," he responded, stopping just short of ruffling her carefully dressed hair. His hand might get caught in all the ribbons needed to tame that same unruly mop of brown curls that he was cursed with, and he might never get free again without the aid of scissors. Looking at the elaborate creation, he didn't envy her maid the task of taming that tangle every morning and was quite thankful he could keep his own cut short and wouldn't have to be bothered with such nonsense.

"And where is your partner in crime?" he asked, looking about for his nephew.

"Oh, he's off with his school chums again, I suppose. That's all he seems to have time for these days," she said, and James could hear the thinly veiled hurt under her feigned disinterest.

Since her brother Andrew had gone away to school, and now to university, James knew they hadn't been able to spend much time together. As young children, they had been nearly inseparable. But time and duty took their toll on everyone, and it appeared Anna was feeling the distance between them more and more.

He took her hand and patted it kindly. "We'll see if we can keep him home at least a little during my visit, yes?"

Her smile brightened a little, and the twinkle came back to her eyes. "He may be home more than any of us cares for, if he isn't more careful," she leaned in and whispered. "He's been getting himself in a bit of trouble at the club, losing money hand over fist, and you know how Father feels about gambling. Another night like he had last week and he'll spend the rest of the season confined to his rooms."

"Oh dear," James said, chuckling. "Let us hope we can save him from *that* fate, at the very least. But for now, imp, I am all over dirt from my journey and wish to go to my rooms to bathe and dress before your mother sets eyes on me. By your leave of course, Miss Ashton?"

"By all means, *my lord.*" She curtsied in response to his formal bow and stepped out of the way for him to climb the stairs.

"I will inform Lady Ashton of your arrival," she called after him archly before turning with a swish of her skirts to scurry in a most unladylike manner toward the back of the house.

James shook his head and smiled as he continued to his rooms. No, his world was just as it should be, and there was no reason to wish for anything else.

Chapter
Two

AS JAMES stepped out of his coach and into the crowd in front of the Sutcliffes' sprawling house, he tugged distractedly at his new waistcoat. Meyer had done an excellent job, as always, and his clothes fit him to perfection, but he couldn't help feeling uncomfortable in his new finery. He would much rather be in his buckskins and worn wool hunting jacket, sitting comfortably in his library, than dressed up like a dandy on display for the London vultures. But tonight was the Sutcliffes' annual end-of-season ball, one of the most coveted invitations in town, and Charlotte had insisted he attend and that he look his best. As Lord and Lady Sutcliffe were old family friends and distant relations, he could hardly refuse.

He tugged unnecessarily on his coat and gloves once more before joining the crowd making their way up the steps to the house. He stood nearly a head taller than everyone in the crowd, and, as usual, his size garnered him much more attention than he would have liked. It was damned difficult for him to go unnoticed at the best of times, and tonight he'd have to use every bit of cunning he had if his plans for later that evening were to come off without a hitch.

He'd been in town nearly two weeks now and had yet to find an evening to sneak away from his family to see to some of his more *pressing* needs. Charlotte had commandeered nearly every waking moment of his time with visits and parties, everyone giving a last gasp before quitting London, he supposed. But as much as he loved his family, he hadn't had the touch of anyone but his own right hand in over a year, and his body was making it quite clear to him that he wouldn't be able to wait much longer.

Tonight would be the night he rectified that situation. With the crush of people attending the ball, he would be able to slip away without anyone from his family even noticing his absence. For the sake of propriety, he would spend a few hours fulfilling his obligations; then, when the streets had emptied a little, he would make his way to Madam Renard's and blessed release.

Anticipation made him edgy and impatient, but none of it showed on his face or in his manner as he made it to the front of the receiving line and greeted his hosts warmly. On any other night, he would have been quite pleased to spend the evening visiting with them, but he was much too distracted and they had their guests to attend to, so he merely greeted them briefly and moved on with a promise to call later in the week.

He made his way directly to the nearest tray of filled glasses before beginning a random circuit of the rooms. The Sutcliffes always served the best wines, and he was in need of something to calm his nerves. He was as edgy as a maiden on her wedding night, and the hours were going to feel like days if he didn't find something to distract himself. He finished his first glass before he even made it out of the room and retrieved another before continuing on. He spoke briefly with friends and acquaintances here and there, but avoided staying with any group too long.

The time passed painfully slowly despite the multitude of distractions at his disposal. He must have checked his pocket watch at least a dozen times in the hour he'd been there, and he even held it to his ear once or twice just to make sure it hadn't stopped on him. It was at times like this that he thought perhaps one trip to London a year wasn't enough, but then all he had to do was look about him at the throng of idle, bored, pompous, backbiting, dull-witted people milling about the ballroom to remind himself why he stayed in the country. Any more than a few weeks a year and he'd definitely say or do something that would scandalize his family.

He downed the rest of his glass and plastered on his best smile as he was hailed by one of the aforementioned gentlemen, Sir William

Archer, a tedious but relatively harmless friend of his brother-in-law's. He allowed himself to be drawn into a discussion on horses and the results of the Ascot earlier that summer. As he dabbled a little in breeding, it helped distract him for a time, but when he found himself checking his watch again, he decided it was time to move on to another distraction.

Putting his watch firmly back in his pocket in disgust, he selected another glass of wine from a nearby tray, made an excuse to Sir William, and set out for the parlor, where tables had been set up for games. He should probably slow down on the wine or he'd be staggering out of the ball instead of just sneaking.

James hovered about the parlor for several moments before giving up on the idea of joining the play. He was much too preoccupied to be able to do anything but fill the purse of one of his peers, and the thought didn't appeal to him.

Instead, he decided he should seek out his family and see how they were enjoying the evening. They'd come separately, as the Ashtons' barouche only held four comfortably, and James had yet to spot them in the crush. The twins were young enough that balls of this kind were still a source of great excitement, so perhaps some of their enthusiasm might rub off on him and help keep his mind off what was to come.

After a bit of hunting, he finally spotted both Anna and Andrew on the far side of the ballroom and began to make his way toward them through the press of bodies. It took every ounce of grace and agility he had to make his way through the crowd without spilling his wine or treading on anyone. A man his size, even in slippers, could do a great deal of damage to delicate, flimsily clad toes if he weren't careful.

He lost sight of them twice and had started to sweat by the time he was able to finally close the distance enough to see their smiling faces. He couldn't help but smile himself as he saw Anna laugh merrily and bring her fan up in front of her face to cover her blush, though his smile quickly turned to a frown when he realized it was a stranger she was fluttering her eyelashes at.

Could his little hoyden actually be flirting with someone?

James was a little startled at her behavior. Feeling protective and a little jealous all at once, he looked to see who could have inspired such behavior in his niece and nearly dropped his own wine glass at the sight that met his eyes. Standing in front of Anna, not ten feet away from him, was what had to be the most beautiful young man James had ever seen, and he couldn't help but halt in his tracks and stare stupidly at him, all thoughts of his niece flown from his head.

Good God, who are you? And would you take it greatly amiss if I threw you over my shoulder and carried you off to my carriage?

Shocked by his own thoughts, he took a step backward and shook his head. Unfortunately, the move brought him into contact with several other party guests, and this time he *did* spill his wine, forcing him to take his eyes off the vision across the room and apologize profusely to the injured parties. After the appropriate amount of groveling had been seen to and he'd wiped the wine from his hands, he looked up to find the cause of his difficulties walking away behind a tall, blond man. Anna and her brother had moved on as well, leaving him torn as to which direction to follow.

His feet, however, had no trouble making up his mind for him. Of their own accord, they turned and followed the young man and his companion out of the room. His mind reasoned that, as a protective uncle, he was only following so he could find out more about the young man who had captured his niece's attentions, but deep down, he knew that that was only an excuse.

Eventually, he caught up with the two men near the card tables. They were conversing with a small group and apparently awaiting their turn at play, giving James a perfect opportunity to study the young man without being noticed. He skirted the edge of the room so that he could watch without making a spectacle of himself and leaned back against the wall, partially concealed by a column.

Closer examination only confirmed his earlier reaction. The young man was absolutely stunning. Black curls, longer on top and clipped close to an elegantly arched neck, caught flashes of blue from the dozens of lamps and candles in the room. He wasn't tall, perhaps the same height as Andrew, and his lean frame spoke more of grace than strength, in better keeping with the current fashion than James's hulking build. His pale, flawless complexion showed only the smallest hint of shadow along a delicate jaw and pointed chin, and his slender brows arched above a small, straight nose and sculpted cheekbones. James was reminded of the stories of fairies and elves his old nurse used to tease him with before putting him to bed.

As he continued to watch, the object of his less-than-innocent regard accepted a glass of wine from a passing footman and brought it to his lips, causing James to bite back a groan. Those lips… *good God they were sinful*. Full, pouting lower lip topped by a slender, bow-shaped upper, both of which just begged to be nibbled on.

James quickly looked away before any sign of his thoughts could manifest on his person, and his eyes landed on the young man's companion. The other man was older than his friend, taller and broader too, though nowhere near James's size. His face was somewhat pinched and hard to James's eyes, and, after a moment, James realized he recognized him.

Victor Weir. The name rose from his memory, bringing with it little pleasure. They'd only met once or twice in passing. He was a gentleman of some means and considerable connections among the peerage, if rumor could be believed, but James had never warmed to him. He'd always thought of him as a bit of a cold fish, and the manner in which he was ignoring his beautiful companion didn't improve James's opinion of him in the slightest.

Deciding that the thought of Weir had cooled his blood enough to risk another look, James turned his attention back to the young man at his side, and a pair of startled green eyes met his own. The moment their eyes met, he felt himself fall into a sea of emerald and gold, and he couldn't have looked away even if he had wanted to.

James didn't know how long their gazes remained locked before the young man jerked and turned his head to the man next to him. Looking down, James could see Weir had taken his companion's elbow and was staring angrily in James's direction. He was fairly certain the man didn't recognize him, for the scowl remained on his face, and he made no attempt to cover it. He knew if Weir could see him clearly, he would never have dared to show open hostility to a man of his rank.

The young man at Weir's side had paled and was looking pointedly at his shoes, biting at his lower lip nervously, making James wonder at the cause of his distress. They'd only shared a glance, nothing more, no reason for such a reaction. There must be something more going on than he was aware of, and he was surprised at the concern he felt. Before he could even begin to understand what was happening, however, Weir was steering the young man across the room by the elbow and the two of them were disappearing into the crush in the main hall.

James was tempted for a moment to go after them. He even took a step in that direction before reason reasserted itself and he stopped. What would be the point of going after them? He didn't like Weir, and presuming on their limited acquaintance for an introduction to his companion would not go unnoticed. Even if they were introduced, what could he possibly gain by becoming better acquainted with him?

A great many sleepless nights and the distinct possibility of making an arse out of myself, that's what.

No, in the interests of his sanity, he needed to walk away now and forget he ever saw the man. He was acting like a fool, and he had no excuse for it. The mere sight of a beautiful young man shouldn't have caused him to abandon his wits in a crowd of his peers. He needed to get to Madam Renard's *now* before he let his body lead him into any more potentially embarrassing situations.

His mind made up, James turned on his heel and attempted to casually make his way to the front of the house. If he moved with too much purpose, people would notice and whisper, and he didn't want to cause the slightest stir. It was earlier than he had planned to leave, but there was no help for it. No good would come of his staying at the ball any longer.

He called for his hat at the door and made his way into the street to find his coach. He didn't want to risk waiting for it to be called. It would be just his luck for Charlotte or the twins to come through the hall while he was waiting at the door.

He found the coach a few blocks away, and after rousing his surprised servants, was finally on his way to the night of debauchery he'd promised himself. Once his body was sated, he felt certain his reaction at the ball would be easily explained away as the temporary madness of a man too long deprived.

KYLE was in trouble. He knew it by the pinched look about Victor's mouth and the painful grip his lover had on his elbow as he steered him through Lord and Lady Sutcliffe's ballroom. What he didn't know was *why*, and therein lay the cause of his anxiety. If he couldn't puzzle out what he'd done before the end of the night, Victor would be even angrier at his stupidity.

When they stopped at the edge of the ballroom and Victor released his arm, Kyle rubbed the tender spot with his palm and looked expectantly toward his lover, but Victor had already turned away from him and was speaking casually to a friend, leaving Kyle feeling even more anxious.

The truth was, he couldn't seem to do anything that made Victor happy anymore. Ever since they'd come to London, everything he did or said seemed to be wrong. The only thing he *could* do that seemed to please his lover was dress in the fine clothes that were bought for him, play the pianoforte for his guests, and remain silent unless spoken to. Kyle had learned to say as little as possible in the past few months lest he open himself, or Victor, to ridicule for his lack of refinement.

As Victor continued to ignore him, Kyle decided he'd best spend his time sifting through the events of the evening, trying to figure out what he'd done wrong. He didn't think he'd said anything untoward. He'd been polite when addressed but otherwise kept his thoughts to himself. In fact, the evening had seemed to be going quite well. Victor had had plenty of opportunities to speak with his friends and conduct a little business, which always seemed to make him happy.

Kyle let his mind and eyes wander about the room, still puzzling over Victor's sudden change in mood, until he realized he was looking for someone in particular and a sudden guilty thought occurred to him. The man in the ballroom. Had Victor caught him staring at the other man?

Kyle swallowed nervously and looked to his lover. He knew Victor had seen the other man looking in their direction. Victor always noticed things like that, most of the time long before Kyle did. His lover told him frequently that men watched him when they were out together, though Kyle never saw them, and usually the idea seemed to make Victor happy. He would say that he liked that other men wanted what was his. Kyle had never liked being referred to as a possession, but he'd learned to keep those feelings to himself. Nothing good ever came from arguing with Victor.

Maybe Victor was angry because this time Kyle had been the one doing the looking. Kyle bit his lip as his stomach fluttered nervously. It had only been a look, nothing else. He'd been bored and a little anxious, as he always was at formal gatherings, just looking about the room for something to distract himself. He hadn't been focused on anyone or anything in particular until he caught sight of the giant of a man against the wall. He hadn't really meant to stare at him, but when those intense brown eyes had met his, he hadn't been able to look away.

Who was he?

He had thought at the time that he looked vaguely familiar but was sure he would have remembered if he'd ever seen the man before. It wasn't just that he was handsome, though that certainly hadn't escaped his notice. But his eyes were what Kyle remembered more than anything else. They were warm and deep, kind and strong and so many other things Kyle couldn't name. In that moment, he'd had the fantastic notion that he could get lost in them forever if he were given half a chance. Now, out from under their spell and standing next to an irritated Victor, Kyle felt foolish for his fanciful notions. Victor was right. He'd been reading too many of Mrs. Radcliffe's novels.

Thinking of Victor brought him back to the present and the realization that perhaps he was indeed at fault for Victor's anger. Kyle sighed to himself and settled in for another miserable night. He could do nothing about it now except try to avoid any other mistakes and hope Victor's anger would cool after a few more hours. Perhaps if he played one of Victor's favorite songs when they returned home or he thought of something special to do for him in their bedchamber.

A small part of him winced a little in shame at the mewling tone of his thoughts. He shouldn't have to grovel. He hadn't really done anything wrong, but he quickly pushed the feeling aside. Things were just a little tense between them right now. Victor had a great many responsibilities weighing on his mind, and all Kyle had to do was try a little harder to be more understanding and things between them would get better again. The fact that this line of reasoning had run through his mind all too often of late did occur to him briefly, but it was also quickly smothered before it could take root.

What other choice did he have?

JAMES woke to the chime of bells above his head and a sharp pain in his neck.

What…? Where…? What time is it?

It took only moments to answer his half-formed questions as he glanced about the room and the clock on the mantle chimed a second time. He remembered now. He had gone to the library rather than his bedchamber after returning from his foray into the seedier parts of London. The rest of the family hadn't come home yet from the ball, and the house had been empty and much too quiet. He'd been too agitated to sleep, so he'd decided to read for a while before turning in. He must have been more tired than he thought, for he hadn't made it more than a couple of pages into the book before falling asleep.

Now, unfortunately, he was wide awake, the house was still too quiet, and his neck was protesting the abuse he'd heaped on it by falling asleep in a chair rather than his comfortable bed. He leaned forward in the chair and rubbed at his neck as the past few hours replayed in his mind.

His carriage had taken him directly to Madam Renard's from the ball. His coachman knew the way quite well after so many years, and he also knew where to wait until he was sent for whilst his master "attended to his business." His servants knew the kind of establishment it was, but even they didn't know the particulars of the type of companionship he procured there.

Madam Renard was an extremely intelligent and canny woman who did not limit her services to any one type of depravity. If a man had a need and the coin to pay for it, she would see that he was satisfied by whatever means necessary, thus ensuring she had patrons from every great house in England and, consequently, would never be raided by anyone who wished to have a career afterward. It was one of the many reasons James patronized her establishment and hers alone.

At his knock, the plump, motherly madam in her simple, if a little low-cut, bombazine gown greeted him at the door and led him to a small parlor. She poured him a glass of brandy and, playing out the now-familiar routine, gently asked what else she might provide for him. It was a scene that he'd enacted with her enough times on his trips to London that he felt certain she could have spoken his lines for him, but he answered anyway, requesting his usual companion. In short order, he was led to his customary room, and he settled into the deep, comfortable chair to wait.

Elias was prompt as always. After a quiet knock, he entered, closing and bolting the door behind him. Dressed only in a loose shirt and fawn trousers, he looked every bit as tempting as James remembered. Without a word, the young man crossed the few steps to James's side and slid gracefully to his knees next to the chair.

James smiled and threaded his fingers through Elias's soft blond curls, closing his eyes and enjoying the simple pleasure of it. Unfortunately, with his eyes closed, the warm silk of the Elias's hair took on a decidedly darker hue in his mind's eye. Blond became blue-black and blue eyes warmed to green despite his best efforts to dispel the image.

Frowning in consternation, James opened his eyes and focused his attentions at the young man by his side. Elias remained silent, on his knees, waiting patiently. They had been together enough times that they were quite comfortable with one another. It was one of the reasons James always requested him. Elias knew what he liked and what he didn't. There would be no awkwardness or need to instruct. Add to that his sweet smile, cherubic features, and lean, slim body, and Elias was the perfect companion to ease the need he'd built up over the past year… or so he would have said only a few hours ago. Now he wasn't so certain.

And *that* thought truly puzzled him. In the past, he'd been attracted almost exclusively to soft-featured blonds, not black-haired, almost fey beauties, but there was no denying his reactions at the ball. Even now, with a delectable morsel like Elias kneeling in front of him, he couldn't seem to get the other young man or his haunted green eyes out of his mind.

James shook his head and gritted his teeth. Elias was right in front of him, ready and willing, and he probably would never see the other young man again. He didn't know what was the matter with him, but it had to stop, and he knew the best way to distract himself.

He slid his hand further down to cup Elias's head and drew the young man into his lap. Elias smiled and cuddled against him, sliding his hand up to James's cravat, undoing it with nimble fingers.

"It's good ta' see you again, m'lord. It's been too long," he said, then moved his hands to the buttons of James's waistcoat.

"Yes, it has," James replied, taking Elias's lips in a gentle kiss. The soft lips parted beneath his, and a warm tongue darted forward to tease him. James groaned. Oh yes, it *had* been too long. This was just what he needed.

He leaned in, tightening his hold in Elias's hair and pulling him in for a deeper kiss. As their tongues tangled and explored, James slid his hands to Elias's waist and drew his shirt up. Leaning forward, he nipped at the younger man's chest, making him moan and writhe in James's lap. The feel of that firm rump wriggling against his already straining cock nearly sent him over the edge.

Standing abruptly, he nearly threw Elias toward the bed. As he tumbled onto the mattress, Elias laughed. "I have indeed missed you, m'lord. How will you have me?"

"I will have you unclothed first," James replied, leaning against the bedpost and crossing his arms over his chest. He took a breath to calm himself as Elias rose up to his knees and pulled his shirt over his head.

"As m'lord wishes, a'course." Elias's eyes never left his as he slid hands down his chest to the front of his trousers, unbuttoning them slowly and sliding them down over his slim hips. He wore nothing beneath, and his long, slender cock sprang free of its confines, fully hard and waiting for him. The sight sent another pulse of warmth straight to his manhood, and James had to struggle again to control himself.

Elias lay back on the bed and extended his legs toward James, his trousers bunched around his knees. James unfolded his arms and tugged them off, leaving the man bare, spread wantonly across the counterpane.

James wasted no time admiring and crawled across the bed, stretching himself full-length against that tempting body. He took Elias's mouth again, more fiercely this time, sliding his hands over that sleek body, grabbing and squeezing the firm globes of his arse and pressing their groins together and pumping his hips.

He wanted to just lie there and feel the simple comfort of a warm body pressed against his own, but his body was crying out for release and wouldn't allow him to be patient. The frustrations of a year of celibacy, coupled with the events of the evening, made games of any kind impossible. He was fooling himself to think otherwise.

Rolling off of Elias to stand, he quickly removed the rest of his clothes and slid back on the bed. Sensing his urgency, Elias slid his hand down and gripped James's throbbing cock firmly in his rough hand.

"I'm already prepared for you, m'lord, if you'd prefer to skip the pleasantries," he said with a knowing smile.

"You know me too well, my boy," James said, grinning in relief and flipping Elias onto his stomach. He pulled the young man up by the hips and slid his hands over that tempting arse, spreading him wide with his thumbs and plunging himself into that tight heat in one stroke.

Elias cried out at the suddenness of the penetration but was soon rocking back against him, matching his frantic pace and moaning. The tight, slick channel felt incredible surrounding him. Perhaps a little too incredible. It was at times like this that James wondered how he managed to go without for so long.

The first time was never slow and sweet, no matter his intentions. He drove into that tight arse over and over, straining for release, knowing it wouldn't be long at all. The sound of their bodies slapping together filled the room as James felt the pressure begin to build in his bollocks.

He blew out a quick breath and slowed his frantic pace enough to pull back from the brink as he reached around to grasp Elias's rigid shaft in a firm grip. No matter how strong his need or the nature of their relationship, James always tried to be a considerate lover. His pride wouldn't allow him to find release without taking his partner with him.

He soon increased the pace of his thrusts again, stroking Elias in time, and the punishing rhythm began anew. He came first, spilling inside that sweet haven with a roar, and if, in that moment, someone else's face swam before his eyes, well, he was sure Elias wouldn't have minded.

He felt Elias follow him a moment after, clenching and trembling around him, squeezing the last bit of seed from his softening cock. They collapsed in a breathless tangle on the bed, and James withdrew, lying back on the bed to catch his breath. Elias went to the washstand and cleaned them both up with the flannel before stretching along his side and smiling at him fondly.

They lay there for a time in silence, Elias running his hands gently over James's body as James tried to relax under his ministrations.

"Up for another go, m'lord?" Elias said, motioning toward James's semi-erect cock.

"Almost," he said, chuckling. "I want to relax for a little while first. Are you in a rush?"

"'Course not. Not when m' favorite lord has returned to me at last." The young man smiled and curled more tightly against him.

"Your favorite, hmm? I'll have to remember that." James smiled and rested his chin on Elias's head, absently trailing the backs of his fingers down his chest.

"Please do," Elias said, and there was an odd note to his voice.

When James pulled back and raised his brows in question, Elias looked up at him and shrugged, saying, "I've always admired you, m'lord. Yer a truly good soul. I meet 'em rare enough in my work to appreciate 'em when I do."

"So serious tonight, Elias. Is something the matter? Are you in trouble?" James asked, concerned.

"You see?" Elias laughed. "You actually care enough to ask if your whore is hurt or in trouble. Yer a treasure, m'lord!"

"Elias...."

"No, no, m'lord. I'm not in any trouble, quite the opposite. If I may speak freely...?"

"Of course. We've known one another long enough, and *intimately* enough, that I think a little informality can be excused," James said with a wry grin, still concerned at Elias's serious tone. The young man was usually so light-hearted and jolly.

"Thank you, m'lord. I haven't told no one but Madam and now you. I'm leavin' London, England in fact, in a few weeks. I got family in America, an' they promised me a home and work, respectable work, if I make the passage," he said, smiling brightly.

"That's wonderful. I'm happy for you, Eli, truly," James replied, relieved and a little disappointed at the news.

"I wanted you to know afore I left and was glad to hear you'd come. You've been so good to me, m'lord, and I always felt a little sad that I couldn'a' done more to cheer you," he said, taking James's hand in his.

"You've cheered me plenty, lad, never doubt it," he responded with a chuckle.

"No, no, I haven't, not truly," Elias said, looking earnestly into his eyes. "There's a sadness in you that I ne'er could touch, and I just wanted you to know that you deserve more. You deserve t'be happy if any man e'er did, an' that's the truth."

James was touched by his words and didn't know quite how to respond to them, but Elias took pity on him and ended his struggles with a kiss, then another and another, sliding down his body as he went. As warm wetness and a clever tongue surrounded his cock, the tender mood was replaced by something far more heated, and James surrendered to it happily.

The second time, his climax was slower to build, and he was able to make the pleasure last much longer, in part because he was so distracted. Ordinarily he would have spent at least another hour with Elias before heading home, but tonight he simply couldn't shake the strange mood that had settled on him after their conversation.

Elias's words hit him harder than he would have expected, and he wasn't certain why. Add to that the strange melancholy that had come over him when he had first arrived in town and his reaction to the young man at the ball, and he was beginning to think he was going a little mad.

Grimacing at himself, James decided he needed to stop this foolishness. Useless pining over should-bes and could-have-beens was not the way he should be spending his time.

What on earth was the matter with him of late?

He slid out from under a surprised Elias and began to dress himself. When he was finished, he leaned in and bid Elias good night with a gentle kiss and a promise to return at least once more before returning to the country, hoping to soothe away any concern Elias might feel over his odd behavior.

On the ride back to the townhouse, he continued to try to shake the strange and anxious humor. He was truly happy for Elias, glad that the young man had a chance at a better life. The only thing he should have been regretting was the fact that he'd have to find a new companion on his next visit to town. Nothing else had changed. His life was exactly as it had been and as it should be, but still he was plagued with strange thoughts and vague longings that he couldn't quite put a name to.

Even now, after a good nap in the quiet and comfort of his sister's home, the queer humor wouldn't let him go. He shook his head once more to clear it and stood up from the once comfortable chair in his brother-in-law's library, stretching to put some blood back into his legs and ease the pain in his neck.

Time to go to bed before you swoon and crash into the depths of despair. All this brooding isn't good for you.

Just then, he heard voices coming from the hall and realized his family must have finally returned from the ball. Thankful for the distraction, he straightened his clothing, grabbed the lamp, and went to welcome them. He had just opened his mouth to do so when his sister's voice cut him off.

"Anna." Charlotte sounded angry.

His niece paused on the stairs and turned large, innocent eyes back to her mother. "Yes, Mother?"

"It's late, I'm tired, and I'm not in the mood to play out this farce. You have been out of sorts since we left the ball and completely silent for the entirety of the carriage-ride home. This, of course, *never* happens. So I must therefore deduce that there is something you *don't* want to say, else it will get you, or your brother, into trouble."

Charlotte was tapping her foot now, which James knew was never a good sign. The action, so un-ladylike and lacking of her normal grace and poise, would only serve to worsen her temper when she realized she was doing it.

Attempting to beat a hasty retreat, James turned but only managed a few steps before he was spotted.

"Uncle James!" Anna rushed to him like a lifeline. "How was your evening? Where did you go?"

"Don't try to use your uncle to change the subject, Anna," his sister chastised. They both turned reluctantly back to Charlotte and watched as her warm brown eyes, identical to their own, turned sharp and narrowed in speculation.

"It's your brother, isn't it? He is not staying with his friends at the Sutcliffes'. He's snuck off somewhere, hasn't he?"

Feeling storm clouds lowering, James tried to extricate himself from his niece's embrace. As her fingers tightened on his arm, he sighed and gave up the fight.

"Out with it, young lady." Obviously taking Anna's silence as a confirmation, Charlotte continued the interrogation. "Where is he and what is he up to?"

James felt Anna stiffen for a moment, then slump her shoulders and turn to her mother.

Wise child. She obviously took after her father in that, as the man was even now hiding in the shadows by the door trying to move as little as possible else he draw his wife's attentions.

"All right, I'll tell you. But he's just trying to help out a friend, so please don't be too angry with him. *Please?*" Her mother was silent, so Anna took a deep breath and continued. "He's gone to Boodles with Mr. Kyle Allen," she confessed in a pained rush.

James didn't recognize the man's name, as unusual as it was, but he definitely recognized the place and winced, wishing for the tenth time in as many minutes that he'd gone to his bedchamber instead of the library.

Charlotte's eyes narrowed, her lips thinned, and her jaw clenched as she absorbed her daughter's confession. When she finally spoke, her words were quiet and clipped. "So, you are telling me that, only *three* days after your father and I forbid Andrew from visiting such establishments for at least a fortnight, as punishment for the mess he made the *last* time he did such a thing, he chose to ignore our wishes and then lie to us about it?"

Oh, no. Maybe James could make his escape now that all eyes were focused on Anna. No such luck. Anna grabbed hold of his hand and squeezed. Rolling his eyes, James knew there was no help for it.

Breaking the charged silence in the hall, he said, "Why don't we move into the drawing room for a bit of a chat?" His sister's eyes followed his pointed gaze to the footmen and Wilton, their butler, attending them in the hall.

Not that it will make much difference, he mused, as the servants would most likely hear it all anyway, but it would allow those servants that wished to get their rest to do so and give his sister the illusion of privacy.

Not waiting for a response, James led the four of them toward the back of the house. He was still carrying his lamp and placed it on the table in the middle of the room. Wilton followed, placing a second lamp on the mantel above the fireplace.

"Thank you, Wilton," Charlotte said. "That will be all for the evening. We will take care of the lamps before we turn in. And tell Margaret and Woods that Lord Ashton and I will take care of ourselves this evening, so they may go to bed as well."

"Very good, my lady," Wilton said, and he backed out of the room, closing the doors.

"Now." Charlotte turned on her daughter with a not-so-pleasant smile. "Please do continue with your confession, my dear."

Anna visibly swallowed and said, "There isn't much else to say. Andrew and I found Mr. Allen later in the evening, um, outside the ballroom, and he seemed to be in great distress. He told us he needed to leave London. He said he needed to get to his aunt in Suffolk but wasn't sure how he would manage it. Andrew came up with a plan to help him, and they, and they… left together. That's all!" she concluded lamely.

"Your brother's idea of helping this young man was to take him gambling?" her mother said incredulously.

"I, I told him it wasn't a good plan, but we couldn't seem to think of another one. And you know how Andrew gets when he's got a scheme brewing." Anna looked between all three adults pleadingly. Hoping someone would throw her a lifeline, James supposed.

His lips quirked, and before he could stop himself, a short bark of laughter erupted from his chest. His sister looked at him like he'd grown another head. She was not amused, but he couldn't seem to help himself. Out of the corner of his eye, he could see a small smile forcing its way along his brother-in-law's lips as well, despite what seemed a Herculean effort to keep them straight, and James couldn't keep another chuckle from escaping.

"Well, dear brother"—his sister's ire transferred to him temporarily—"since you seem to think this is so amusing, *you* can be the one who goes to get him from that place and bring him home before he can get himself, and this young man, into any more trouble."

"Oh, Char, have a heart, dearest." His brother-in-law, William, spoke up at last. "Your brother looks like he's only just returned home himself. We can't make him pile back into a carriage so soon."

"No, no, William," James said, managing to sober himself. "It's all right. You have been out and about all evening whilst I have been lounging in the library for at least an hour. I'll go get the scamp and drag him home for his beating."

If it gets me out before Charlotte really loses her temper, it will be well worth it.

As he made his way out of the parlor, his sister confirmed his reasoning when she began, "Now then, young lady, we must discuss *your* behavior...."

The Ashtons' carriage hadn't been put away yet, so it came around quickly when sent for. They reached St. James's Street in short order, and he instructed the driver to turn the carriage and wait across the street for him. It wouldn't take long to collect his nephew and be on his way. At least, that was what he hoped. It had been a busy night for him, and he was starting to feel it. Muscles in his body that hadn't been used in over a year were protesting loudly that he needed to get home and rest. He smiled, remembering how they'd gotten that way, then sobered, focusing on his mission.

He entered the club but waved off the servant who greeted him at the door and kept his hat. The rooms were thick with conversation and smoke as he passed several tables in search of his nephew. He was hailed here and there by acquaintances lounging in plush chairs or waiting their turn at the tables, but he gave only the briefest of greetings before passing on. He was tired, and he felt the beginnings of a headache coming on now that he was in the crowded, smoke-filled rooms.

He finally found Andrew near the back at a small table. Relieved, he made his way around the table, attempting to quietly draw his nephew's attention. When he came close enough to recognize some of his nephew's opponents, he caught sight of the young man sitting directly across from Andrew and nearly forgot why he was there.

The very person he'd been trying *not* to think about for the past few hours was sitting at the table not ten feet from him, and for the second time that night, all thoughts of his family fled from his head.

He rolled his eyes heavenward in a plea for strength and gritted his teeth. For God's sake, his evening with Elias was supposed to sate his passions, not send them raging out of control. Yet here he was again devouring the lad with his eyes like he was a banquet spread before a starving man.

Oh dear lord, get hold of yourself before someone sees the way you're staring at him.

At least his reason didn't completely desert him, and this time, when thoughts of carrying young men off in carriages came to mind, they brought him back to the room with a jolt, reminding him that his brother-in-law's carriage was waiting outside for him to discharge his commission. With that thought held firmly in mind, James was finally able to tear his thoughts away from the distraction at the table and focus on his nephew.

Andrew must have followed the other player's gaze, because his eyes met James's over the table and widened. When James gestured to the front doors with his head, Andrew closed his eyes and grimaced. His tablemates must have taken note of his reaction, because curious gazes turned in James's direction, and some nodded and chuckled quietly, perhaps surmising the reason for his appearance.

The first part of his charge accomplished, James moved a discreet distance from the table and leaned back against a paneled wall, waiting for them to finish their play. There were plenty of other gentlemen close by who'd be more than willing to sit in, so James knew his nephew would be able to extricate himself from the game with a minimum of fuss.

The wait didn't bother him in the least. It gave him a chance to calm himself and hopefully allow some of his blood to return to his head. It wasn't easy. More than once, temptation won out and his eyes strayed back to the young man across from Andrew.

The young beauty continued to play but seemed preoccupied, glancing worriedly between him and Andrew. By this James finally surmised that he must be the infamous Mr. Allen, the friend that Andrew was trying to help with his dunderheaded scheme. The thought did not give him comfort. He wondered what could have happened in the few short hours after he left the ball. Why did Allen need to leave London, and where was Victor Weir?

These questions and more plagued him as he continued to watch the play. He was surprised to note how well Allen played despite his distraction, and James had to admit he was impressed. From the look of him he couldn't be much older than Andrew, yet he was holding his own quite well against several older gentlemen at the table. Though *that* thought made him grimace the moment it popped into his head. The "older" men at the table were close to his own age, so what did that make him?

He's your nephew's friend, for God's sake, barely half your age. Show a little restraint.

James was becoming disgusted with himself. Perhaps going to see Elias had been a bad idea after all. It certainly hadn't helped.

James glanced around the room, hoping for a distraction. It was a bad idea, for in doing so, he couldn't help noticing more than one man's attention drifting back to that table over and over. Apparently he wasn't the only man in the room so affected, and the surge of jealousy he felt at that realization caught him off guard.

James closed his eyes this time. *That's enough. You haven't even met the man, and already you're feeling possessive? Collect your nephew and go home before you make a fool of yourself.*

The round concluded, and Andrew and Mr. Allen stepped away from the table, each giving their apologies. James turned and moved toward the front doors without looking to see if they were following. The thought that the young man might be joining them in the carriage sent equal parts anticipation and anxiety coursing through him, adding to his self-disgust.

Out in the street, he walked to the carriage and climbed in without a word. The other two followed shortly after and settled onto the seat opposite him. No one broke the silence, for which James would be eternally grateful. The carriage took off as soon as the footman climbed on, and in short order they were on their merry way home.

FOR Kyle, it was the longest and most uncomfortable carriage ride he had ever experienced. Any other night, he would have thrilled at the beauty of the carriage itself, positively the finest he'd ever been allowed to ride in. But the pleasant haze from the brandy Andrew had shared with him only an hour before was gone, and the pain from the jostling of the carriage was forcibly reminding him of the nightmare his life had become.

As he tried to find a more comfortable position on the bench, he felt the strange, empty calm he'd managed to maintain slipping away and the reality of his situation, and Victor's betrayal, descend on him. His stomach twisted, and he broke out into a cold sweat as he struggled to hide his reaction from the other two men in the carriage.

Oh please, someone say something, he pleaded mentally. Neither man had spoken since they'd left the club, and the silence was becoming deafening.

He was so close to coming apart now. When he'd been playing at the tables, he'd been able to distract himself. But now, with the strange, intense man sitting across from him and Ashton sitting sullenly next to him, obviously in trouble, his composure was slipping away at an alarming rate.

He looked back and forth between the two other men, hoping to distract himself, and in the light from the passing streetlamps, a detached part of his mind finally realized why the older man had seemed familiar at the ball. It was obvious that he and Ashton were related. They had the same warm brown hair and eyes, the same strong nose and chin, but there the similarities ended. Ashton was nowhere near as imposing as his relation. The older man's head nearly brushed the roof of the carriage, and his shoulders and chest were so broad Kyle felt sure the man could break him in two if he wished to. The thought sent a strange shiver through him.

The silence in the carriage continued until Kyle felt sure he would break under its weight when, finally, Ashton came to his rescue.

"Were Mother and Father really angry, Uncle?" he asked meekly, confirming Kyle's supposition.

The man across from them simply raised his brows and glanced briefly in Kyle's direction before returning his gaze to Ashton.

"Oh, I'm terribly sorry." Ashton blushed. "Uncle, this is my friend Mr. Kyle Allen. Mr. Allen, please allow me to introduce you to my uncle, Lord James Warren, Viscount Sudbury."

"A pleasure to meet you, Mr. Allen," a surprisingly deep voice murmured.

"The pleasure is mine, my lord," Kyle replied. His voice was much weaker than he had intended, perhaps due to what the other man's voice was doing to his innards.

Lord Warren continued to frown sternly at his nephew for another few moments before he raised a hand to rub his forehead. Then, like the sun cutting through the clouds, his face split into a smile, and he chuckled, causing Kyle to catch his breath.

"Ah, nephew, don't look so glum," Warren said, clapping Ashton on the knee. "You know it's not the gallows or the pillory for you. You'll face your mother's wrath, serve your sentence, and be back out with your friends in no time, I'm sure."

His brief glance at Kyle set his heart pounding, and all he could do was stare at the man. Warren's teasing and merriment had transformed his face from simply handsome to nearly breathtaking. Lines had appeared at the corners of his mouth and eyes, showing that he must smile and laugh often, and the warmth radiating from his voice and eyes spilled out into the rest of the carriage, making Kyle's skin tingle.

Of a sudden, all he could think of was basking in that warmth, of what it would feel like to have that smile directed at him.

Where did that *come from? And what is* wrong *with me?* he wondered for the hundredth time that night. *After everything that has happened to me, how can I be thinking such things?*

He closed his eyes and leaned a little further back in his seat, hoping his heart would slow and the pounding in his ears would cease. He felt miserable, sick and confused to the point where he wasn't even certain of who he was anymore.

I'm just tired, he decided. *It's just the shock and worry that has me thinking this way. What Victor did to me....* Kyle's mind flinched away from the memory, and he sat further back in his seat, trying to think of something, *anything* else.

They arrived at their destination before Kyle could finish collecting himself, and Warren stepped out without waiting for the footman. Ashton followed, stepping into the street before turning to look back as Kyle hesitated in the doorway.

"Ashton, wait," Kyle said shakily. "I... can't go in with you." His words stumbled to a halt under Lord Warren's raised brows, and Kyle kept his eyes firmly fixed on Ashton before he broke out into tears and shamed himself in front of them.

Ashton didn't seem to know what to say as he looked up to the house and then back at Kyle. But he gathered his wits quickly and responded, "Oh, of course, Allen, I understand completely. You must be done-in after... well... I'm, I'm sure the coachman will take you wherever you wish to go." There was a question in his eyes, if not in his words.

"Thank you so very much for all your assistance, Ashton. I will, of course, send word when I'm settled, to both you and your sister. Thank her for me as well, will you? I don't know what I would've done if it weren't for your kindness."

Ashton just looked at him for a moment and then nodded his understanding, much to Kyle's relief. He didn't look happy about it, but his new friend wasn't going to fight him on this.

Thank you. It will be better for everyone if I leave now and let you get back to your lives. I've caused enough trouble with my stupidity and weakness.

"Good night, my lord. Good night, Ashton," Kyle said, nodding to both men and retreating back into the carriage. He was sure there was more he should have said or done, but he couldn't think, and he needed to get away before he fell apart completely.

As the footman closed the door, Kyle instructed him to tell the coachman to drive out the northern end of the square and up four more blocks. He had no idea where he was. Victor's rooms were nowhere near this part of town, and he hadn't been in London long enough to familiarize himself with other areas. He was too tired to think, and he was running on the last shreds of his strength as it was. He only hoped his instructions were enough not to inspire concern or suspicion in the servants.

When the carriage stopped, Kyle was let out in front of another row of townhouses. He waved the coachman off when he would've waited, which he was sure would seem suspicious, but he didn't know what else to do. After the coach turned the corner, he headed into a small park he'd seen from the carriage window.

Finding a secluded corner as far away from the street as he could, Kyle hunched down against a tree and wrapped his coat more tightly around himself. The late summer nights were still quite warm, but he couldn't seem to shake the chill that had settled into his bones. Wrapping his arms around his knees, he began to shiver uncontrollably as tears stung his eyes. He didn't have the strength to stop them anymore. He'd used what little he had left keeping his composure in front of Ashton and his uncle, and now he was limp with exhaustion.

With no defenses left, the memories he'd been fighting swamped him, images of Victor's cold, almost inhuman face in the dark, memories of being all but dragged to an empty room, forced over the back of a couch, and held down while Victor…. Kyle's stomach revolted and he stumbled onto his knees, retching in the bushes before falling back against the tree. Alone in the dark, he relived every moment of Victor's betrayal in painful detail, too weak to do anything more than whimper.

He didn't know how long he stayed like that before exhaustion finally claimed him and he surrendered into a blessedly dreamless sleep. It wasn't until he woke, several hours later, shivering and damp, that he realized Ashton still had his purse.

Chapter Four

JAMES hadn't slept well at all, despite how tired he was. After the carriage had pulled away, taking Mr. Allen with it, Andrew and he had climbed the stairs and let themselves into the house. He had put his arm around his nephew's shoulder as they had made their way directly to the drawing room, where Andrew's parents waited.

After assuring herself that her son was none the worse for his adventures, Charlotte had launched into a lecture of epic proportions, and James had taken the first opportunity to excuse himself, claiming exhaustion. Charlotte had mercifully let him go, barely breaking her tirade long enough to nod in his direction.

But though he hadn't been exaggerating his claim, sleep simply would not come. As he lay in his bed, staring at the ceiling, his mind kept returning to the beautiful young man he'd collected with his nephew, his own unusual reaction, and the mystery surrounding Allen's troubles.

He supposed it was understandable that the young man wouldn't want to come inside and experience the wrath of Lady Ashton in full temper, but why had he been so pale and agitated? Charlotte wasn't *that* frightening, after all. And why had the young men's parting exchange been so mysterious?

James had had the feeling there was a world of meaning in the few words the boys had exchanged that he was not privy to, and it worried him. What had happened? Why did Allen need to leave

London?

The twins were being surprisingly circumspect about the whole affair, and it left him more than a little concerned, and not just for the sake of his family. Allen had looked so lost and miserable across from him in the carriage that he'd wanted *badly* to reach out and gather him up, to cradle him in his arms until that lost look left his eyes.

That thought, and the riot of emotions the young man inspired in him, had kept him scowling out the window of the carriage and at his nephew for far longer than he might ordinarily have done. But, realizing he was probably making the situation worse, he decided to lighten the mood and allow some of his natural good humor to show through. Teasing his nephew had put him back on familiar ground and eased the tension within the carriage a bit.

He was glad he'd made the effort when he saw both young men relax. However, though he'd coaxed a smile out of Andrew, Allen's lips had remained pinched and his eyes worried. That had disappointed him more than he'd wanted to admit, even to himself. He'd really wanted to see the young man smile.

Which, of course, brought his thoughts full circle, back to the feelings he'd been trying to push out of his head since the moment he'd met the man.

James rolled his eyes at himself and finally gave up trying to sleep. He'd brooded for hours, his mind going 'round in circles, to no avail. It was not his nature to spend hours in contemplation. His sister called him a man of action, just like their father, and he'd have to admit that most of the time, she was right. He didn't know what it was about Allen that had gotten him so spun up, beyond the obvious, but he was damned sure he wasn't going to keep on like this. Mooning around like some fool boy was just damned childish and beneath him... and he'd done more of it in the past few weeks than in all of the past few years combined.

Pulling himself together, he washed and dressed, choosing not to wake his valet. He donned his coat and decided a brisk walk in the pre-dawn air would be just the thing to put him in a better humor. There were a few servants about on the main floor, but he knew it would be hours before the family rose for the day. He would have plenty of time for a walk before he would be missed by anyone. Wilton let him out the front door without comment, and he set off at a brisk pace in no particular direction.

He was feeling immensely better by the time he returned to the square. The slightly cool, damp air and the exercise had helped him decide that the mysteries of last night simply weren't his business. His niece and nephew were old and wise enough to be trusted to ask for help if they were in any real trouble, and their parents would likewise keep them safe, so there was really no reason for him to involve himself further. Allen would be leaving London soon; in fact, he was probably already on his way out of town, and there would be an end on it. Mystery or no mystery, there was absolutely no good reason for him to get involved.

He thought he'd convinced himself of this line of reasoning right up until the very moment he spotted Mr. Allen waiting outside their house, at which point his stomach flipped, his breath caught, and he named himself a fool.

When Allen spotted him in the pre-dawn light, he visibly started as well, then seemed to collect himself and bowed formally in James's direction.

"Good morning, my lord." His voice still sounded weak and uncertain as James returned the bow with a nod, approaching the younger man slowly.

"Good morning, Mr. Allen," James replied. "What can I do for you this fine morning?" He hoped he sounded more composed than he felt.

As the man was waiting outside their home when the sun had barely crested the horizon, James assumed his reasons were urgent enough that he would appreciate dispensing with the usual pleasantries.

"Please, my lord, I, that is." Allen took a breath. "Would it be possible to speak to Mr. Ashton for a moment, do you think? I know it's early for a call, but I only need a moment of his time, and then I will not trouble any of you further."

"I'm sorry, Mr. Allen, I fear my nephew will still be abed. Perhaps you can call back later," James answered honestly.

"Oh. I...." Kyle seemed shaken but rallied once more. "I... w-would it be possible for you to give him a message for me? I would not impose on you like this, but I truly must speak with him as soon as possible."

"Certainly, if you wish, though I'm sure he won't be kept from receiving or returning letters should you choose to send one," James suggested.

"Thank you, my lord, but I fear I haven't time for a letter, it's just...." Allen stopped again, and when he didn't continue, James decided to take pity on him.

"Very well. You may give me the message and I will be happy to see that Andrew receives it," James offered with an encouraging smile.

Allen, however, didn't seem to know how to proceed, because he simply stared at James for a few moments before swallowing and looking at his boots.

"Mr. Allen?" James coaxed.

The young man took a deep breath and, with flaming cheeks, said, "I fear I didn't realize, when we parted last night, that Andrew still had my purse in his keeping. I wouldn't have troubled any of you like this, but I fear it was all I had, and I am in need of it at the moment."

"Ah, I see," James responded. "Well, perhaps I can simplify the situation for all of us. If you would tell me how much Andrew was carrying for you, I can simply give it to you now and have my nephew return it to me when he wakes. The purse itself can be sent to you when you're settled. Would that be satisfactory?"

James doubted the young man was lying about the money, but even if he were, he looked so miserable that James wouldn't mind the loss of a small sum of money if it helped the poor man out and sent him on his way before James did something he'd regret.

"Oh, thank you, my lord. That would be more than generous of you." The look of gratitude in his eyes reaffirmed James's conviction that this was the proper course, even if it fueled a few less-than-noble thoughts in the process.

"How much was he carrying for you?" James prompted.

"Six guineas, my lord. Thank you, my lord," Allen said, looking embarrassed again.

"Very well," James said as he pulled out his purse and handed over the coins. "There you are. That should take care of it."

The exchange of monies between himself and a strange young man on the street in front of his sister's house might have set a few tongues wagging had it not been for the relative quiet of the early hour. James was thankful for the privacy, for both their sakes, but to be on the safe side, it would be best if he ended their exchange now.

"Good day to you, Mr. Allen," James said with a nod. But the young man's flinch let him know it had come out a little more harshly than he'd intended, so he added, "And please do find time to write to my nephew, when you can. He and my niece both seemed most anxious for your welfare and will worry if they do not hear from you."

"Oh, of course, my lord. Thank you, my lord," Allen replied hurriedly, then bowed again as James turned to make his way up the stairs.

He'd just entered the hall and leaned his back against the door when his niece came running down the main stair, all fluttering pink ribbons and white muslin.

"Oh, good morning, Uncle! Excuse me, Uncle!" she gasped as she made her way toward the back of the house.

"Good morning, Anna. Wait a moment, what's the rush?" James asked, pushing himself away from the door and reaching for her hand.

"Sorry, Uncle, I need to talk to Mott about something. It can't wait!" she said as she attempted to pull her hand from his.

"Anna, stop just one moment, young lady. Why is it so important for you to speak to your father's coachman?" He was getting swallowed into the mystery again, he was sure of it, and he was also sure he wasn't going to like it.

Anna bit her lip, then answered in a rush, "I went to talk to Andrew first thing when I woke. Andrew was supposed to look out for Mr. Allen last night. He was supposed to help him, and it's my fault that Mother and Father found out and Andrew got dragged back home. But at least Andrew could've made sure Mr. Allen had somewhere to stay before letting him go off alone in the carriage, and I just want to make sure he made it somewhere safe and he's going to be all right. And Mott can tell me where they let him off. So that's why I need to speak with him."

"Take a breath, sweet. All is well, I assure you. I just this moment finished speaking with Mr. Allen right outside this house. He seemed well enough. There's no reason for you to be so overwrought." James spoke calmingly while stroking his thumb over the back of her hand.

"Outside? Just now? Oh, thank heaven!" she cried before rushing around him and out the front door before he could react.

He caught up to her at the bottom of the stairs and followed her gaze to Allen's retreating back. The young man was almost to the corner when a tall blond man grabbed his arm and started dragging him across the street. In the dim light it was hard to see his face, but James was fairly certain it was Weir.

"Oh no!" Anna exclaimed, and she started to rush after them.

James managed to catch her arm before she'd gone more than a step. "Hold on, young lady. What do you think you're doing?"

"Uncle James, please, we have to help him! That man is going to hurt him again. I just know it. Please, please hurry!" she cried, trying to pull away and follow the two men as they disappeared down a side street.

"Stay here!" he commanded. "Promise me you won't move from this spot or neither one of us is going anywhere."

Her anxiety had infected him, and he was a bit startled when his heart lurched at the thought that Allen might be in danger. But no matter how strongly he wished to rush after him, his first responsibility was to his family, and he certainly wasn't going to allow his niece to be in any kind of danger, either.

"I promise! Just, please hurry, Uncle!" she pleaded.

"Go back inside," he ordered, before charging off down the street.

He caught up with them in a dark alley leading to the stables behind the houses. As he closed in on them, the taller man pushed Allen hard against the brick wall next to them and pinned him there by the shoulders.

"You little shit!" Weir hissed. "How dare you disappear on me like that? Obviously you didn't learn your lesson last night and you're in need of another. Did you actually think you could simply walk away from me? After all I've done for you? After all I've given you? Stupid, ungrateful little tart."

James's anger and concern quickly turned to confusion. *What the hell is going on?*

Weir was a *gentleman*, for God's sake. Though James had never liked the man, bullying a young man in an alley only a few yards away from the prying eyes and ears of the servants in the stables just didn't fit with anything he'd heard of him.

"It was embarrassingly easy to find you, you know," Weir continued, almost casually.

He was now holding Allen's wrists above his head in one hand while running the other down the front of his coat. "All I had to do was ask a footman if they'd seen you leave and who you'd left with. It took no time at all to find the home of your little friend, and lo and behold, there you were, right out in front of the house, just waiting for me. What did you offer the boy to get him to take you in, hmmm? Did you get on your knees for him? Did you let him ride you? He must not have been particularly satisfied with you since he cast you out before dawn. Not surprising."

As James listened in shocked disbelief at what he was hearing, he saw Allen's face fade from pale to completely white. James had heard enough. Money and connections or no, *this* man was no gentleman. His rage returned full force.

"Let him go, Weir!" James shouted down the alley as he walked toward them.

Weir whipped around, face set in fury, only to have his eyes widen in recognition.

"Lord Warren!" He recovered quickly, his scowl relaxing into a bland smile as he released Allen's wrists and bowed. "My apologies, my lord. I hadn't seen you there. I... oh goodness, I suppose this does look rather queer, doesn't it? I assure you, my lord, you need not have troubled yourself. This is simply a small misunderstanding between my young friend here and I. Isn't that right, Allen?" Weir hadn't stepped away from him, and Allen remained silent, his wide eyes darting between the two of them. The only reaction James could see were two spots of bright red that appeared on his white cheeks.

"I heard enough, Weir," James growled. "I say again. Let him go." Part of him hoped that Weir would defy him so he could give the man a good thrashing, but a more rational part of his mind feared, as angry as he was, that once he began, he might not be able to stop.

"Oh, of course, my lord, as I said, there's no call for any concern. We were simply having a small misunderstanding. We can of course discuss it some other time, as my lord wishes." Turning to Allen, he said, "We'll finish our little chat another time, my boy. Good day to you both."

Weir practically scurried past him out of the alley, bowing to James as he passed.

Wise choice, coward!

Allen remained frozen for a moment but for the heavy rise and fall of his chest, then straightened and dropped his eyes. He was still deathly pale, and James feared he might crumple to the ground at any moment, but he made no move toward him. The desire to hold him was swamping his senses again, and he feared if he got any closer he wouldn't be able to control himself. The lad was obviously mortified, and James wanted to spare him some dignity.

The silence stretched painfully as James fought for control and Allen stared determinedly at his boots. James wanted to offer words of comfort, but he knew that would only add to his mortification, so instead he said, "Mr. Allen, my niece was most concerned for your welfare and asked that I come to check on you. Would you do me the courtesy of accompanying me back to the house so that she may see I have discharged my commission?"

"Miss Ashton?" Allen asked dazedly.

"Yes. Please come." James gestured back the way he had come.

The young man pushed himself away from the wall and took two steps toward him before he started to crumple. James lurched forward, catching him under the arms and drawing him against his chest for support. He felt Allen stiffen in his arms a moment before melting against him. The move made James's heart pound in his chest and his arms spasm involuntarily, tightening his grip on the slender body, drawing him closer. This was most definitely a bad idea, but he couldn't help noticing how good Allen felt in his arms.

Allen kept his face buried against James's chest, so he felt rather than heard the sob that rocked the younger man's body. James's hand slid of its own accord into that silken black hair, cradling Allen's head against his chest, offering the comfort he'd longed to since the previous night. His heart ached for the man, and he raged inwardly at Weir.

To have his emotions so far out of his control was most upsetting, but he couldn't deny them any more than he could deny his body's reaction to the man in his arms.

Embarrassed, he shifted position a little before Allen felt the evidence of his regard and took a breath to master himself. They were still in an open alley and could be seen at any moment. The young man had just been accosted and probably worse the night before, and now here he was, holding him like a lover. He had to take control of the situation before things got out of hand and they became the objects of dangerous gossip.

Clenching his teeth, he pulled Allen away from his chest and held him at arm's length while the lad regained his balance.

When those beautiful, sad eyes met his, his resolve faltered, and he was on the verge of pulling him back into his arms when Allen seemed to rally, raising his head and saying, "I'm so terribly sorry, my lord, I didn't wish to be any more trouble to you. I should not have taken such liberties."

"Think nothing of it, Allen." James was proud his voice didn't shake. "My niece will be beside herself with worry by now. We should get back, if you feel well enough."

"Yes, of course. If you would just give me a moment, please," Allen responded. He straightened a little further, taking a deep breath, and James reluctantly released his arms. When he took a few steps and didn't appear on the brink of another collapse, James relaxed and stepped further away from him.

They headed back to the house side by side, James hanging back a little just in case he was needed. In his distress, Allen didn't seem to notice, which was perfectly satisfactory for James, as he was still trying to salvage both their dignities. He was not proud of his failure to control himself where this young man was concerned, and he needed to remind himself of who he was.

Anna hadn't gone inside as he had ordered, but he decided to let the matter drop. When she spotted them, she came running down the walk in a manner that would have her mother in fits. But, thank heaven for small favors, she stopped short of launching herself at them on the street.

"Kyle, I mean Mr. Allen, are you well?" She blushed.

"Yes, thank you, Miss Ashton, I'm quite well. I must apologize for any distress I may have caused. I had no wish to worry you," Kyle replied, and James was relieved that his voice sounded a little stronger.

He was proud of the man for his efforts, but his pale skin and slightly breathy reply gave lie to his words, and James wasn't surprised at the disbelieving frown that crossed his niece's face.

"Come, let us avoid creating any more of a spectacle for our neighbors and return to the house," James said, staring pointedly at his niece. At least she had the decency to blush. "I believe there is more we need to discuss; however, it can wait for more privacy." Without waiting for a response, he led the way back to the house and held the door for both Anna and Allen to enter.

After allowing a somewhat disgruntled Wilton to close the doors, James led them into the front parlor and gestured for Allen to take a seat on one of the chairs near the fireplace.

James was thankful Charlotte and William were still abed, as it would give him time to think before he had to explain himself to his sister. James bade Wilton to see that some tea and scones be brought for Anna and Allen and some coffee be brought for himself. Though his sister and her family hated coffee, they always kept a good supply in the kitchens for him, knowing that some mornings he could be quite unpleasant without it… and this was definitely going to be one of those mornings.

After Wilton left, James settled back into the chair opposite Allen's and closed his eyes, hoping the other two would take the hint and remain silent until the tea arrived. Anna had perched herself on the edge of a low settee between them. She looked distraught but thankfully said nothing.

So, what now, sir knight? You've rescued yon fair maiden from the evil villain, now what are you going to do with him? Don't answer that.

As James sat quietly with his eyes closed, Weir's words began to sink in, and he was finally able to make some sense of the events of the past several hours.

Weir and Allen must be lovers. He grimaced in distaste... and perhaps jealousy.

He couldn't imagine anyone choosing a cold fish like Weir for a companion. And while, under other circumstances, he would have been delighted to find that Allen shared his preferences, thinking of what else Weir had implied left him cold.

"Obviously you didn't learn your lesson last night," Weir had said.

So, something unpleasant happened between them at the ball. Weir did something to Allen.

His mind shied away from exactly what that might be; otherwise he might be tempted go back out to find Weir, for Allen's sake as well as for whatever harm witnessing it had done to his niece and nephew. At least he now had an answer as to why they were so reluctant to speak of Allen's troubles.

The rest of what Weir had implied regarding Allen's supposed payment for their help James knew to be utter nonsense. Firstly, the twins would never have asked for payment if they thought they were doing someone a good turn. They were too kind-hearted and had been brought up too well for that. And secondly, Andrew was most definitely *not* interested in young men in that manner. James would have known. He was sure of it. So the thought that such a thing would even occur to his nephew was preposterous.

The tea and coffee arrived, forcing him from his thoughts, and

Anna dismissed the servant and set about serving them like a proper little hostess. It struck him again how much she'd grown. He missed his little hoyden.

It was unfair of him to want to keep her a child forever. He knew that. But he couldn't help missing the little girl with dirt under her fingernails and twigs in her hair who would climb into his lap and cajole and wheedle until he read her a story or got down on the floor to play the part of her pony.

Her eyes met his over the service, and she answered his fond smile with one of her own, the twinkle in her eyes letting him know that perhaps the little girl wasn't so very long gone after all.

James was reluctant to start the inevitable conversation, even after they had refreshed themselves. Allen had gotten a little of his color back, but he still looked done-in. Perhaps it would be better if he gave the young man some time to rest and gather his wits. The sun had finally come up, and James hadn't missed that the clothes he was wearing were the same he had had on the night before, and looking far the worse for wear.

Where did he spend the night? he wondered, recalling his niece's concern from earlier.

"Well, I believe I can speak for all of us when I say we have had quite enough excitement for one morning. Don't you agree?" James said, forcing his tone to be light and bantering. "I would therefore like to propose a rest, for all of us, before we decide what is to be done about all of this. Mr. Allen, if you would be so good as to accept our hospitality, we will find you a room, a bath, and perhaps a fresh change of clothes for you to wear whilst yours are being cleaned. My nephew should have something to fit you."

Kyle's eyes widened, and he said, "Oh, no, thank you, my lord, but I couldn't possibly impose on you any further. You have already been so kind to me. I could not, in good conscience, ask any more of you."

James leaned forward and, in all earnestness, replied, "Mr. Allen, it is no trouble, we assure you. My niece and my nephew have named you 'friend' and as you are such, I won't hear of you leaving before you've had a good rest and a decent meal. You'll be able to see things much more clearly when you've slept and had a chance to recover from the trials of last night and this morning. Please, do us the honor of accepting our hospitality."

"Yes, please, Mr. Allen, don't go until we've had a chance to keep our promises to you. It will all work out. You'll see," Anna chimed in, her eyes pleading and intense, making James a little concerned at the possible strength of her feelings for the young man.

Allen seemed to want to refuse but thought better of it. "I... yes, all right, thank you, thank you so much, my lord, Miss Ashton. I cannot tell you how grateful I am to have met you all. I am humbled by your generosity," he said with an acutely embarrassed look on his face.

"We certainly can't have that, now can we?" James said, chuckling, some of his good humor returning in the wave of relief he felt at Allen's acceptance. "Let's get you settled and we'll have our chat when you come back down. Don't hurry on our account, though. Sleep as long as you like; we'll send someone to wake you if you aren't down by dinner."

James directed a footman to take Allen to a guest room and send up a bath. With that done, he left his niece to her own devices and made his way to his nephew's rooms.

Uncomfortable as the conversation would be, he needed to find out what the twins had witnessed the night before and whether Charlotte would need to be told. He dearly hoped not, but if there were delicate matters that needed to be explained to his niece, James would certainly not be the one doing it.

Gritting his teeth, James knocked on his nephew's door and said, "Andrew, may I come in?"

"Of course, Uncle, please," came the sleepy reply.

Andrew was sitting in his dressing gown at a table near the window of the small antechamber in his suite. James remembered his nephew had chosen these rooms specifically for the view to the garden below.

His nephew's valet was in the bedchamber arranging Andrew's clothes for the day, so James turned to speak with the man first.

"Young man?" he said. James couldn't remember the valet's

name. He'd only seen him once or twice since he'd been hired for Andrew.

"Timms, my lord," he said, bowing and coming forward anxiously.

"Timms. We have a guest in the green room, a Mr. Allen. He will need to borrow some nightclothes and a suit of evening clothes, as well as any other necessities you can think of, from Mr. Ashton. Will you please see to it and allow me and my nephew a few moments alone?" James instructed. Andrew raised his eyebrows but remained silent.

"Yes, my lord. Excuse me, my lord." Timms bowed, retreated to the bedchamber to gather the requested clothing, and closed the door.

"He's here?" Andrew asked after Timms had left.

"Yes, he's here, and we've had quite an eventful morning," James replied.

Taking the chair opposite his nephew, he waited for the sounds of the outer door and Timms's retreating footsteps before satisfying his nephew's curiosity. Starting with his conversation with Allen in front of the house and ending with Allen's acceptance of his offer of hospitality, he related the tale of the morning's events, leaving out only what Weir had said and the conclusions he had drawn as a result.

No need to fill in any holes in my nephew's education if it isn't absolutely necessary.

"What I would like to know now, nephew, is what *exactly* happened last evening and what it was you and your sister witnessed that led to you offer aid to this young man, whom you'd only just met," James continued.

"We didn't actually *see* anything, really," his nephew replied, much to James's relief. "Anna and I were just looking for a bit of quiet time together. So, just like old times, we went upstairs to some of the unused rooms at the back of the house, where we used to play with the Sutcliffes' children. We heard someone in the hall, and when we looked, it was Mr. Weir and Mr. Allen. They went into one of the other rooms, and we could hear them arguing. After a few minutes, Weir came out, told Mr. Allen to meet him downstairs, and left."

Here Andrew paused, and when it seemed he wasn't going to

continue, James prompted, "So what made you decide to interfere?"

Andrew's neck flushed crimson above the opening to his dressing gown, and he said, "Uh, well, it was the *way* Weir said it, and his clothes were in disarray. His trousers were…." Andrew swallowed and looked away, unable to complete the sentence and blushing furiously all the way up to his hairline.

Well, obviously my nephew has *learned a few things they don't teach at university.*

"I was still trying to decide whether we should leave or check on Mr. Allen when Anna pushed past me and entered the room, and then I *had* to follow," Andrew said, turning back to meet his uncle's gaze. "He was turned away from us, lying on his side, and he wasn't moving. We feared the worst, but when he heard us, he leapt up. He was shaking and pale, and his clothes were…."

James took pity on him. "I understand, Andrew, you don't have to go into details." In fact, it would be better for both of them if he didn't, as James's gut was already churning and a black fury was beginning to pulse through his veins again. *Weir, you filthy cur!* he fumed silently.

"Thank you," Andrew continued with a relieved sigh, seemingly unaware of the violence of his uncle's reaction. "Well, he looked so mortified, I thought perhaps we should excuse ourselves and leave him his dignity, but Anna wouldn't hear of it." He smiled ruefully. "I don't believe Anna truly understood what had happened. But he was so pale and obviously unwell that she wouldn't hear of leaving him alone."

When Andrew fell silent again, James took a moment to look away and compose himself. He had never in his life felt this level of protectiveness for anyone outside of his own family, and it confused and frightened him.

"So the three of you came up with a grand scheme to help him and off you went?" James finished for him, swallowing his discomfort.

"Almost," Andrew admitted. "Boodle's was my idea. Anna didn't think it was a good one, but he needed money, and he didn't want anyone else to know what had happened. He told us his father had disowned him because of Weir, and he had no other friends or family in town. There's an aunt at Bury St. Edmunds that he hoped might aid him if he could get enough to pay for the journey. It seemed like an excellent plan at the time," he finished defensively.

"One would have thought, with nineteen years of experience and a first-rate education, that you would have learned to never underestimate your mother's nose for mischief," James commented sardonically.

Andrew chuckled. "I suppose you're right, Uncle. If I ever get too high in the instep, all it takes is one word from Mother and I'm back in a skeleton suit with dirt on my nose." He laughed again, seeming to relax from his earlier discomfort.

"Yes, well, perhaps you're wiser than I thought." James chuckled. His own unease hadn't abated, but his nephew didn't need to know that. "Thank you for being honest with me, nephew. You and your sister were right to try to help, though there were perhaps better ways for you to have gone about it. I'll have a talk with Mr. Allen after he's rested and see if we can get this sorted out," James finished, and he stood to go.

"Uncle." Andrew stood with him and grabbed James's shoulder. "He really is a decent fellow. We had time to talk on our way to Boodle's, and I, I truly believe he's a good chap. He didn't deserve what happened to him, no matter what anyone says about... *that* sort. He seems a decent man to me, and I don't think who he chooses to... anyway, I don't think it should matter among friends," he finished lamely.

"I *do* understand, nephew, though I'm surprised to hear you say it. You have a good heart," James said, smiling fondly at his nephew.

"I don't know about all that, Uncle, but, to quote Voltaire, tolerance 'is the consequence of humanity. We are all formed in frailty and error; let us pardon reciprocally each other's folly—that is the first law of nature'," Andrew said as an embarrassed flush crept up his face. "Don't understand it at all myself, but it's the nineteenth century, for God's sake, modern ideals and all that."

"It seems you have been paying attention in school. I'm proud of you, Andrew. We'll talk again after dinner," James said, pulling Andrew into a brief hug before releasing him and heading out of the room. He needed to get to the privacy of his own rooms, *now*.

He was almost choking on the intensity of his emotions, and he needed quiet and solitude before he broke down and embarrassed himself in front of his nephew.

God, I need a drink, he thought as he entered his bedchamber. Thankfully, his own valet, Edwards, was nowhere to be seen. He needed to collect himself before anyone else set eyes on him.

Folding himself into a plush chair by his own set of windows overlooking the garden, he closed his eyes and leaned his aching head against the back. He was not ordinarily such an emotional man, and the strain of the morning made him feel very old indeed.

Yet another reason why I should never leave the country. His estate and his home were so peaceful, the rhythm of his life undisturbed with all this emotional upheaval.

It was time to sort through his churning emotions like the sensible man he was. He thought back to the last words he and his nephew had shared and smiled.

He wouldn't be able to explain to Andrew why his easy acceptance of Allen had meant so much to him. His own inclinations were simply not a subject he discussed with his family, or anyone, for that matter. There was no need. The possibility that he could be open about that part of himself with anyone in his family was something he'd never entertained.

He sometimes thought that Charlotte must have guessed, but they never spoke of it. He was always discreet, and his lack of bride and children made her son his heir, so, he supposed, she should have little reason to object, but it was not a risk he was willing to take.

Still, Andrew's words eased a tightness inside him he hadn't realized was there, and he couldn't keep a few wistful imaginings from playing across his mind, thoughts he hadn't entertained in over fifteen years.

There had been a time, long ago, when he had considered sharing his life with someone, before he had become *Lord* Warren. He'd fallen in love with a boy at school.

Jonathan. Blond, blue-eyed, angelic Jonathan.

They'd been friends for more than a year before they'd

discovered they shared more than that. They'd come together in a set of unused rooms at the back of the school one glorious afternoon shortly before the summer holiday. They hadn't known what they were doing, of course, but the innocence of their time together still held a special place in his memories, completely unsullied by anything that came after.

Jonathan had been his first and only love, and they had given themselves to each other in secret all that next year, declaring their love with words and deeds every chance they found. It had been a wonderful dream, but all dreams are destined to end, and, toward the end of that year, it had.

He remembered the day had been quite warm, and he and Jonathan had just returned from a long walk, among other things, in the woods when he was summoned to the dean's office. He'd been a little concerned at the summons, but still flushed with the excitement of a stolen tumble in the grass, he hadn't even considered that anything could so completely crush the joy he felt.

The letter informing him of his parents' deaths had caught him completely off-guard, like a blow to the gut, sending him to his knees in the dean's office, unable to breathe. It had taken him a long time to gather himself up and stumble off to his bed, and, once there, he hadn't been able to leave it for a day and a night. Even now, more than fifteen years later, the memory of that day had the power to make his stomach clench and his chest hurt.

He and his parents had always been close, closer than any of his friends would ever claim to be with their own families, including Jonathan. The depth of his grief had not been understood by anyone, not even the boy he loved. When the closeness he and his lover had shared could do nothing to ease his grief, he had withdrawn into himself and Jonathan had lashed out at the perceived rejection.

Their parting had been ugly and bitter. At the time, he had been so tangled in his own grief and guilt and fear that he hadn't even tried to make his lover understand.

His duty had been the lifeline he clung to during those first terrible months, and over time, he realized that that was where his future lay, not in the fantasy he and Jonathan had been playing out. The carefree, happy boy he'd been at school simply couldn't stand against the harsh reality of the world outside, and there would be no going back to a love that never could have lasted in the first place.

The slight ache those memories caused was as familiar to him now as breathing. It had dulled over the years, leaving only a small emptiness that he knew would never truly disappear.

Jonathan had written to him a few years after their parting, on the eve of his marriage to some Scottish heiress. He'd apologized for any misunderstandings they might have had and assured him that he now understood the weight of duty and honor. He had even gone so far as to ramble on, at some length, about the virtues of marriage in general, and his soon-to-be bride in particular, to the point where James had almost thrown the letter into the fire without finishing it.

Even now, he still wasn't sure whom Jonathan had been trying to convince. James supposed he had written the letter seeking some sort of closure to that time in his life, and perhaps he had wanted James to do the same. But the formal and stilted tone of the letter had only left James feeling cold and unhappy for both of them.

He'd never harbored any hopes that anything could ever happen between them again, but he would have been quite content to leave that door open and the dream in place for the rest of his days. There would never be anyone in his life again like that.

But *that* thought inevitably led him to the other reason he was hiding in his rooms: Mr. Kyle Allen, beautiful, bright, good-natured, and in need of his aid.

James sighed. He simply didn't have any energy left to deal with whatever he was feeling for the man. There wasn't any point, really. The poor young man had been through hell, and anything he might be feeling beyond concern was completely inappropriate… and impossible. He would do what he could for the lad, and that would be an end on it. Wistful imaginings aside, even if they'd met under better circumstances, he couldn't risk acting on his feelings for the same reasons he'd chosen to live his life as he had.

England had not changed, so neither could he.

Weir was another matter. He would have to think on what to do about the blackguard, and soon. In all conscience, he couldn't allow Weir to get away with what he'd done nor leave him free to do it to someone else, at least not and be able to live with himself.

But not right now, he supposed. He was too tired to come up with a plan that would punish Weir *without* causing a scandal. His fatigued brain could only come up with finding the man in a dark alley and pounding him into the ground. But unless he killed the man, that wouldn't be any kind of permanent solution. And, despite his thoughts from earlier, he wasn't a murderer, so that wouldn't do at all.

Pistols at dawn, perhaps? He chuckled wryly. Charlotte would kill him if Weir didn't.

Sleep and then a bath were what he needed now. His hands, his neck, and his head all ached from suppressed fury and other feelings. It was time he did something about it before he became an absolute *bear*.

Stretching, he rose and rang for Edwards. The man arrived in short order, and after helping him undress, with more than one disparaging look at the cravat James had tied for himself, Edwards left, taking the offending cravat and the rest of James's clothes with him. James left instructions for him to assure his sister that he was well but would not be joining them until the afternoon and to wake him with a bath in a few hours, then slid under the crisp linens of his bed and forced himself to fall asleep.

Chapter Five

KYLE sat on the edge of the large four-poster bed in a daze. He had been led to a lovely room decorated completely in shades of green: the walls, the furnishings, and counterpane were all in soft, calming greens. It was quite lovely, but he was hardly in any condition to appreciate it.

He had been brought a bath, and Ashton's valet, Timms, as he'd introduced himself, had brought him some of Ashton's clothes, instructing him to ring when he was ready to be dressed for dinner. Then, after Kyle had assured him he didn't need anything else, Timms had left him to his own devices, closing the door behind him.

Kyle was happy to be alone. As the son of a country curate, he'd never had a manservant to wait on him or help him dress before coming to London, and he was still uncomfortable with the idea. At home, they'd had only two or three servants in the house most of the time, and being in a house this grand made him feel small and shabby.

After he'd bathed and changed into the nightshirt and dressing gown, more servants had come to take away the bath and his soiled clothes, and now he was sitting numbly on the edge of the bed, feeling pale, hollow, and insubstantial.

A small part of his mind kept urging him to pull back the linens and surrender to sleep, but he couldn't seem to dredge up the strength to obey. He was almost too tired to sleep. He was numb all over except for a sharp ache he didn't want to think about. He'd had to suppress a yelp on entering the bath when the warm, soapy water had stung his abused body. And now, clean and dressed in Andrew's fine shirt, he couldn't seem to take that final step that would allow him to fall into oblivion.

Tears stung his eyes as the events of the past twelve hours began to play themselves out in his head again. He didn't want to think about it, but he still didn't have any answers, and it seemed his mind would continue to torture him until he did.

What did I do that was so wrong?

There must have been something awful that he missed for Victor to use him with such violence. One minute they'd been standing in the ballroom with Victor's friends; the next Victor was leading him up the stairs, away from the other guests. He'd been startled by Victor's strange behavior, but at the time, he'd just assumed that Victor had decided not to wait to give him a tongue-lashing.

Thinking back to the last few minutes in the ballroom, he had to admit he hadn't been paying much attention to the conversation. Perhaps there had been something said that made Victor even angrier with him than he already was. But that didn't make any sense. Kyle felt sure that if the conversation had had anything to do with him, he would have noticed. Even the words Victor had said as he'd forced Kyle over the back of the couch and torn into him hadn't made any sense. Though he had to admit, he'd stopped hearing them as soon as the shock of what was happening to him set in.

There was something about his friend Wells? And this morning he called me a tart.

Kyle shook his head. He didn't *want* to remember. He wanted to sink into blessed insubstantiality, a sweet grayness without memory or feeling, but the nightmare wouldn't let him go.

How could he have done this to me? He told me he loved me, that we belonged together and that he would take care of me. He was whining again, and the less forgiving part of his mind chose that moment to flare into life.

You were a weak fool! he railed silently at himself in a voice that sounded suspiciously like his father's. *You watched him change toward you day after day and you said nothing! You* did *nothing but cower and simper and grovel like a dog, hoping for a pat on the head, and when you didn't get it, you* still *did nothing!*

He couldn't even use their coupling as an excuse for the way he'd allowed himself to be treated. Victor hadn't shown much interest in Kyle's pleasure after their first few times together and had even become a bit rough with him since they'd been in London, though he'd never truly hurt him before. Kyle was so confused, sick and filled with self-loathing, he didn't know what to do.

Sleep, another voice said. *Just sleep. Perhaps you'll find this was all a dream, a horrible dream. You'll wake in your own room, back home in Atcham, and none of this will have ever happened.*

Dredging up what energy he had left, Kyle finally surrendered to the one voice in his head that promised peace, climbed under the crisp linens, and fell into blessed oblivion.

When he woke to the chiming of a small clock, it was three in the afternoon. He was not home in his own bed, it had not all been a dream, and he was still going to have to face the ugliness of his situation. The realization made him groan and roll out of the bed.

After ringing the bell for Timms, he went to the basin and ewer for a quick wash before the man arrived to help him dress. He felt stiff and uncoordinated, but at least he wasn't shaking anymore.

Ashton's clothes were a little too large for him, but not terribly, he decided as he checked his appearance in the glass. Timms had done an excellent job, and Kyle had thanked him profusely, though the man had seemed embarrassed with the praise.

At least I'll look *respectable when I face my rescuers and the rest of the family.*

Timms left after informing him that a footman waited outside to take him to the library, where Lord Warren waited for him.

Well, you've stalled long enough. Time to go down and face the mess you've created.

Kyle gathered himself together, took a deep breath, and joined the footman in the hall. As he followed the servant to the study, he could feel himself breaking into a sweat. He was dreading seeing the man again. It was bad enough that he had witnessed Kyle's humiliation in the alley, but then he'd flung himself at the man and wept on his chest. His shame knew no bounds, and now he had to try to look the man in the eye.

"I heard enough, Weir," Warren had said.

Kyle cringed in remembered shame. The things Victor had said were bad enough, but to know that Warren, of all the people in the world, had heard them was enough to make him want to bury himself in a hole and never crawl back out again.

What did the twins tell him? Kyle wondered with a twist of his gut. *How much does he know? And, more importantly, how am I ever going to face him knowing what he must at least suspect? He must think I'm the most pathetic wretch he's ever had the misfortune to meet.*

Kyle took another breath to steady his nerves, trying to find comfort in the fact that the lord had been nothing but kind to him. He had assured Kyle that he would help him and had even granted him hospitality in his sister's home. Even if he believed Kyle was unworthy, he had still taken pity on him.

Somehow that thought didn't bring him as much comfort as he would have liked. Pity was not something he wanted from that man. He desperately wanted his good opinion, though he couldn't have said why it mattered so much to him. He would probably never see the man again after today.

The footman knocked on a large oak door and opened it after a short bark of "Come" from the room beyond.

He found himself ushered into a small room lined from floor to ceiling with bookshelves, packed with handsomely bound volumes. The student in him was distracted for a moment reading titles and wondering at the number of books, until movement by the windows snapped him back to the moment.

Lord Warren was seated at an escritoire in front of a large bank of windows. He looked every bit the nobleman in tan trousers, a gold and brown striped silk waistcoat, and a rich brown wool coat. The colors were understated, but they suited him somehow, and the quality of the material was undeniable.

Sunlight streaming in the windows caught gold highlights in his thick brown hair, and, coupled with the smooth texture of the fine wool of his coat, Kyle was reminded of the warmth of the man's arms around him in the alley. He suddenly longed to bury his face in that coat, to feel that fine wool on his skin, thread his fingers through that hair and curl up in that warmth.

Dear God, what is the matter with me?

Here he was, in the worst tangle he had ever been in in his entire life, and he was fantasizing about throwing himself at the man who might be the only thing standing between him and ruin.

If he decided to cast you out into the street this moment, you would well deserve it! he berated himself. *You're here to swallow what little pride you have left and beg this man for his aid, not curl up in his lap!*

Biting his cheek and stepping forward, he bowed to the viscount and waited for him to speak.

EVERYTHING that James had planned to say to Allen fled from him the moment the young man entered the room. Rested and dressed for dinner in a combination of grays and greens, he looked even more beautiful than James had remembered. The pallor from earlier had left his cheeks, and the colors of his borrowed finery accentuated the beauty of his fair complexion and extraordinary green eyes.

Though he couldn't do it in truth, James was sorely tempted to send for Timms and shake his hand in gratitude for his selections. The man certainly knew what he was about.

Though perhaps I shouldn't be so grateful, as now I can't seem to remember my own name.

James stood as Allen bowed in greeting. Clearing his throat, he motioned Allen toward the chairs by the fireplace. Once the young man was seated, James asked if he would care for any refreshment.

"No, thank you, my lord, I fear I have no stomach for anything at present," Allen replied.

"I believe I can understand that. You've had quite a night," James said, seating himself in the chair opposite Allen, regretting the words the moment he saw the man wince.

Taking a breath and remembering why they were there, James said, "Well then, we are alone here, so, if it would not offend you too greatly, Mr. Allen, I would like to dispense with formality and talk candidly with you about your situation." James waited for Allen's nod, then continued. "Excellent. I fear, spending as much time in the country as I do, I have to ape the polish of my more fashionable peers when I'm in London, and it's damned tedious for me at times. If I can get away with it, I'm normally a plain-speaking man." He smiled, trying to put Allen at ease.

It must have worked, because Allen gave him a small smile in return and said, "As am I, to own the truth, my lord. As the son of a country curate, I fear I've been frightfully out of place in London."

"I'm sure that's not true, but whatever the case, I will give you leave to speak plainly, if you will do the same for me." Allen smiled again, and James could sense his gratitude. It left a warm feeling in his chest that he worked hard to ignore.

"So, back to the business at hand." James forced his mind back to the topic of their conversation. "I have spoken with my nephew, and he told me some of your troubles. At least, those I didn't witness myself this morning."

At those words, the smile fell from Allen's face, and his eyes dropped to his boots. James noticed the lad's hands shaking at his sides before they were clenched tightly into fists. He had every right to be afraid, James knew. He wasn't a peer and had no connections. If any of what he knew ended up in the wrong hands, the young man could go to prison or the pillory, at the very least. At the worst... well, he didn't want to think about that.

Again the intense desire to comfort and reassure the lad rushed through him, but there really was no way for him to give that comfort without endangering his own reputation, so instead he clenched his fists and pressed on.

"I am aware of your desire for secrecy, and I will honor that. Though Weir should be held accountable for his actions, I understand your reticence for the facts of the case to be made public, as getting the law involved in these matters could prove dangerous. You have my word that I shall not speak of what I know to anyone. I gather from my nephew that Mr. Weir was your only friend in London and that your father has disowned you. Is that correct?"

"Yes, my lord," Allen answered in a near-whisper as more of the color washed from his face.

James was on the verge of giving Kyle permission to call him by his given name, at least in private, when he stopped himself. That would be much too much familiarity, and Allen would wonder at it. Also, he wanted to hear his name on those lips a little too strongly for his own good. It would be best for both of them if he left things as they were.

So instead he asked, "You have an aunt in Suffolk that you believe may aid you, yes?"

"Yes, my lord. She is my father's sister, though they are not close. I have never met her, but I hope, if I can go to her and speak to her myself, that she will take pity on me and offer me aid. She's the only family I have that might even consider helping me, I think," Allen replied, looking up.

"No one else?" James asked. "What of your mother's family?"

"My mother is from Ireland, my lord, and she has never spoken much of her family there. I suppose my father doesn't approve of them. His eldest brother is Sir Edward Allen, Baron Barwick, a man of some distinction, and my father has always been very proud. I believe my uncle will have already received news from him, so I know I will find no welcome there. My only hope is that, because of their estrangement, my aunt won't have received any news of me and might be willing to see me."

"And what will you do if she refuses you?" James asked.

At that, Allen sighed and looked back at his boots. "I don't know, my lord," he whispered. That lost look from the night before had returned, and with it, James's protective feelings.

"I see," James responded as he rose and took the few steps to the fireplace, leaning his back against the mantle. He needed to put a little distance between them, as the desire to gather the other man into his arms was on him again.

Crossing his arms to keep from reaching out to Allen, he said, "That won't do, will it? I think perhaps you should send a letter to this aunt of yours before using your last farthing on a journey that may prove fruitless. You don't have to tell her everything, just that you have had a disagreement with your father and would like to visit her and speak with her directly regarding your prospects. Then, at least, you'll know if she will refuse to even see you before you've stranded yourself in the country."

"That would perhaps make more sense, my lord; however, I don't have anywhere to stay while I wait for her reply," Allen said, shaking his head.

"Do you think us so heartless that we would throw you out in the streets, Mr. Allen?" James said, raising his brow.

"Oh no, my lord, never that! But I could not possibly ask you to do any more for me than you have already done. You, my lord, and your whole family, have been more generous to me than I can ever possibly repay."

"Don't think on it. As I told you before, my nephew has named you his friend, and if you would permit me, I would do the same. So what kind of men would we be if we didn't offer aid to our friends when they were in need of it, hmm?" James waited for his words to sink in and was well rewarded when shocked and hopeful eyes met his own.

"I do not know what to say, my lord," Allen replied.

James smiled and turned to pace a few more steps away before turning back to him. He needed the added distance.

Clearing his throat and willing his body to behave itself, he said, "No need to say anything. And now that that is settled, the only problem I foresee with your awaiting your aunt's letter *here* is that Mr. Weir knows where you are. And while I should think he would not dare attempt to accost you again, given his behavior of the past two days, I cannot be certain of that. So this puts a bit of a difficulty before us."

"Oh no! I had not thought of that." Allen also stood and took a few agitated steps of his own. Looking at James, he said, "I would not think of putting any of your family in danger or at risk of a scandal, my lord. Yesterday I would have said he was not capable of any such thing, but after this morning, and last night, I... I suppose I don't know him at all." Allen's mouth twisted in a pained frown, and his eyes dropped again to the floor.

"Weir has a great many men fooled, Mr. Allen. There's no need to punish yourself for that," James said quietly, cursing Weir again for a scoundrel.

In that moment, James made up his mind what to do. His decision would most likely be the source of a good deal of discomfort for him over the next several days, but he couldn't stand seeing Allen so miserable a second longer.

I can control myself long enough to see this young man through his current trial. Then I'll simply have to come back to town and find Elias or someone else willing to let me plow them through a wall for several nights running.

Keeping a rueful smile off his lips, he said, "I believe I have a solution to our current situation, and I want you to hear me out before you say anything." James raised his brows in question, and Allen nodded warily.

"We are agreed that you should send a letter to your aunt and await her reply. We are also agreed that your staying here could prove problematic. So my solution is for you to quit London and accompany me to my estate in Suffolk until you receive word from your aunt." When Allen opened his mouth to interrupt, James raised his hand.

"You agreed to hear me out, remember." Allen closed his mouth again, and James continued, "I come to town late in the season for a reason, Mr. Allen, and any excuse to leave again for the quiet and comfort of my home is always welcome. Also, Kentwood Hall is perhaps fifteen miles from Bury St. Edmunds, so you would be a great deal nearer to your goal there than here. And last, but certainly not least, my niece and nephew often join me for a short holiday on my return to Kentwood, and I believe they would be most grateful for your company there. So you see, there's absolutely every reason for you to accept and no reason for you to refuse."

Allen remained silent after James had finished, hope and concern warring in his eyes. It appeared that hope won, because his eyes got suspiciously bright, and he chuckled weakly.

"I suppose I cannot refuse an offer like that, even if I should wish to," he said.

"No, you cannot," James answered, smiling in return.

But if you continue to smile at me like that, this is going to be a very long journey indeed.

KYLE'S head was still reeling from the events of the last few days as Lord Warren's coach finally won clear of the London streets and set a steady pace on the road to Suffolk.

After their rather unbelievable conversation in the study, Warren had gone to speak with Lord and Lady Ashton regarding his plan, and Kyle had been shown to the drawing room.

He still felt uncomfortable with accepting such generosity, but the truth of the matter was that he didn't have much choice. He couldn't go back to Victor. He didn't have enough money to travel to his aunt's and buy clothing enough so that he would be fit to be seen when he got there. And even if he had, Warren was right. If his aunt refused him, he might be stranded penniless in a strange town.

The twins were waiting for him in the drawing room, and his entire conversation with their uncle was dragged out of him in barely a minute's time. They seemed to think it was a brilliant plan and were, Kyle thought, genuinely pleased about the prospect of spending their holiday with him.

"I knew my uncle would fix everything. He is the best and most generous of men," Anna had said, smiling warmly. "I knew he wouldn't let anything bad happen to you."

Kyle had to agree with her. He'd never met anyone quite like Lord Warren and was quite certain he never would again. He hadn't known what to expect from the man when he'd entered the library that morning, but he certainly had never dared to hope that he would be met with such compassion and understanding.

He asked to call me his friend! he thought wonderingly.

Kyle knew he could be in prison right now with what Lord Warren knew of him, and the relief he felt at the man's acceptance of him had left him weak and on the verge of tears for nearly their entire interview. He never would have forgiven himself if he'd broken down in front of the man again, so he'd fought it with everything he had.

When Lord Warren and the twins' parents joined them shortly before dinner, Kyle had been relieved to find them as charming and unaffected as the rest of the family. Warren had promised to keep his secrets, so Kyle was fairly certain they knew nothing of his failings, but the mere fact that they could be so open and welcoming to a stranger in their home touched him deeply. In that moment, he felt he'd never met a better family and vowed silently that he would do everything in his power to pay them back for their kindness as soon as he could manage it.

Dinner had passed quickly, with the family making plans for their departure from town. He tried to say as little as possible, falling back on old habits to keep him from making himself look any more the bumpkin in front of his new friends.

During dinner he learned that Lord and Lady Ashton would not be accompanying their children to Warren's estate. They still had engagements in London. But he was assured that this was the case every year, so he need not feel responsible.

Though he didn't say why, Lord Warren had determined it best that they leave in two days' time, and as the twins were already engaged for a ball that evening, it was decided that Kyle and Lord Warren would travel together in his carriage and the twins would follow the next morning, in their own.

The next day, Ashton had accompanied him to Savile Row, where he'd been fitted for new clothes that would be sent on to Kentwood Hall for him. When Kyle had protested, he'd been assured that an accounting would be kept, and, when he was able, he could repay the viscount every penny, with interest, if he felt it necessary. Somewhat mollified, Kyle agreed, and upon returning to the townhouse, was given a few more of Andrew's clothes to wear until his could arrive.

Afterward, he had had another pleasant evening with the family, though, much to his disappointment, Lord Warren had not joined them, and the following morning, he and the small trunk he had been given were packed into the lord's carriage, and off they went.

Everything had happened so fast, Kyle hadn't even had a chance to think, but now, seated in the viscount's comfortable carriage, with Warren napping in the seat across from him, there were no more distractions to keep his thoughts at bay. They came tumbling over one another in his head, making him almost dizzy and a little sick as he gazed out the window at the passing countryside.

I had a good home, a decent education, decent prospects, and parents who, while perhaps not particularly loving or affectionate, were at least willing to do their duty and see me properly situated. And what did I do with it?

The thought of his parents reminded him of the warm and loving relationship he'd seen among the Ashtons, and he couldn't help but compare it to his own family. His mother had sometimes been affectionate with him, at least as a young boy, he remembered, but as he had grown, and more markedly, after the death of his elder brother George, it had become harder and harder to earn her affection.

He'd learned to play the pianoforte and sing Irish folk songs specifically because he knew it pleased her, and it had been one of the few ways to keep her attention. His father had allowed it because it meant he could also play for church services. The time he'd spent sitting next to his mother while she'd taught him to play had been the happiest of his life.

He'd never been allowed to associate with the village children because his father, in his pride, had thought them beneath him, so music had been his only real joy in an otherwise rather lonely childhood. George had died when Kyle was very young, so he hadn't ever really known his elder brother, though his parents had never failed to tell him about how wonderful George had been and how far Kyle was lacking in comparison.

Music was the only talent he had had that George hadn't, and so he'd clung to it like a lifeline. Victor had loved to hear him play and sing. It was one of the few things he could do that Victor *hadn't* found fault with.

Yes, pretty bird, you sang and sang without even knowing you'd been put in a cage. Kyle flinched at the turn of his thoughts.

The more Kyle thought about his months with Victor, the more disgusted he became with himself.

How could I have been so blind? How could I not have seen what was happening until it was too late? He'd been chipping away at me, little by little, until there wasn't anything left but the pretty shell he wanted on his arm. And I let him do it!

Kyle began to rub his temples, trying to ease the ache that had begun there. He had to think of something else or he'd go mad or start sobbing or pull his hair out, he didn't know which. Turning his head from the window, he looked over at his traveling companion. While the lord slept, Kyle had the perfect opportunity to look his fill without the man knowing he was doing it.

Much more pleasant to think about than Victor and my own folly.

James. He spoke the name in his mind, a thrill of guilt at the familiarity. The man exuded an air of strength and certitude even in his sleep. His head and broad shoulders were relaxed against the back of the seat, with his large hands clasped across his chest. Kyle was struck again with the memory of what it felt like to lean against that chest and feel those hands holding him close.

Shaking his head, he tried to change the direction of his thoughts yet again before they ventured any further into where they shouldn't. He still couldn't believe he was traveling with a viscount, in his carriage, as an invited guest to his estate. It was almost too fantastic. This handsome, kind, powerful man had rescued him from Victor, given him sanctuary, then offered him a place as a guest in his home after knowing him only a few hours. Coming after the betrayal of the night before, it was almost too much. Part of him was afraid to trust in his good fortune.

Just then, the subject of his thoughts grunted in his sleep and his head fell on his shoulder, a small smile curling his lips. Kyle's heart stuttered a little at the sweetness of it, and he longed to run his fingertips over that smile. The compulsion, and the tender feeling behind it, surprised him.

He'd never experienced this kind of feeling with Victor. Oh, he had bent like a reed under the storm of Victor's passion. He'd longed to please him, to garner his attention and approval, but he never remembered feeling any tenderness for him, not like this.

Don't be a fool, he scolded himself. *The man is helping you out of pity and a fondness for his nephew, and you're mooning over him like a lovesick girl. After you hear from your aunt, you'll probably never see the man again, and he'll be well rid of you.*

But the man *was* a pleasure to look at. Kyle could at least admit that to himself without guilt. So look at him he did. He just had to keep a tighter rein on his errant thoughts, that was all.

In time, the pleasant view and the rhythmic bouncing of the carriage eased the ache in his head and allowed him to relax and simply enjoy his journey in the well-appointed carriage. The heat of the day made him drowsy, and it wasn't long before his own head was nodding.

Somehow all will turn out right, he thought hopefully. *And I* will *figure out some way to repay all the kindnesses I have received. I* will!

Those were his last thoughts before he fell asleep.

JAMES was a bit too warm but as comfortable as one could be in a carriage bouncing over rutted roads. He'd been drowsing nearly since they'd climbed into the carriage that morning, just allowing himself to drift in semi-consciousness as they had passed through the city and out onto the road. He hadn't slept well the night before, and he knew he wasn't going to be pleasant company, so he decided to take advantage of the long hours in the carriage and relax, keeping his mind purposely blank.

He must have fallen asleep at some point, because it wasn't until he felt slightly cooler air on areas that had been almost uncomfortably warm before that he realized his waistcoat had been opened and pushed aside. Looking down in surprise, he found green eyes flecked with gold staring back at him from beneath a mop of short black curls. On his knees on the floorboards of the carriage, between James's spread thighs, Allen was busily unbuttoning his trousers.

"What...?" he said in confusion, trying to shake the cobwebs from his head.

"Shhhh," Allen said. "It's all right. Let me."

Stunned, James couldn't think of anything to say, and as he felt Allen's warm hand slide into his trousers and those long, elegant fingers wrap around his quickly hardening cock, any thought of speaking left him entirely.

A gentle tug from that hand pulled him free of his clothes, and he could feel the slight breeze from the window kiss the tip of his shaft. Before he could become used to the sensation, however, another warm hand joined the first, higher up, pulling down gently to expose his crown, and a warm wet tongue circled and dipped into his slit. Eyes never leaving James's, Kyle ran his tongue in an ever-widening circle around the crown of his cock, then dipped to tease the length of his shaft in lazy circles with the pointed tip.

James groaned, aching to feel that warm mouth surround him even in the summer heat, and bucked his hips to show his impatience with the teasing. Another time, he would have gladly held still and let the man torment him as long as possible, but he wanted this too much. He'd been fantasizing about this particular mouth since the first moment he'd laid eyes on Allen, and, knowing he wasn't going to last long, he wanted to be in it before he spent.

Allen took his not-so-subtle hint and cupped his tongue around James's shaft, sliding back up to the crown before pursing those sweet lips and pulling him inside that deliciously wet haven.

James groaned again as he felt himself slide all the way in and brush the back of Allen's throat before being pulled back to edge of those lips. As he watched, Allen set a steady rhythm with his hand and mouth, the occasional jostling of the carriage over ruts and bumps in the road creating a not-unpleasant counterpoint, but James still wanted more. Bracing one arm against the side of the carriage and threading the other into Allen's hair, he angled his hips further forward.

"Harder," he growled, hand clenching in Allen's damp black curls and knees braced on either side of his slim hips to steady him.

The suction and rhythm increased as Allen's eyes closed and his head dipped lower. James felt the pressure building in his bollocks, and his hand clenched tighter as he felt Allen brace himself against James's thighs and move his other hand lower to cup James's sac.

Oh God, yes! was all the thought he could manage as he teetered on the brink of release.

He was only a moment away from surrendering to that joyous end when a sharp horn blast split the air and he was startled awake. As he watched another carriage pass by, James shook himself fully awake, looked blearily around him, and realized several very depressing things at once: he was alone on his side of the carriage, he was still fully clothed, Allen was asleep across from him, and he was painfully erect and unsatisfied.

A dream. He scowled, then shifted uncomfortably in his seat, making sure the drape of his coat kept his condition hidden should Allen wake. *And I have hours ahead of me before I'll be able to find some privacy to take care of myself.*

He gritted his teeth. *Looks like a nap was not the best means of improving my temper.* James sighed and straightened in his seat, trying to find a more comfortable position. It was going to be a long day.

When Allen awoke a short time later, James hoped no evidence of his dream remained on his face or his person. The last thing he wanted was for the young man to be afraid he'd escaped the clutches of one scoundrel only to fall into those of another. James had known before he even proposed his plan that this was not going to be easy on him. But he'd be damned if his inability to control himself would make things any more difficult for Allen. Weir had done enough damage to the lad.

At least I have the satisfaction of knowing I did something on that score, he thought, recalling how he'd spent the day before their departure.

While Allen and his nephew had gone to the tailor's, James had taken the opportunity to pay a call on an old friend, Lord Robert Morton, sixth Earl of Harrow, a man of some influence and unimpeachable character who just happened to share some of the same interest in companions as he, though no one outside of a very small circle of friends knew of it. The earl's own wife and four children were no small proof against that.

He and Harrow had shared a brief liaison many years ago, when James had come to London, only a few short months after receiving that goodbye letter from Jonathan. He had been vulnerable and lonely and had come to town seeking distraction. The older man had taught him a great deal about discretion, as well as many other things, before the end of their affair. They had remained friends, and James always knew he would receive good counsel from the man, as well as help, if he needed it. So, unsure about what to do about Weir, James had sent a small note to his old friend and had been invited to call.

In short order, James had apprised his friend of the situation, though he'd left Allen's name and whereabouts out of it. And though Harrow had seemed surprised, he had assured James that he would keep his eyes and ears open regarding Weir. He had even gone so far as to promise he would discreetly hire a few runners to quietly check into the man's affairs.

When James had protested that that was going above and beyond, his friend had assured him that it was in all of their best interests that Weir be contained before he did or said anything that could not be hushed up. Weir had too many connections, skirting their own small circle a little too closely, to be allowed to be involved in a scandal of that magnitude. And, though their respective ranks would prevent any lasting harm from coming to either James or himself, they had other friends who might not be so fortunate. Harrow's philosophy had always been that you could never be too careful, and James couldn't fault his friend's reasoning.

After expressing his gratitude and spending the evening catching up over dinner, James had said his farewells and called for his hat and gloves.

"I will keep you apprised of anything the runners dig up," Harrow had assured him when the servant had gone to get his things. "And *do* let me know how things turn out with your young man."

"He is not *my* young man," he had replied, chuckling at the knowing smile on his friend's lips.

"Oh?" the earl had replied, smiling wider, then sobered. "You can't fool me, old friend. We've known each other a long time, and I have never seen the look on your face that I witnessed when you were speaking of this mystery man. It was good to see it. Whether you're fooling *yourself* in the matter or not, you cannot fool me."

"The lad has just been through hell, old friend. I will not take advantage of his vulnerability. And, as you well know, I never dally outside the confines of Madam Renard's. I will see him safe to his aunt's, and that will be an end on it, I assure you," James replied, still smiling at his friend's doubtful look.

"As you say, Warren, as you say," he had said, shaking James's hand and accompanying him to the door. "Until next time."

Bowing his farewell, James had headed home to see to the final preparations for their departure with a much lighter step.

He'll find something we can use against Weir if anyone can.

Now, with the object of their discourse sitting awake and silent across from him, James decided he needed to say something before things became uncomfortable.

"We should arrive at Chelmsford within the hour. We'll stop at an inn there for the night to rest the horses and resume the second leg our journey tomorrow morning. Ordinarily there would be a change of horses waiting for us but, as my return is a little earlier than expected, I didn't have time to have them sent. There's no harm in staying the night, though, and having a leisurely journey," James said.

Allen smiled and looked relieved enough that James thought he must be suffering from the same twinges in his bladder that James was beginning to feel, especially now that another part of his anatomy had stopped screaming at him.

"I'm glad, my lord. I'm afraid I'm not used to this much traveling. Before coming to London, the farthest I had been from home was to school in Shrewsbury," Allen admitted.

"And how did you like it?" James asked, wanting to keep the young man engaged and distracted from whatever thoughts brought that sad look to his eyes.

"The school? Oh, well enough, my lord, I suppose. It was situated near the river Severn, and when we weren't at our studies, most of the boys would spend time on the banks or in the boats. It's lovely country," Kyle said fondly.

"I'm sure, like most young men, you spent more time with your friends than at your studies," James prompted.

Kyle's face turned a little sad then, and James was sorry he'd said it. "I fear I didn't have many friends at school, my lord. I suppose I was never very good at making friends. Perhaps it comes from growing up without any brothers or sisters, I don't know. My elder brother George died when I was very young, and I was my parents' only other child."

"I'm sorry for your loss," James said for lack of anything else.

"Thank you, my lord. But as I said, I was very young, and I barely remember him. My father gave me his name after his passing."

"George?" James asked, confused.

"My given name is actually George Frederick Kyle Allen. My father is George. 'Kyle' was my mother's family name, and I believe my father only allowed it because I was the second son and to avoid a row with her. It was the name she had for me."

"I like it. It suits you," James admitted.

Allen smiled and blushed. "You may use it if you wish, my lord. Truthfully, I prefer it to Allen, though I suppose it is ungrateful of me to say so. 'Allen' reminds me of my father, and I look for him in the room every time someone calls me by it."

"Then, if you prefer it, that is what I will call you," he said, charmed at the hint of wit Kyle was displaying now that he'd relaxed a little. "Your mother's family is in Ireland?"

"I believe so, though I know little of them. I think perhaps my father felt my mother's family beneath him somehow. My mother never spoke of them. But I'm sure you don't want to hear about any of that," Kyle continued shyly.

"I wouldn't have asked if I hadn't, Kyle," James replied, smiling to soften the words. "We have another long carriage ride ahead of us tomorrow and a couple of days at Kentwood Hall after that before my niece and nephew arrive. If I am to do all the talking, I can promise you it will feel even longer." James was rewarded with a quiet chuckle and a sparkle in Kyle's eyes.

"Well then, my lord, as I cannot allow that to happen, how am I to entertain you?" Kyle asked, a teasing note entering his voice again.

Kyle's playful side surprised him and encouraged him to answer in kind, but he was most certainly *not* going to answer that question truthfully, so instead he said, "I would not be the one in need of entertainment, Kyle. I assure you. But tell me more about this school of yours. Did they teach you anything other than playing on riverbanks and the rowing of boats?"

And so their journey continued while they chatted companionably, lapsing into comfortable silences from time to time. Kyle spoke of his studies and time in Shrewsbury, and James answered questions about the lands they passed through as well as his estate and Kentwood Hall. The time passed quickly, and he found he understood how Andrew could have developed so deep a regard for Kyle in so short a time. He was bright and articulate, with a playful sense of humor that was most endearing. James couldn't help but come to like the young man more and more as their trip continued.

And if, once or twice, he was more fascinated with Kyle's mouth and hands than the words and gestures they produced, well, that couldn't be helped, really.

There was no real harm in *looking*, after all.

The night in Chelmsford passed without incident. They ate in the inn's dining hall and retired early to their rooms. James was still tired, and after sitting across from Kyle for most of the day, he needed to find some privacy to take care of a few personal matters. They left the following morning after a fine breakfast, and late in the afternoon, they reached his estate.

James watched Kyle's face as they came up the long drive to Kentwood Hall and was rewarded with the awe and pleasure he read in the young man's widened eyes and slightly open mouth.

James had always loved his home, a sprawling three-story redbrick Tudor surrounded by manicured lawns, gardens, and a revetted moat. When he was a child, the corner turrets and murky moat had formed the perfect stage for his mock battles and daring rescues. He had been the bane of the gardeners' existence with his jousting tournaments against the carefully trimmed bushes, to the point where they had given up on trying to shape them into animals of any kind.

"Do you approve, Kyle?" James asked, smiling as the carriage crossed the west bridge into the main courtyard.

"Oh yes, of course, my lord. It's magnificent!" Kyle said, with an artlessness that James had come to covet in their short time together, for it meant that Kyle was moved enough to forget proper reserve for a time and simply be himself.

"I'm glad. I am rather fond of it myself," James responded, his voice warming with pleasure. "Perhaps now you can see why I don't choose to leave it often, even with the siren song of London's many delights."

"Oh yes, my lord," he said again. "If I lived in such a place, I should think I would never want to leave it."

Nor would I want you to, James thought, then chided himself. Such thoughts were not going to do either of them any good. But it pleased him more than he wanted to admit that Kyle admired his home.

"Let's get you settled and rested, and afterwards I will give you a tour of the house and grounds. How does that sound?"

"That would be wonderful, my lord, thank you. But you don't need to entertain me if you have affairs to attend to. I wouldn't want to keep you," Kyle said, his reserve returning.

"As to that, I believe you will learn in time that, when I am at home, I rarely offer to do that which I do not wish to. I was not expected home for some few days yet, so I think my household can manage a few more hours without my interference. And I promise you, it will give me great pleasure to show you my home," James assured him with a smile.

Kyle relaxed a little and returned his smile, saying, "Then thank you, my lord, I would like that very much."

"Excellent," James said.

By then they had stopped in the large square courtyard, and several liveried footmen descended on the carriage. James stepped out once the door was opened for him, mounted the stairs to the main doors, and greeted Ellis, his butler, who stood at the head of a small crowd of servants.

"Good afternoon, Ellis. This is Mr. Allen; he will be staying with us for some few days. Will you show him to the green room and order baths drawn for him and myself?"

Ellis had been with his family for longer than James had been alive. When he had been left alone to manage the estate after his parents' funeral, Ellis had been a strong shoulder to lean on as well as a trusted advisor. He'd felt so unprepared for enormity of his responsibilities that he had depended on the man day and night for those first horrible months. Since that time, the distinction of rank had always been preserved between them, but he still thought of the man as a good friend and the best butler a man could ask for.

"Yes, my lord. Welcome home, my lord," Ellis said, a warm smile on his face. Any tension that James might still have felt from his time in London always seemed to fade whenever he was in the presence of that smile. Though Ellis was graying a bit at the temples and his face had more wrinkles every year, there always seemed to be some secret delight twinkling behind his eyes that never failed to lighten James's mood. He'd missed the old man.

"Thank you, Ellis. It's good to be home," he replied, giving him a warm smile in return and walking through the main doors into the hall.

Turning back to Kyle, he noticed a strange smile on the young man's face and asked, "Is there something amiss, Mr. Allen?"

The young man chuckled and shook his head. "No, my lord. It's just that this will be the second green room that you've sent me to."

"Perhaps because of your eyes," he murmured, then he decided he should quickly change the subject, as Kyle's cheeks flushed and his eyes widened.

Clearing his throat and casting a glance aside at Ellis, wondering if he'd noticed the exchange, he said, "Well then, Mr. Allen, I shall leave you in Ellis's capable hands. When you are rested and refreshed, ring the bell and someone will show you to the library. Then we may begin our tour." With a nod to Kyle, James allowed him to be taken up the main stairs by Ellis, followed by a footman with his trunk. He would take a few moments to peruse his letters before going upstairs himself. If he kept a decent distance between himself and his young guest, he might just make it through the next few days with his sanity intact.

Chapter Seven

AFTER the servants had come and gone with his bath, Kyle was too excited to lie down. Kentwood Hall was incredible. Kyle had been enchanted from the moment they passed the gatehouses and he'd gotten his first view of the house.

It has a moat, *for heaven's sake.*

He felt like he'd stepped into the pages of a novel, and he couldn't wait a moment longer to get on with the adventure.

After he rang the bell, a footman led him to the library, a large room lined floor to ceiling in bookshelves made of a wood so dark as to be almost black. A huge Persian carpet covered most of the floor in deep red tones, sprawling beneath heavy, dark, roughly carved wood furniture, all adding to the masculine and somewhat gothic feel of the room. Warren was seated in a tufted dark red velvet chair, staring into the fireplace with a large leather-bound book in his lap, looking every bit the brooding lord of his castle.

I have *been reading too many novels,* he thought, rolling his eyes.

Victor had introduced him to Mrs. Radcliffe's work when they first met in Shropshire, and Kyle had to confess that he had developed a voracious appetite for them. They were something his father would have never allowed in his house, and reading them had been a delicious sort of rebellion for him at the time.

As Kyle continued into the room, however, Warren looked up and smiled that warm smile that seemed to touch him everywhere at once, and the illusion was dispelled. This was no tortured, brooding villain, and his home was certainly no haunted ruin.

"You're down much earlier than I expected, Kyle. Was your room to your liking?" Lord Warren asked.

"Oh yes, thank you, my lord," Kyle answered. "My room is wonderful. I simply wasn't very tired and was eager to see the rest of the house." He bit his lip then, wishing he hadn't said that. He didn't want to seem too eager.

Always the little bumpkin. Victor's voice echoed inside his head. But Warren only smiled in pleasure at his eagerness. Victor would have laughed at him.

But Warren is not Victor. Victor is not here, and he won't be if you stop thinking about him!

Warren must have seen a change in his expression, for he asked, "Is everything all right, Kyle?"

He didn't seem convinced at Kyle's nod, but he continued anyway. "As we are here already, I suppose we can start your tour with the library, if that meets with your approval?" Again Kyle nodded, trying to bring a smile back to his face.

Warren stood and gestured about the room. "This room was a project begun by my grandfather, the third Viscount Sudbury, and in the intervening years, both my father and I have continued to add to it. If it weren't for my sister's influence, these would probably be the only improvements made to Kentwood in my lifetime. I fear I love the old place too much as it is to think about expanding drawing rooms and adding ballrooms and the like. As you've probably guessed, I don't entertain often unless my family is visiting."

Warren continued to detail some of the work that had been done, then took a moment to assure Kyle that he was welcome to read anything he chose before he glanced out the windows and said, "Well, perhaps we should move outdoors so you can get a feel for the place before the sun abandons us completely."

Warren led him through the hall, back down the stairs into the courtyard, and around the east wing of the house. Kyle couldn't help but notice the change in the man's manner after only a few hours in his home. He seemed so much more relaxed and happy than he had in London. Unfortunately for Kyle, the change in him only served to enhance his already undeniable appeal, and he was hard-pressed to keep his mind from wandering down avenues it should not be wandering.

As he was led through the flower gardens and across the sprawling lawns, Kyle also couldn't help but note the similarities between the lord and his home. It seemed to Kyle to be a living extension of the man. The open lawns, neatly laid gardens, and simply shaped trees and shrubs had an air of quiet elegance that reminded him of their lord. There was nothing overly ornate or garish, no riots of colors or fantastical shapes, just nature simply arranged and neatly kept. The size and grandeur of the house were a little intimidating, as was the man himself, but not in any calculated fashion. It was more an air of harnessed power and quiet confidence that drew Kyle at the same time that it made him feel completely out of his depth.

When Warren determined that the sun had gone too far below the horizon for Kyle to see properly, he led him back to the house to continue their tour indoors. He was shown through the great hall with its plastered walls, rich tapestries, and minstrel's gallery to a well-appointed dining room in the modern style with white-trimmed bright lemon walls, gleaming delicate furniture, and brocade-covered seat cushions. As they walked, it felt a little like traveling through time, as the styles changed sometimes drastically from room to room.

When Warren noticed Kyle's reaction to the mix of periods, he stopped his speech on the history of the house and chuckled. "I mentioned my sister's influence? Well…." He waved his hand around. "While there are some rooms I won't let her touch, I need to give in every once in a while, else I'll never hear the end of it."

Kyle smiled at his jesting tone and said, "It's wonderful, my lord," and he meant it. It had a character the pristine homes he'd seen in London lacked, a sense of history that drew him and made him wish for years to explore every nook and cranny.

Letting his pleasure show openly on his face, he turned to find the lord of the house staring at him with a very odd look. As Kyle watched, the older man took a single step toward him, then halted, opening his mouth, but before he could say whatever it was he was going to say, Ellis entered through the doors at the far end of the room.

"My lord, dinner is prepared. May I serve?" he asked.

With another somewhat breathless chuckle, Warren said, "Ellis, your timing is impeccable, as always. Well, Mr. Allen, as we are already in the dining room, are you prepared to dine?"

"Yes, my lord, I am quite prepared," Kyle said with a laugh of his own.

He wondered what had prompted the odd look on the other man's face and what he had been about to say, but it seemed the moment had passed, and he didn't want to let it interfere with his enjoyment of their banter. He knew he was perhaps being too familiar with Warren, teasing the way he was, but he couldn't seem to help himself.

From the moment they'd entered the Hall, Warren had gone out of his way to make Kyle feel welcome and relaxed, and he couldn't help but allow it to happen. The stress of his days in London and the worry about his situation were fading in a dream of fragrant gardens and tapestry-covered walls. He was losing himself in the pleasant fantasy of a kind, handsome lord in his charming red brick castle as if he belonged there.

He knew, deep down, that all too soon he would receive a reply to the letter he had sent before they left London, and the dream would be over. He also knew he'd done nothing to deserve this holiday. But for now, he would accept it and cherish it as the gift it was, knowing it would likely be a very long time before he would have another, and certainly none so grand as this.

As they ate, Warren told him more of the history of the house and the neighboring villages, and Kyle was content simply to let that deep voice wash over him. They ended the evening by returning to the library and drinking port over a game of billiards, which of course Kyle lost, as he had very little experience with the game. The light banter they'd exchanged throughout dinner continued over the table, and as Kyle sipped his way through a second glass of port, he was feeling quite warm and content.

When Warren sat down by the fireplace to finish his port, Kyle happily moved to join him. He was tired, and the drink wasn't helping, but he didn't want the evening to end, and he couldn't seem to bring himself to leave the other man's company just yet.

Warren seemed preoccupied as he sat and sipped at his glass, and after a few moments Kyle began to feel that perhaps he'd overstayed his welcome. He was about to excuse himself when the older man spoke.

"So, Kyle, now you've had a few days to rest and recover, what are your hopes for your future?" he asked without looking up from the glass he held.

"I, I don't know, my lord. I suppose it depends greatly on whether or not my aunt will see me. If she will, then… I suppose I will accept whatever position she is able to secure for me," Kyle replied, caught a little off guard with the weighty turn of the conversation.

"Is there nothing in particular that you hope for?" he asked, looking up and meeting Kyle's gaze with an intensity that set Kyle's heart pounding.

Kyle had to take a moment and swallow the rest of the contents in his glass to wet his suddenly parched mouth before he could answer.

"No, my lord. I… I've never really thought about it, to own the truth. Father intended me for the church, but I don't believe that will happen now," he said, feeling some of the shame begin to creep back on him. He had to look down at his lap and away from that intense gaze to gather what few wits he had left.

"I must confess, I never really wanted a career in the church," he continued, fidgeting nervously with the empty glass in his hand. "But now that I no longer have that choice, I don't know what kind of career I should wish for or would be particularly suited to."

"I see," the other man said quietly, and Kyle felt as if he'd failed some sort of test.

His stomach twisted as it had so many times with Victor and his father, and he looked up, dreading the look of disappointment he fully expected to see on Warren's face. When he read only sympathy and understanding in the other man's face, he was so surprised that all he could do was stare.

"I know the demands of duty and family as well as any, Kyle," Warren said quietly. "I am on the path set for me by my father, and my father's father before him, myself. I know what it's like to live knowing only one future has been ordained for you. I was simply curious to know, now that you've been freed from that path, what you would choose for yourself," he said with a small smile.

Kyle continued to stare at Warren for several long moments, and before he could think of a response, the older man frowned and rose suddenly, saying, "Perhaps it was presumptuous of me to ask. Forgive me. I will claim weariness as my only excuse for the lapse and bid you good night."

"Oh no, my lord, there was no offense, truly. I only wish I had been able to give a better answer," Kyle rushed to say in his confusion, not wanting Warren to be upset with him. He didn't know how the mood had changed so quickly from the jolly time they had been having, but he was sure somehow it was his fault.

"Well… I'm glad I did not offend you, Kyle, but I am indeed very tired, so I think it best we say good night. Until tomorrow," the lord replied, his frown easing back into a somewhat sad smile before he turned and headed for the door.

"I'm a little tired myself, my lord. So I think I will join you," Kyle said, following him out, still feeling a little uncertain.

They made their way up the main staircase together in silence and turned right to enter the west wing. After giving Kyle leave to make use of any of the rooms on the main floor he chose, Warren bid him good night again and continued down the hall.

Before closing his door, Kyle was a little startled to discover that Warren was entering a room on the opposite side of the hall, only a few doors down from his own. That he'd been put so close to the family rooms surprised him a little and helped ease the knot that had formed in his belly during their last conversation. The relief he felt, combined with the unusual amount of spirits he'd imbibed, allowed him to fall asleep not long after his head hit the pillows.

The next day dawned bright and sunny, and though he was a little parched and his head hurt, he couldn't help the thrill of anticipation he felt at spending another day in Warren's company. Yesterday had been wonderful despite the few times his host had seemed preoccupied and perhaps a little displeased with him, and Kyle vowed to be extra vigilant today and not say anything that might ruin their time together. The man's good opinion meant more to him with every moment they spent together, and he wanted everything to be perfect for however much longer he was allowed to stay.

If this was going to be his last dream before the prosaic reality of his new life, then he was going to enjoy it as much as he could. Warren seemed to have forgiven him for his lapse in London, so as long as he was careful, there would be no more embarrassing episodes to mar his time here.

After taking care of his ablutions, Kyle dressed and headed for the stairs. Ellis had offered him the services of a valet, but Kyle had declined. Victor had insisted on a valet to make sure Kyle was the picture of perfection at all times in London, and he didn't want to be reminded of Victor in this place. He had dressed himself for years at home, and he would be doing so again once he started his new life.

Best to remember old habits, he thought as he straightened his borrowed coat and headed for the stairs.

Warren was nowhere to be found when he reached the main floor, though Ellis found *him* before he'd gone more than a few steps into the hall. The man had preternatural abilities, Kyle was sure of it, and though they'd only exchanged a few words so far, Kyle had immediately taken a liking to the man.

Ellis was a middle-aged, slightly bowlegged man of about Kyle's height whose warm smile and sparkling blue-gray eyes hinted at some secret delight that the man was always laughing at. Though impeccably dressed, he didn't have the cold hauteur of many of the butlers Kyle had met in London, and, just like his lord, he'd seemed to go out of his way to make Kyle feel welcome from the very first moment.

Smiling, Kyle greeted the man and received a grin in return.

"Good morning, Mr. Allen. Would you care for some breakfast?" Ellis asked.

"Yes, thank you, Ellis. That would be wonderful," he replied. He was starving, and just the thought of breakfast made his dry mouth water. The food at dinner had been marvelous, and he couldn't wait to taste what the Hall's cook prepared for breakfast.

"Excellent. If you will follow me," Ellis said, leading the way to a room they hadn't reached on his tour last evening. "If you'll wait in the drawing room, I'll bring you a tray as soon as it is ready."

"Thank you, Ellis, that's very kind of you," Kyle replied, receiving another of those wonderful smiles in return.

After Ellis left, Kyle took a moment to look around and was delighted to learn that the drawing room doubled as the music room, and a large corner of it was taken up by a gleaming pianoforte. Kyle's fingers itched to try it out. It was a beautiful instrument, not as large as many he'd seen, but obviously of good quality and well maintained.

He went immediately to the shelf of music behind it and was leafing through a stack of sheets when Ellis returned with his breakfast. The smells coming from the tray were enough to distract him from his discovery, though he took the stack with him when he crossed to the small table where Ellis had placed the tray.

"Thank you, Ellis. This smells wonderful," Kyle said with enthusiasm.

Ellis smiled, and the lines around his eyes deepened. "Thank you, sir. My wife, Mrs. Ellis, is the cook and will be glad to hear your praise." He paused a moment, considering, then said, "Sir, I see your interest in the music. If I may ask, do you play?"

Kyle smiled shyly and said, "Yes, I learned to play when I was a boy, and it has been a passion of mine ever since. Do you think Lord Warren would mind if I made use of the pianoforte?"

"Oh no, sir, I think my lord would be most pleased to hear you play. He is quite fond of music, though he does not play himself, and the instrument is rarely used. Miss Ashton plays, but not often, when they're here. We had it serviced in anticipation of her arrival, so it should be in excellent sound for you." He paused again, then smiled and leaned in a little, saying quietly, "And, if you don't mind me saying, the staff wouldn't mind a bit of music livening up the old place, either."

"Is there anything the staff would like to hear in particular, Ellis?" Kyle asked with a grin of his own.

Kyle was flattered that the man felt comfortable enough around him already to speak so informally, and he wanted to encourage it if he could. The man and his lord seemed closer than master and servant, and Kyle had the feeling the older man held a special place in Warren's affections.

Ellis put his hand to his chin and seemed to think about it for a moment. "Well, I don't know much about fine music," he said, "but a country dance would do a good turn at livening up the place a bit." Then, seeming to remember himself, he straightened his shoulders and said, "Will there be anything else, sir?"

"No, Ellis, thank you. I'll see what I can find in here, " Kyle said, laying his palm on the stack of music. "I'll have to warm myself up with some slower tunes first, though, as it's been a little while since I last played."

"Very good, sir. Thank you, sir," he said, bowing himself out of the room.

By the time Kyle had finished his meal, he had selected several sheets of music from the stack, some he knew and some he'd like to learn. He sat down to the pianoforte and began playing "The Pricklie Bush," a song he'd learned long ago that was familiar enough that he wouldn't necessarily need the sheet music. It was a simple tune and perfect to warm up his hands. Relaxing into the familiar feel of the keys beneath his fingers, he lost himself in the music.

JAMES was enchanted the moment the first notes began echoing through the Hall. He'd spent the morning catching up on estate business and correspondence, avoiding his guest. Another day like the one they had had yesterday and he wouldn't be able to stop himself from pouncing on the man and ravishing him. He had had no idea of the effect having Kyle in his home would have on him. If he had, he never would have suggested he bring him here alone.

He was territorial about his home, he knew that, but he had no idea that that would extend to anyone within his home, and the feeling was hard to ignore. Seeing Kyle in *his* library, at *his* table, and walking *his* grounds had the word "mine" echoing in his head. Throughout the day, he was tortured with vivid images of throwing the young man over the nearest piece of furniture and claiming him, marking him in any way he could. The almost savage compulsion unsettled him no little amount, as he'd never thought himself that kind of man.

You've never brought a beautiful, sweet, and charming young man home with you before, either.

It seemed peace of mind would not be his again until Kyle left for his aunt's, so he'd hidden himself in his study, hoping the day would pass quickly and his niece and nephew would arrive, putting some much needed distance between the two of them.

But now, with music drifting through his halls, he found himself irresistibly drawn to the sound and made his way out of his office toward the drawing room. James watched for a time from the doorway so as not to break the spell Kyle seemed to have woven for himself. The young man's head was bowed over the keyboard, black curls falling across his forehead and his lower lip clasped between his teeth as his elegant fingers glided across the keys. James thought Kyle had never looked more beautiful, and he was content for the moment to just lean against the lintel and watch.

Besides, if I get any closer, he won't be able to continue playing, as I'll have him bent over the side of the damn thing.

Closing his eyes, James forced himself to stand still and just enjoy the music. Kyle seemed to be moving randomly through songs. Slow, mournful ballads were followed by lively dances and back with no obvious pattern, but all were played with remarkable skill and those bursts of emotion the young man so rarely showed.

Only when the music stopped did he open his eyes to find Kyle staring at him with an unreadable expression. While James wondered what was passing behind those amazing eyes of his, the silence stretched, and he decided he needed to break it, and soon.

He cleared his throat and said, "That was excellent, Kyle. If I had known you played so well, I would have brought you here *first* on our tour last evening."

Kyle blushed at the compliment, and James nearly groaned aloud as other ways to bring a flush to that face played across his mind. It was going to be another very long day. The more he found out about this young man, the more he liked him, and the harder it was to remember all the reasons he shouldn't do what he *really* wanted to do with him.

Taking another breath, he reminded himself his family would be arriving soon. He just hoped it would be soon enough to save his sanity.

"Thank you, my lord; it is a beautiful instrument. I don't know that I've ever played on one finer," Kyle said, bringing him out of his thoughts.

"It's good to see it in the hands of someone who truly appreciates it. I purchased it for my niece, but I don't believe she has the passion for playing that you seem to," James replied, not moving any closer. "Please don't let me interrupt you if you'd like to continue. I had thought we might go riding after I finished my business this morning. It appears to be a glorious day. But it can wait until later if you would prefer."

Now, why on earth did I just say that?

He could have simply left word with Ellis that he'd gone riding, and he would have had a painless gallop across the fields to clear his head. Instead, he'd allowed his desires to overcome his reason, and now the ride would most definitely *not* be painless.

"Oh no, my lord, I'd love to go riding," Kyle answered. "The music can always wait for this evening. Perhaps, if Miss Ashton isn't too tired after her journey, we can play a duet after dinner."

Kyle stood and straightened the sheets of music before moving toward him and the door, smiling in a manner James was certain would be the death of him. He turned before Kyle got too close and led the way toward the front hall.

Rather than wait for the horses to be brought 'round, he decided it would be a better idea to keep moving, so he continued out the main doors into the courtyard.

As he crossed the main bridge over the moat and walked along the drive toward the stables, he said over his shoulder, "As your clothes haven't arrived yet, we'll both just make do with what we have on, if that's all right with you?"

"Yes, thank you, my lord," Kyle answered as he caught up.

When the grooms brought out their horses, he introduced Kyle to his mount for the day, Guinevere, or Gwinny, and gave them a moment to get acquainted, trying very hard not to watch too closely as Kyle mounted.

"My niece and nephew name the foals, so we never know what we'll end up with any given year," he said, as much to distract himself as to entertain his guest, then mounted his own gelding, Percival, or Percy, and led the way out of the stable yard toward the open fields to the west of the main house.

When they'd cleared the lawn and reached the fields, he quickened their pace, and when Kyle seemed to have no trouble keeping up, he let Percy have his head. They galloped across the open fields, and James surrendered to the visceral pleasure of it for a time. All too soon, however, they approached his reserve, and he was forced to slow them to a trot.

When they reached the trees, they slowed again to a walk, and he led the way along a deer track he knew well, enjoying the shade and allowing the horses to cool off a bit. The heat wasn't as oppressive as it had been in London, but the sun was still quite strong, and the shade was a welcome relief.

As the track widened to a more heavily used path, James took the opportunity to drop back next to Kyle and let the horses walk abreast for a while. Kyle's cheeks were flushed from the ride, and his eyes were dancing in a way that James found irresistible. He'd never seen Kyle like this, so open and unguarded, and though he knew it was a bad idea to stay this close, he couldn't seem to help himself.

"Thank you, my lord," Kyle said, a little breathless. "It has been a very long time since I had the pleasure of a ride on so fine a horse."

"My pleasure, Kyle. You may take her out anytime you wish. The twins will probably want to go out first thing tomorrow after they've rested from their journey, so you will not lack for company whenever you wish to ride," he replied.

"I look forward to it. Your park is beautiful." Kyle smiled, and James caught his breath. His smile was wide and bright, untainted by worry or shame, reaching all the way to his eyes, and in that moment, James realized it was the first genuinely happy smile he'd ever seen on Kyle's face. It was dazzling.

"I'm glad you like it," he managed, shifting in his saddle and forcing himself to watch the scenery rather than his companion.

They continued on in silence for a time, the wood hushed and peaceful around them, and James let the serenity of the moment wash over him. With the only sounds the muffled clop of the horses' hooves and the occasional bird or insect, it felt like they'd left the rest of the world behind.

"Do Mr. and Miss Ashton visit you often?" Kyle asked, his almost-whisper breaking quietly into James's reverie.

"Not as often as I might wish," he replied just as quietly, surprising himself with the wistful tone in his voice. It seemed they were both affected by the spell the wood had woven around them.

What was it about Kyle that unsettled him so, that made him want to pour out feelings so long buried he didn't even remember they were there?

He understood his body's reactions. Kyle was beautiful, there was no escaping that, but he barely knew the young man. They'd spent little more than a few days in each other's company, yet he felt drawn to him so strongly he could barely contain himself.

"Do you have any other family?" Kyle asked him, and there was a certain wistfulness in his voice as well.

"No, none close, at any rate," he replied. "We have cousins across the length and breadth of England, of course, but my sister and her family are the only close relations I have left since our parents' deaths many years ago."

"Is it lonely for you here, when they're gone?" Kyle asked, and

James had to close his eyes on the wash of emotion that moved through him.

Kyle was so close that all he had to do was reach out and he could touch that cheek. He felt sure if he looked into Kyle's eyes right then, he'd see an answering loneliness mirrored there, for he could hear it in his voice.

James clenched his hands to keep himself from doing any such thing, and Kyle must have mistaken his reaction for anger or displeasure, because he halted Gwinny and said, "I, I'm so sorry. Forgive me, my lord. It was impertinent of me to ask such a question."

When he mastered himself enough to turn and look back at Kyle, James noted the stricken expression on his face and hastily replied, "You don't need to apologize, Kyle. I was simply uncertain how to answer, that is all."

Kyle's face relaxed a little as those lovely green eyes earnestly studied his face before dropping back to his saddle. His voice was a little shaky and his countenance grave as he said, "My lord, I... I just wanted to say again how grateful I am for all you've done for me. I never would have expected so much kindness and generosity from anyone I just met, and I want you to know that, though I don't deserve it, I will do all in my power to repay your kindnesses to me."

"Don't be silly, Kyle. We've only shared a little hospitality with you, and there should be no talk of you not being deserving of such a thing."

James was getting uncomfortable again. The spell the wood had woven around him was making him careless, and the earnestness of Kyle's gaze and his obvious vulnerability were making his arms ache to grab the younger man and reassure him.

He nudged his horse a little ahead to put some distance between them and said, "Come on. If we hurry, we can make the full circuit around the park before my niece and nephew arrive."

When he looked back, however, Kyle was biting his lip and his eyes were sparkling for a different reason.

That did it, he thought, groaning inwardly, and turned his horse around. *How can a man resist that lost puppy look?* James's chest tightened and his throat closed as he faced the younger man.

Pulling up beside Kyle so that their legs brushed, he managed to say, "Come on, Kyle. Everything will be all right. Trust me."

"I'm sorry, my lord, I don't mean to be such trouble. I've made such a mess of things, and I've been so foolish. I can't even fathom why any of you would want to help me. I'm such a coward. What you must think of me," he cried, lowering his head.

James didn't even stop to think about the folly of what he was doing this time. He simply reached out and cupped Kyle's chin gently in his palms. Holding Percy in place with his knees, he brushed at the tears trickling down Kyle's cheeks with his thumbs.

"Kyle," he said, his voice sounding thick even to his own ears. "I think very highly of you. I assure you. You are a wonderfully bright, charming, kind and talented young man. You have no reason to be ashamed of who you are. You're braver than you know. Don't let anyone ever tell you differently… or I'll be forced to thrash you for calling me a liar."

Kyle's tear-filled eyes met his, and for an eternity, he got lost in liquid emerald and gold. It took every ounce of his willpower to stop himself from letting his lips follow where his thumbs had gone, to force himself to let go of that lovely face, and settle back into his saddle.

"We're friends, are we not?" James continued, trying to slow his hammering heart and nudging Percy away. "You're just going to have to trust that your friends have enough discernment to know a good man when they meet one. Now come on, let's see if Gwinny and Percy have gotten their wind back, shall we?" James turned Percy around again and headed toward the track he knew would take them back toward the Hall.

Looking back over his shoulder, he was relieved to see that, after a moment's hesitation, Kyle nudged Gwinny into a canter to catch him up.

Dear God. Too close, much too close.

Touching Kyle again had been a mistake. Now his hands knew the feel of that cheek and the warmth of it still lingered in his palms.

The twins can't get here soon enough. Bloody Hell! He cursed himself as he urged his mount into another gallop once they'd cleared the trees.

He checked behind him to make sure Kyle was still following before heading toward the drive that would take them back to the Hall and nearly fainted with relief at the sight that met him when he turned onto the drive. Like a gift from heaven, the Ashtons' carriage was sitting outside the stables, and he could see his niece and nephew walking out the main doors of the Hall to meet him.

Oh, thank you, God.

"Uncle, Mr. Allen!" Anna called by way of a greeting, coming down the steps into the courtyard. "Glorious day for a ride. Sorry we came too late to join you."

Not as sorry as I am.

"We've been sitting in that blasted carriage for hours, sister. I hardly think sitting ahorse sounds particularly agreeable to me at the moment," Andrew put in, grinning and rubbing his rear end in demonstration as he followed his sister down the stairs.

"Brother!" Anna gasped, then she dropped all pretense and giggled. Looking at Kyle, she said, "It seems the country air agrees with you, Mr. Allen. Your color is so much better."

As the blush crept over Kyle's cheeks, James thought it best to change the subject. "When did you arrive?"

"Oh, only a quarter of an hour ago, Uncle," Andrew replied. "Mrs. Holt is in the drawing room, and we were just about to order tea when we heard you coming up the drive."

"Well then, by all means, let's all go in and catch up over tea," James said, almost giddy with relief.

At least now that the twins had arrived, he could make himself scarce and not have to worry about it being obvious he was avoiding his guest. His niece and nephew and Anna's chaperone, Mrs. Holt, would keep Kyle entertained while James could hide in his study and remind himself of all the reasons why he lived alone.

After greeting Mrs. Holt and sitting down to tea, they all chatted amiably about the twins' journey and the assembly they had attended before they left London. He caught Kyle looking at him strangely once or twice during the conversation, but other than that, the time passed easily enough.

When he considered he'd stayed long enough to be polite, he stood and excused himself, giving estate business as the reason. He retreated to his study at what would have been a run, if he didn't have his dignity to preserve.

Thirty-four years old and you're running away like a child. How pathetic. You need to get hold of yourself, man! Just a few more days and he'll be on his way and life will settle back into customary quietude.

If he truly expected the thought to bring him comfort, he was disappointed.

Chapter Eight

KYLE was in misery. For the entirety of his ride back to the Hall, he had been desperately trying to come up with some way to salvage Warren's opinion of him after his outburst. He'd almost dredged up the courage to broach the subject again when he saw the twins' carriage and his spirits fell even further. Glad as he was to see them, he could have wished for a few more hours alone with Warren to try to salvage his dignity and bring back the comfortable intimacy he and the older man had begun.

Before I shamed myself in front of him again.

Because he had no choice, he did his best to hide his discomposure and followed everyone else into the drawing room, joining in the conversation as best he could.

As everyone sat down to tea, he tried to make polite conversation, but he couldn't help sneaking looks at Warren, hoping to see some hint as to what the man was thinking.

When Warren stood and left not long after they finished their tea, Kyle was afraid he had his answer and could barely hide his shame and disappointment. The twins continued to chat as if nothing was amiss, and he kept up his part of the conversation, though his mind was far away.

He couldn't help returning to the ride with James over and over in his head, trying to understand what had happened, hoping he could think of a way to win back Warren's good opinion.

It had felt so glorious to set Gwinny free and race across the fields. He'd felt like he was flying, moving so fast that nothing but joy would ever be able to catch him. When they'd slowed to take the sun-dappled track through the woods, it had been so peaceful and idyllic that he'd been overwhelmed with gratitude to be given such a lovely afternoon. He'd felt completely happy and at peace right up until the moment he'd opened his mouth and ruined everything, breaking down like a child in front of the last man on earth he ever wanted to see his shame… *again.*

He didn't understand it. There had been no warning. He hadn't been prepared for it. The sudden flood of pain and shame caught him off-guard and spilled out of his eyes before he could do anything to stop it, and knowing that Warren had seen it only made it worse.

He'd been fighting desperately to stem the tide and preserve what little dignity he had left when he'd felt those strong hands cradle his face and that deep, reassuring voice envelop him. Looking up in shock, he'd fallen into those caring brown eyes and forgotten everything else.

He'd barely heard a word that the man had said to him, only his tone, gentle and reassuring. When the hands on his face had brushed away his tears, something had clenched tight in his belly, and when those eyes had continued to stare into his, warmth had pooled lower still. Oh, how he'd wanted those hands to keep touching him.

I must be going mad, he couldn't help thinking now.

There was simply no other excuse for the riot of emotions he'd been experiencing over the past few days. He was bouncing between misery and desire, need and shame, so rapidly it was making his head spin. His body and his heart were betraying him, and he couldn't seem to stop them any more than he could take back what had happened to him. He wished desperately that he had someone to talk to about everything that he was feeling.

But there is no one, he realized. *I have to rely on myself now.*

He couldn't even confide in his new friends because his feelings for their uncle were most of his difficulties.

Oh Aunt, please write soon, he pleaded silently. *I need to leave here before I ruin the best thing that's happened to me in so very long, before I make another stupid mistake. If I do anything to taint the friendship I've found with this family, I'll never forgive myself.*

He had to be strong. He had to take control of himself before he did something unforgivable. He took a deep breath and tried to still his thoughts.

It's just the shock of everything happening all at once, he tried to console himself. *My life was so quiet before I met Victor. I had everything planned out for me on a staid and predictable path, and now I simply don't know what to do with myself, that's all.*

"…isn't that right, Mr. Allen?" Anna said, pulling him out of his thoughts.

"I'm sorry, Miss Ashton, I didn't hear you," Kyle replied, chagrined.

"I know you didn't," she said, laughing. "I said I thought that purple hair was quite the fashion for a young girl, just to see if you were listening. Are you feeling ill?" she asked, sobering.

"Oh no, I am well. I fear I have a lot on my mind these days, what with everything that has happened," he replied, trying to be as truthful as he could with his new friends.

"Would you like to talk about it?" she asked.

"Or would you like a distraction?" Ashton offered, shooting his sister a quelling look.

"A distraction would be wonderful," he said, grateful to Andrew for giving him an out.

"How about a game of Ombre or Whist, if Mrs. Holt will join us?" Andrew suggested over Anna's pout.

"Or how about we sing a few songs?" she shot back at him. "I noticed that some of the music has been pulled out. That must have been you, Mr. Allen, for I know my uncle wouldn't have done it. Do you play?" Anna asked cheerfully over Andrew's eye roll.

"Yes, Miss Ashton. I do indeed play. In fact, I promised your uncle a duet after dinner if you were feeling up to it. Shall we practice?" Kyle replied, feeling better by the moment. The twins' playful bickering was helping his mood considerably.

While Kyle and Anna sat down to practice playing and singing together on the pianoforte, Ashton sighed and pulled out a deck of cards to practice shuffling and dealing the way he'd seen some of the true cardsharps do in London.

Mrs. Holt soon excused herself to visit with Mrs. Ellis, an old school friend of hers and the real reason for her willingness to act as Anna's chaperone, at least according to Anna. An hour or so after she left, they all took a long walk out in the gardens before retiring to their rooms before dinner.

Some of Kyle's new clothes were ready by the time the twins left London, so they had brought the box with them when they traveled to Suffolk. He now had a new suit, his own dressing gown, a nightshirt, and two more linen shirts and trousers.

Anxious to try on his new finery, Kyle quickly bathed and changed for dinner. The black jacket and green and black flocked satin waistcoat were perhaps a little formal for their quiet country dinner, but they were all he had for now, and he had to admit he liked how he looked in them. He was being a little vain and he knew it, but part of him hoped the lord of the house would like how he looked as well.

"It seems Meyer did his usual best, Allen, you look quite sharp," Ashton said as Kyle joined the family on their way to the dining room. Ellis had just called them to dinner when Kyle reached the bottom of the main stairs.

"Thank you, Ashton, I believe he did. I'm well pleased with the fit, and now I cannot wait for the rest of the order to arrive," Kyle said, smiling in response. "I'm very grateful to you for the loan of your clothes, but it's nice to have my own again."

"Think nothing of it, Allen. I understand how you feel," Ashton said, waving a dismissive hand before offering his arm to his sister and leading her to the dining room.

Anna, for once, was completely silent, and Kyle was surprised at it. When he smiled and made her a bow, she merely blushed and bobbed a small curtsy before allowing her brother to lead her away.

Kyle looked at Warren for a moment before continuing on to the dining room himself, hoping for a smile or a word of approbation, but he was sadly disappointed. The lord of the house was as conspicuously silent as his niece this evening and barely looked at him as he followed them. Kyle tried to swallow around the lump in his throat and felt like a fool for his earlier vanity over his new clothes.

Mrs. Holt was waiting for them in the dining room, and after Anna seemed to rally from her earlier shyness, the two ladies managed to keep conversation continuous and light despite the fact that two of the men at the table did little to help.

As the evening progressed and Warren said less and less, hardly looking in his direction, Kyle became more and more convinced that he had indeed offended the man. He ate very little, as the realization soured his stomach, and he couldn't wait for the meal to end. His earlier resolve to show some fortitude and fix whatever he had done was being swamped by self-doubt.

He regrets bringing me here. I know it. Perhaps Victor was right, I really can't do anything right, he thought with an accompanying pain in his chest.

As the meal ended, Mrs. Holt excused herself and bid them good night, and Kyle nearly ran for the drawing room and the pianoforte. His one solace as a child and the only means of keeping his mother's attention called to him with all the promise of comfort it always had.

Warren had said he enjoyed Kyle's playing. At this point, he was desperate for anything that might erase his shame from the afternoon and make the lord of the house smile and joke with him again.

Anna joined him on the bench, and they began the duet they had practiced earlier. After that, Anna played and sang a few songs while Kyle turned the pages, casting furtive glances at the two other men as they sat talking quietly by the fireplace, but Warren never once looked in his direction unless it was to applaud his niece's efforts.

Kyle took over after her, but instead of playing one of the melodies he'd selected from the stack of sheets, he chose to play some of the old Irish melodies he had learned for his mother. Getting lost in the comfort of bittersweet memories of his childhood while singing the familiar tunes, he hoped to ease some of his shame and humiliation and soothe his nerves.

He'd just finished "Cliffs of Doneen," his mother's favorite, when he heard Anna speak close to his ear.

"Oh, Mr. Allen, that was lovely," Anna said, and her eyes were suspiciously bright in the lamplight.

Kyle looked up after the last notes had faded and smiled at her. "Thank you, Miss Ashton. The songs were some of my mother's favorites. It has been a long while since I played them."

He couldn't help another glance at the two by the fire, and this time he found Warren gazing intently at him, an unreadable expression on his face. Their eyes met, and Kyle wished with all his heart that he could know what the older man was thinking. Suddenly, Warren looked away, breaking their gaze, and stood, leaving Kyle feeling bereft.

Appearing to address no one in particular, he said, "Well, it has been a long day for me, and I believe I will retire for the evening. Please don't let me stop you young people from enjoying yourselves, though. I will bid you good night."

Kyle and Ashton stood, nodding good night to him as Anna said, "Good night, Uncle. I believe it's been a long day for me as well, so I think I will say good night to you all also."

When they had left, Ashton offered Kyle a glass of port, and Kyle decided that that would be a wonderful idea. The object of his obsessive thoughts had gone to bed, and there was little else he could do but wait until morning to try and win the man's favor again. He also needed something to calm his nerves and help him sleep tonight.

While they drank, he and Ashton talked about nothing in particular. Ashton bragged of his exploits at the card tables, and Kyle joked that he would have to witness that for himself. As they talked, Kyle was reminded of how much he really liked Ashton. His feelings for his new friend weren't nearly as confusing as they were for his uncle, and he hoped very much that they could remain friends once he began his new life.

Well into their third glass of port, Ashton grimaced suddenly and said, "I wanted to tell you something, but I wasn't sure how exactly to do it. I don't have my sister's talent for this sort of thing, so I'll be blunt, if I may?"

When Kyle nodded warily, he said, "I saw Weir at the assembly we attended before we left London. He had the ruddy cheek to ask me about you when he caught me alone, and, when I wouldn't answer, he gave me a message for you. I thought perhaps I wouldn't tell you, but I decided you really ought to know and it was not my place to keep it from you. He told me to tell you that he did not consider your debts to him discharged and that he would find a way to collect and soon."

Ashton paused for a moment and waited, but when Kyle didn't say anything, he leaned in with concerned eyes and said, "Allen? Are you all right?"

Kyle shook himself out of the panic Ashton's word put him in and cleared his throat, managing to croak, "Yes, thank you, Ashton, I am well. I suppose I should have expected that he wouldn't let go so easily. I had hoped he would but never really believed it."

"If you would not consider it impertinent of me, may I ask of what debts he speaks? Is there aught we could do to pay him off so he'll leave you alone?"

Now Kyle felt himself blush, though the rest of him remained cold. Clearing his throat again, he said, "No, Ashton. I, um, I don't believe he means money." Noting Andrew's blush of embarrassment, he said quickly, "Thank you for giving me the message. You were right to do so. I'm so sorry to have caused your family so much trouble. I never wanted to be such a burden."

"Don't trouble yourself over it, Allen. You know my sister and I are quite fond of you, and our uncle now as well. We will do what we can to help you. Everyone deserves a good turn now and again, and next time around, you can return the favor," Ashton said, smiling.

"I will do everything in my power to make sure I do just that. Thank you again," Kyle said earnestly over the lump in his throat. "But now I believe I should go to bed myself. It has been a long day, and I look forward to spending tomorrow with you and your sister, so I had better get my rest."

Andrew still looked concerned, but he only said, "I look forward to it too. Good night, Allen."

"Good night," Kyle replied, heading for his rooms before his knees wouldn't carry him anymore.

He hadn't realized the dream he'd been floating in at Kentwood was quite so fragile. After the upsets of the afternoon and Warren's distant behavior that evening, all it took was one mention of Victor, and the fantasy had shattered into a thousand tiny little pieces. He'd been a fool to think he could escape so easily, and he hadn't drunk nearly enough port to give him a peaceful night's sleep.

YET again, James couldn't sleep. If he kept on like this, he'd fall off his horse or end up facedown in his soup at dinner.

Perhaps some brandy to ease the way. He donned his dressing gown and went to the library in search of it.

After his third glass of brandy, however, he was beginning to believe that nothing would stop the thoughts in his head from their merry dance.

He'd managed to find a measure of peace this afternoon by immersing himself in boring estate affairs and more letter writing, to the point where he'd felt much better collected when he'd gone to join the others for dinner.

Then Kyle had descended the stairs in his new finery, and James's pitiful illusion of calm had fallen apart in seconds. The man had looked even more strikingly beautiful than ever, and after the closeness they'd shared in the woods, he was finding it extremely difficult to think of anything other than touching him again.

So he'd done his best to keep his distance and remained quiet throughout the meal, lest he give away his feelings to his family and his guests. He'd managed to maintain his composure throughout the evening until Kyle had begun singing in that achingly beautiful tenor. At that point, he had lost what little control he had and fled the room as quickly as he could.

Bloody hell! he swore, not for the first time that night. *My will, my reason, and my sanity all seem to have abandoned me the moment I met the man. What happened to my perfectly content and comfortable life?*

Sighing, he put back the last of the brandy in his glass, picked up the bottle, and rose to head back to his rooms.

If I'm going to drink myself to sleep, I'd best be in my bed when I do it.

He was in the hall, headed for his bedchamber, when he heard a frightened cry come from Kyle's room. Foxed as he was, he didn't even stop to think about what he was doing, he just pushed open the door and rushed right in.

There was enough light from the nearly full moon outside to see Kyle's thrashing form in the bed, and as he hurried to the bedside, Kyle cried out, "NO!" and flung out his arms.

James caught one arm in mid-swing before it could connect with his head or the bedpost and gently held it, saying, "Kyle, wake up! Come on, now, it's just a dream, you're safe, wake up now."

Kyle started, pulling his arm out of James's grasp and gasping.

Kyle's eyes looked dazed for a moment; then they cleared, and he said, "Oh God, I, I'm so sorry, I…." He shuddered, then seemed to come fully awake. "Just a dream. It was just a dream."

"Yes, Kyle, it was just a dream. You're at Kentwood, among friends. You're safe," James reassured both of them while his heartbeat slowed to something approaching normal.

Jumping back from the bedside, he walked swiftly toward the open door and said, "I heard you cry out from the hall. I apologize for the intrusion. I'll give you your privacy and let you get some rest."

James had almost made it to the door before Kyle made any response, and when he did, he knew he was sunk. Kyle let out a strangled sob, turned his head away, and whispered, "Forgive me, my lord. I'm so ashamed… falling apart twice in one day." Another sob was cut short, but James could see the younger man's shoulders trembling even in the shadows.

Groaning inwardly, he closed the door and made his way back to the bed. He couldn't have stopped himself sitting down and gathering Kyle into his arms any more than he could have stopped the moon from rising that night. He felt the man in his arms resist only for a moment before turning and burying his face in James's shoulder. Wrapping one arm more tightly around Kyle's back, James set down the brandy bottle and threaded his fingers into Kyle's hair, cupping his skull and supporting him against his shoulder.

They sat like that for several long minutes as James listened to Kyle take sobbing breaths until he couldn't take it anymore. He had to do something before he broke down and wept himself.

His hands moved, seemingly of their own accord, to cup Kyle's face, and he pressed his lips to the top of Kyle's head, raining light kisses on those soft black curls. He continued to press kisses down the line of his forehead and along his arched eyebrows, punctuating each soft kiss with reassuring nonsense.

"It's all right, sweet…. No one can hurt you here…. You're safe with me, beautiful boy…. You're all right." If he had been clear-headed and in the full light of day, he'd probably have been appalled at what was coming out of his mouth, but right then, in the moonlight, it was so easy to give in to temptation.

His kisses dropped to wet eyelashes and tear-stained cheeks, and all the while he continued his murmured reassurances. When Kyle moved his face higher in James's grasp, it seemed only natural for their lips to meet. Kyle's soft, trembling lips, salty with his tears, brushed James's once, twice, and a third time before Kyle let out a strangled moan.

He felt Kyle's hands fist in his dressing gown and his mouth open, drawing James's mouth into an almost desperate kiss. Startled, James would have pulled back, but Kyle's grip on his gown tightened, and his kiss became fierce. He felt himself twisted and pressed back against the head of the bed as Kyle leaned his entire body into that kiss, pulling back only long enough to catch short, sobbing breaths before pushing back into James's mouth again.

The young man's fierceness set him on fire, sudden and unexpected as it was, and soon he was kissing him back just as desperately. He wasn't sure how he'd lost control of the situation, but at the moment, he was enjoying it too much to care. Some small part of his mind assured him that, when dawn came and the brandy was gone from his blood, he was going to be a very sorry man, but at the moment, that voice could barely be heard over the pounding in his ears.

Kyle continued to kiss him ravenously, his tongue sweeping every corner of his mouth, before pulling back and sucking hard on his lips. When James felt Kyle's knee press between his thighs, he opened immediately to accommodate it. Kyle's nightshirt rode up his thighs, bunching around his hips, and James's hand connected with the smooth, warm skin of his thigh when it dropped to steady him. He could feel the heat and straining of Kyle's erection through the folds of their clothing, and he groaned into Kyle's mouth as a fresh wave of need flooded his body.

Kyle was still trembling all over as he began moving against James's thigh, though whether from his nightmare or need, James couldn't tell. Kyle's thighs squeezed his almost painfully as he thrust his cock over and over against it, whimpering and mewling against James's mouth. As the thrusts became more desperate, Kyle's teeth clamped down painfully on James's lower lip, and he tasted blood. James grunted at the pain but made no attempt to move as Kyle held on while pumping himself to climax against James's thigh.

Just as he was beginning to feel the pressure build in his own body, his lip was released, and he heard Kyle let out a small cry. The young man's body went rigid, then collapsed against his chest, panting and boneless, and James took that moment to let his own head fall back against the headboard and catch his breath.

He didn't even have time to think about what had just happened before Kyle started sobbing, "I'm sorry, I'm sorry, I'm so sorry" in between ragged breaths and started shaking again, trying to pull away.

James tightened his arms around the younger man's body, not letting him escape, and said, "Don't, sweet. It's all right. Everything will be all right. Calm yourself."

He didn't know if Kyle heard what he said or simply obeyed the needs of his body, but it was only a few moments before the trembling stopped and his breathing slowed. He held on for a while longer before he realized that Kyle had fallen asleep.

Gathering the young man up as carefully as he could, James eased out from beneath him and settled him back under the bed linens. He crept to the door on shaking legs and closed it with a small click behind him.

He only made it a few steps away from the door before his knees threatened mutiny, forcing him to lean his back against the wall and close his eyes. His head was spinning, his lip was throbbing, and his cock was screaming in protest. Kyle's thigh had been stroking him with every thrust of his hips, and now he was being made painfully aware that he had not found release before Kyle had found his own.

He supposed he should be grateful that Kyle had fallen asleep. He didn't know what he would have allowed to happen if Kyle hadn't, but his body was not quite so pleased with the circumstance.

Taking a deep breath to steady himself, he pushed away from the wall and walked the last few feet to his bedchamber, then swore to himself when he realized he'd put his brandy down in Kyle's room. He was in no condition to navigate his way back to the study to find a substitute, and he was certainly not going back in that room.

Damnation! I suppose it serves me right.

Closing the door to his rooms and grumbling uncharitable thoughts to himself about beautiful young men, grown men who should know better, and the unfairness of the world in general, he removed his dressing gown and climbed into his empty bed.

Hiking his own nightshirt up, he grabbed hold of his still throbbing shaft to give himself some cold comfort so he might fall asleep sometime before dawn. Leaning back into the pillows, he allowed more pleasant thoughts to push past his guilt and pique: the silken feel of Kyle's short curls, the salt-sweet taste of his lips, the smell of soap and sweat mixed with the scent of Kyle's spend. Running his tongue over the spot on his lip where Kyle had bitten him, he began to stroke himself in earnest.

This wouldn't take long. He could already feel the pressure building in his bollocks and coiling in his belly as thoughts of those firm, lean thighs squeezing and riding his own slid over him. He could still feel the warmth of that sweet body pressed against his and the surprising strength of those elegant hands clutching at him.

It took only a single sweep of his thumb across his slit before his release rushed over him, spilling out over his hands and onto his thighs and belly. Stifling his own cry, he rode the waves of intense pleasure, stroking until there was nothing left of him.

After cleaning himself with a damp flannel, he lay back against his pillows, giving in to post-climactic lethargy. His mind was already trying to reassert itself as guilt tried to push its way back to the surface, but his body won the fight for the second time that night, and he slipped into a deep, dreamless sleep.

Tomorrow. He'd tear into himself tomorrow. He was just too tired to do it now.

Chapter Nine

KYLE woke with his head set for cracking, his eyes puffy, his mouth dry, and his nightshirt stuck to his body in a most uncomfortable fashion. It only took a moment before his memory returned, and with it a rush of shame.

Oh God, he moaned inwardly. *What have I done?*

He'd gone to bed with his stomach in knots after Ashton's news. Thoughts of Victor had warred with memories of his ride with Warren. Fear had meshed with shame and desire, leaving him sick. He must have fallen asleep at some point, because he remembered dreaming of phantom footsteps following him through foggy streets, and, no matter how hard he ran, they kept getting closer.

Phantom hands had grabbed him, and Victor's voice had whispered in his ear, *"You're mine. You'll never be anything more. You're nothing without me."*

He'd tried to fight, to kick and scream, but the voice and the hands wouldn't let go of him. Then he'd heard another voice, calling his name, telling him everything would be all right, and he had woken to find that beautiful man looking at him with nothing but care and concern. It had proved to be too much.

He'd tried to hold back the shameful outburst long enough for Warren to leave him, but it was too late. The best he could do was turn his head and clench his jaw over the tears that threatened so Warren wouldn't see his weakness. But instead of leaving him alone, strong arms had pulled him against a warm, broad chest, and that wonderful voice had offered him all the comfort and protection he could ever want.

Then what did you do, you bloody fool? he castigated himself. *You threw yourself at him and rutted against him without so much as a "by your leave."*

He remembered the man's grunt of surprise when he'd shoved him back against the bed and claimed his mouth, but at the time, he'd been so wrapped up in his own need that it hadn't even registered. Warren's arms had felt so good around him, and when he had kissed his brow and his cheeks, it had set a fire in Kyle that he'd never felt before. At that moment, he'd wanted that man more than he'd ever wanted anything in his life.

He'd thought Warren was kissing him back when it was happening, but now he wasn't so sure. Going over and over it in his head, Kyle realized the man hadn't done anything but hang on while Kyle rubbed himself to completion on his thigh.

Did I shock him into immobility, or did he desire me too? And even if he wanted it, what did I do for him but rut against him and fall asleep?

Awash in a new rush of shame and confusion, Kyle groaned and put his head in his hands.

I wonder where forcing yourself on your host ranks on the list of social faux pas, he thought without humor. *And will he simply throw me out, or will he thrash me first?*

Opening his eyes, he decided he wouldn't be able to fix anything by lying in bed all day, so he pulled back the linens and stood up. What he would do now, he didn't know.

The man he'd left his home for and allowed to take over his life had betrayed and hurt him and was still somewhere wishing him harm. The man who had taken him in and shown him nothing but kindness, generosity, and tenderness was probably even now preparing to send him away, and all of it was his own damn fault.

No hope for it. He sighed. *I promised myself I would take responsibility for my own life, so I suppose there's no time like the present. Perhaps someday I'll learn my lesson and be able to control myself... if I manage to live so long.*

After washing and dressing in the clothes he'd been wearing the night he'd met Ashton and his sister, Kyle descended the stairs to the main hall and inquired after the lord of the house from a footman. The lord was "in his study and not to be disturbed," but Kyle wasn't sure he'd have the nerve to talk to him if he waited much longer. He couldn't bear the thought of sharing breakfast with the twins without knowing what was to become of him, and he very much doubted he'd be able to keep anything down even if he tried. So, taking what courage he had in both hands, he made his way down the hall to the large oak door that Warren had told him was his private study and knocked.

"What?" was the growled response.

Not a good sign. He winced, swallowing at the lump in his throat.

"My lord, it's Mr. Allen. I would beg a moment of your time to speak with you privately," he said, proud that his voice didn't shake.

There was a long pause, during which Kyle was afraid he would be refused, then a reluctant, "Come."

Kyle opened the heavy door into a small room containing only a desk, two chairs, and bookshelves filled with leather-bound ledgers. Warren was seated behind the desk with a forbidding frown on his face, and Kyle almost lost his nerve and bolted for the door.

Clenching his hands into white-knuckled fists at his sides, he took the last painful steps into the room and closed the door behind him.

"Well?" James said. It appeared as if one-word sentences were all Kyle was going to be getting from him today.

Kyle bit his lip, squared his shoulders, took a deep breath, and began the speech he'd been preparing since he woke. "My lord, I apologize for the intrusion, but I felt I could not wait to speak with you. I know I have no right to ask anything of you at this point, but I beg you to allow me the opportunity to apologize for last night. I am utterly ashamed of the way I behaved. I take full responsibility for the appalling manner in which I acted, and I will accept any punishment you see fit to mete out. I realize you will not want me in your home after what I have done,"—here he faltered, and his voice cracked—

"and I only beg that you not share the whole of the story with Mr. and Miss Ashton."

Warren held up a hand when he paused for breath, and Kyle fell silent.

The other man then closed his eyes and brought both hands up to his face, dragging them down it before opening his eyes again and saying, "Mr. Allen, you weren't the only man in that room last night. If you recall, I was there also, and despite your very noble efforts to take all the blame, I am no innocent maid."

When Kyle looked up in surprise, he smiled rather sourly and continued. "You also seem to have failed to notice that I am more than fifteen years your elder and at least a half a foot taller and broader than you. All of which means that there would be very little you would be able to force me to do if I were not willing."

Kyle's jaw had dropped during James's speech, but he couldn't seem to think of anything to say.

"As for casting you out of my house, I don't think that will be necessary. As long as we come to an understanding about what happened and vow that it will not happen again, I will not speak of it," he continued.

Kyle latched onto some of his words like a lifeline. "But if I didn't force you, then...?"

"No, enough. We will not discuss last night any further," James interrupted, as he stood and rang for a servant. "You are still my guest, and you will remain here while you wait for your letter from your aunt. We will forget that anything else ever happened, and there's an end on it."

Before Kyle could respond, there was a knock, and Ellis entered, saying, "Yes, my lord?"

Warren's scowl turned to a look of surprise when he saw who was at the door. "Ellis, I thought you had business in the village this morning."

"I did, my lord, but seeing as how his lordship ordered that he not be disturbed in so very *firm* a manner this morning, it was requested of me, by the other members of the staff, that I let my business wait so that I could be near should you require anything," Ellis replied, keeping a straight face, though that twinkle that Kyle liked so much was lurking in his gray eyes.

Warren's eyes narrowed at the veiled reproof, but he continued, "Mr. Allen is in need of breakfast, Ellis. Please take him to the drawing room and see that he gets it. Also, I have business in the village myself today, and I won't be back before dinner. Please inform Mrs. Holt and my niece and nephew not to expect me, if you would." Nodding to Kyle, he said, "Good morning, Mr. Allen."

Kyle had been the recipient of enough pointed dismissals in his life to know there was no use in arguing, especially not in front of Ellis, so he said, "Good morning, my lord," and bowed his retreat, preceding Ellis into the hall. He needed the time to think, in any case.

That had to be, without doubt, the strangest conversation he'd ever had. He'd gone in fearing the worst only to be gruffly informed that he wasn't the only one at fault and ordered to remain as a guest of the house.

He supposed he should simply be grateful that he wasn't being shown the door with a boot in his backside, or in the arms of the magistrate, but all he could think of was what else Warren had said.

Could he have wanted it too?

Kyle thought back to their encounter, to the feel of his arms, the smell of his skin and sound of his voice.

He called me "beautiful boy," he remembered suddenly.

He also remembered, now that the pulse of his own need wasn't making him blind to anything else, that, when he'd collapsed against Warren's chest, he'd felt the man's own arousal beneath his hip before sleep had claimed him.

He was hard. He wanted me! Kyle realized wonderingly, the knowledge making him flush with a mixture of pleasure and fear.

He was still trying to sort through his feelings when the twins arrived, joining him for breakfast. He tried to rein in his emotions as much as he could before anything showed on his face. Andrew would attribute any discomposure to his news about Victor, but Anna would probably ask questions, and he wasn't in any condition to answer her.

As Kyle was trying to figure a polite way to excuse himself without drawing their concern, Ellis arrived carrying a letter for him, and all other thoughts fled from his head.

It was the letter he had been waiting for, the one from his aunt that would decide his future. The twins looked at him with equal parts excitement and concern as he excused himself to read it in private. Not sure where to go, he made his way outside to the gardens, and with shaking hands, he broke the plain wax seal and sat down on a small bench to read it.

There wasn't much to read. There were the usual formal greetings, a declaration of concern regarding the difficulty he found himself in, hints that youth and possible character flaws on his part were the root cause of those difficulties, and an invitation to visit as soon as possible so that they might discuss his plight and prospects.

Well, it's better than I feared. At least she's willing to see me.

He reread the letter to make sure that he hadn't missed anything, and his heart sank as he realized something.

She sounds just like Father.

At that disheartening thought, he folded the letter and straightened his shoulders before going to find the twins. They would be waiting for his news and concerned if he took too long.

As if I needed anything more to think about today, he thought as he rubbed at his still lingering headache.

He made his way back inside and found the twins waiting where he'd left them. He quickly told them what the letter contained, and they congratulated him and assured him that all would turn out well.

After pretending more enthusiasm than he felt, he asked if they thought their uncle would mind if he borrowed a horse to ride to Bury St. Edmunds, and they assured him that it would be no trouble. Ashton even offered for Kyle to take Gwinny, if he wanted.

"She's my horse, really," he said. "She was a birthday present, and my uncle keeps her here for my visits. You're welcome to borrow her."

He thanked Ashton for his kindness and decided that he would wait until the morrow before going to visit his aunt. He had too many things on his mind to make the trip that day.

And someone I need to speak with again, privately, before I go.

He was probably making another mistake, but no matter what Warren had said, Kyle couldn't leave things as they were. It would haunt him for the rest of his days if he didn't make some kind of peace with the man.

The rest of the day went much as the day before. Kyle resolved to let himself be distracted by the twins, hoping that the calm he had felt before would return. Warren wouldn't be back until the evening, and he couldn't do anything about his feelings until the man returned, so he might as well do his best to fill the time and show his appreciation to the twins for their hospitality.

They played a little music, then took pity on Ashton and spent some time at cards. The three of them went on an afternoon ride, then retired to bathe and dress for dinner. Despite his resolve, he couldn't help but feel the loss of Warren's company, and his absence made Kyle fully realize how much he'd come to like the man's company… more than like.

After dinner, Kyle excused himself and bid the twins good night, using his journey on the morrow as his excuse for retiring early.

"I fear I may also leave before you wake in the morning, so I will say my farewells now," he said. "I am unsure if I will stay the night or not, as I have no idea what to expect from my aunt, so please don't wait dinner on me. If I return tomorrow night, I will dine before I come."

Turning to leave, he stopped and turned back to them. "I must thank you again for your generosity. You have no idea how much you have given me in the few short days I have known you."

Anna looked for a moment like she would cry, but she simply cleared her throat and said, "Your friendship is the only gratitude we require, Mr. Allen. We are very pleased to know you. Safe journey to you."

"Thank you, Miss Ashton. I will tell you all on my return. Good night."

He took a moment to request brandy be brought to his room

before making his way up the stairs. He purposely kept his mind blank as the footman brought in the tray and left, closing the door behind him. After removing his coat and cravat, Kyle poured himself a drink and then another before settling back in the room's overstuffed chair to think.

Start with the least confusing and work from there, he ordered himself.

There was the business with his aunt. *No choices or decisions to make there.*

He didn't know what to expect from her, but it seemed like she was willing to entertain the idea of helping him. He would have to graciously accept whatever help she offered, and if all went well, he might have a means of securing his future in a few short days.

And that should make me happy, right?

But somehow it didn't, and he knew why. The prospect of leaving Kentwood, of leaving the *lord* of Kentwood and rejoining the real world, left him cold. He knew he had to leave. There was no place for him here. But despite the emotional turmoil he'd been in, every fiber of his being ached to stay right where he was, with the man he had come to care for so deeply in such a short time.

Inevitably, his mind wandered back to the man who had dominated his thoughts for days, despite his efforts to the contrary.

"You weren't the only man in that room," Warren had said.

And then, *"There would be very little you would be able to force me to do if I were not willing."*

He had *been kissing me back. He must have, otherwise he would have denied any part in what happened.*

No one could make a man like Lord Warren do anything he didn't want to.

Unlike me....

Unfortunately, *that* thought made his stomach flip for another, less pleasant, reason. Had it only been a few days since he had been brutalized by the man he thought he loved?

No. He had to be honest with himself now or never. It wasn't true. There hadn't been love. There'd only been lust and a cowardly need for someone to free him from the life that had been chosen for him. A life he didn't want. He'd let Victor sweep him up and carry him away because he'd been too selfish to do his duty to his family and too much of a coward to tell them so himself.

He shook his head, finishing his second glass of brandy. He *had* been weak. He *had* been cowardly… but not anymore. Now it was time to take control of his own life and to pay the price for his foolishness.

He would leave Kentwood. He would take whatever position his aunt could secure, and he would never again allow anyone to take control of his life.

He sighed.

But tomorrow, not tonight. Tonight I will let the dream go on just a little longer, I think… and hope my lord will join me.

The thought made his body tingle and his heart beat faster. Could he do this? Could he risk the man's anger if he had read him wrong?

Feeling his courage rise with each sip of his brandy, he decided he could. This would be his last chance to know joy with another man and to erase the marks Victor had left on him.

After tonight, he could not risk being with a man ever again. He would be a poor clerk or a secretary or some other humble profession, if he was lucky, and keeping such a position, and with it his life, was reliant on his character being above reproach. If he didn't take the chance now, he would never have another.

Perhaps I am a little mad to want this so soon after Victor. But the thought of being with Warren brought him nothing but eager anticipation, no fear, no shame, just longing.

He would never hurt me. I don't know how I know it after so short a time, but I do.

Add to that the fact that the man was handsome, charming, and had the body of Atlas, and it was no wonder Kyle couldn't help but want him. He was strong without being cruel. He had humor and wit, intelligence, and a calm, confident air that drew Kyle like no one else ever had.

Kyle closed his eyes, remembering how those hands had felt on his face, in his hair, on his thigh, and heat pulsed through his veins. Yes, he needed to feel that again, to forget anything that had come before, even if it was just for one night.

As he poured his third glass of brandy, he heard Ashton bidding his sister good night in the hall; then all was quiet. He'd dozed off for a short time only to wake to the sound of footsteps and to hear Warren's voice instructing Ellis to send up a decanter of brandy and informing him that he would be sleeping late and not to disturb him.

At the sound of that voice, butterflies stirred in his stomach, and his hand tightened around his glass. He sat unmoving as the servant came and went, presumably delivering the brandy. He continued to sit as he waited for the house to go silent, until the only sound he could hear was the nervous beating of his heart.

It's now or never.

Rising perhaps a little too quickly, he made his unsteady way down the hall to the man's door. No light came from under it, telling him that Warren must have already gone to bed.

Taking a deep breath to calm himself and clear his spinning head, he carefully turned the knob, thankful that the door was unlocked. He closed the door as quietly as possible before fumbling for the bolt. After sliding it home, he stepped further into the room and looked around him.

Moonlight poured in from a large set of windows to his left, illuminating a small sitting area furnished with two chairs and a small table. Traveling past them, Kyle made his way to the large bedchamber beyond. Another set of windows lit a giant canopied bed in which Warren's still form rested on his side. Swallowing his doubts, Kyle made his way to the bed and looked down on the man's sleeping face.

God, he's beautiful.

Taking a deep breath, he knelt next to the bed and reached out with unsteady fingers to touch that face. He trailed his fingers down the strong jaw, rough with a day's growth of whiskers, and as he watched, Warren's eyes fluttered open, registering surprise and confusion. With his back to the moonlight, Kyle knew Warren couldn't see his face, but it was obvious he knew who it was when he said, "Kyle? What are you doing here? Is something wrong?"

"No, nothing," Kyle said simply, moving his fingers from the man's jaw to slide over his lips. Warren's hand shot up and clasped Kyle's wrist hard, pulling his hand away from his face.

"No," he said firmly. "Go back to bed... now." He didn't immediately let go of Kyle's wrist, however, which gave him the courage to ignore the command.

"Please," Kyle pleaded, "please don't send me away. I want to be with you so much. You want it too, don't you?"

He watched as emotions flitted across Warren's face too quickly to name. The man swallowed and closed his eyes before saying, "We can't do this, Kyle. This can't happen."

It was not a complete denial, and Kyle took heart. As the man had yet to let go of his wrist, Kyle chose to listen to his body rather than his words and leaned forward until his lips hovered just above the other man's.

"Please," Kyle whispered against those lips before closing the final distance and sealing their mouths together.

Warren groaned, and his grip on Kyle's wrist tightened before his lips opened and his tongue shot forward to tangle with Kyle's. He tasted of brandy and something sweeter that had Kyle opening further, hoping for more. Warren's tongue plunged deeper into his mouth before withdrawing to nip and suck on his lips. Kyle felt the grip on his wrist release a moment before strong hands cupped his jaw, holding him in place as his kiss became hard and demanding.

He hadn't given Warren the opportunity to take control of their last encounter, but now his body thrilled at the force with which the other took possession of his mouth. Oh yes! This was what he needed.

JAMES had never wanted something so badly in his life. He'd spent the entire day trying *not* to remember how good Kyle had felt pressed against him, how sweet those lips had been, and how those strong thighs had clenched around him.

Now, in his own bed after a frustrating day spent trying to distract himself, the object of his obsession appeared like a dream, on his knees, begging to be taken. It was too much to resist.

He was not made of stone, nor was he a saint. He was only a man, a man who'd been in a near-constant state of arousal for days. Any and all reasons why he shouldn't be doing what he so desperately wanted to do flew from his head the moment Kyle's lips met his, and there was nothing he could do to stop them.

Surrendering himself completely to the moment, he sat up on the bed and leaned back against the pillows, pulling Kyle up and partially on top of him. Following his lead, the younger man climbed onto the bed and knelt next to him as they explored each other's mouths.

This time, there would be no conflicting desires, no regrets. He was not a man of half measures. Once the decision was made, there would be no going back. He committed himself fully to the experience, and all his doubts disappeared.

Sliding his hands along his lover's throat, he could feel Kyle's pulse beat erratically under his palms, and his own heartbeat sped in answer. When Kyle drew back a little, gasping, James moved his mouth to Kyle's neck, licking and sucking over that pulse, then leaning down to bite the cord of muscle joining it to his shoulder. Kyle moaned and leaned into his mouth, spreading his hands across James's chest for support, and James couldn't help a moan of his own at Kyle's responsiveness.

Frantic to taste more of him, James dropped his hands to Kyle's waist and pulled his shirt free of his trousers. Kyle leaned back and raised his arms to allow it to be drawn over his head, then cursed as the cuffs caught and effectively trapped his arms.

Chuckling quietly, James found himself strangely charmed and aroused at hearing such filthy words coming out of that sweet mouth for the first time. He twisted the shirt a little tighter and drew Kyle's hands down between them, holding them together while he took the opportunity to lean forward and take one of Kyle's nipples in his mouth, sucking and nibbling at it until it hardened under his tongue.

Kyle gasped and pressed his chest harder against James's mouth as his body began to tremble. Encouraged, James moved to the other, teasing until it peaked, taking his time and savoring the flavor and heat of his lover's skin.

When Kyle's hands fidgeted restlessly between them, James pulled back and freed them from the shirt before pulling Kyle close again and reclaiming his mouth. Kyle's hands, now freed, fisted in James's hair, drawing them even closer together. Smiling to himself at Kyle's obvious enthusiasm, he took delight in exploring Kyle's mouth again as his hands caressed his lover's newly bared torso. The lightly muscled planes of his back and flanks slid smooth and warm under his palms as he committed every inch to memory. It was heavenly, but he couldn't help but want more.

He rose up, pulling Kyle against him, molding their bodies from breast to knees. He slid his hands down Kyle's back to the waist of his trousers, pushing them inside, cupping and squeezing his buttocks. The firm, tight globes fit perfectly in his hands, and he used his hold to grind their hips together.

Kyle moaned against his mouth, taut muscles flexing in his palms as the young man rubbed his cock and belly against James's. He could feel Kyle panting against his neck as they strained together, his warm, moist breath heating James's already fevered skin a moment before the younger man drew back to meet his eyes and began tugging at James's nightshirt.

He reluctantly let go of Kyle's arse only when the man began making angry, frustrated noises at the nightshirt, which was trapped beneath his knees.

James chuckled and leaned in to capture those frowning lips, sucking and nibbling at them as he moved to help. Together they managed to free him from his nightshirt, and once bared, James leaned back into the pillows, drawing Kyle on top of him again. As their bodies met, he reached down to grasp Kyle's hips, urging him to move against him. They rocked and rutted for several moments, and soon he could feel Kyle's hands everywhere on his body, frantically stroking one moment and clenching about his shoulders and arms the next.

James couldn't help but find Kyle's urgency contagious. He

wanted to take his time and explore this treasure, but he was fairly certain that that was not going to be possible. He finally had Kyle in his arms, someone he admired as a man as well as desired as a lover, and the intensity of his need was almost overwhelming.

He pulled Kyle closer still, melding their bodies together, pressing his face against Kyle's neck and enjoying the warm, solid body pressed against his. He tried to force himself to slow down then, taking a deep breath and stilling his body, but his lover was having none of it. Kyle began wriggling in his arms, forcing his hand between them and gripping James's shaft. When James felt him run his thumb over the crown, he gasped, and his hand flew to cover Kyle's, holding it still. That was too much.

"Wait," he said through clenched teeth. And to Kyle's confused look, he replied, "Not yet, or we'll be over before we've begun."

Kyle smiled shyly, then gasped as James gripped him by the hips and flipped him onto his back, taking control again. Though he was finding Kyle's combination of aggression and submission surprisingly intoxicating, he needed to take some control of their encounter, or it would be over all too soon.

Pressing Kyle into the mattress and using his weight to hold his lover still, he quickly undid the fastenings of Kyle's trousers and pushed them down around his hips. Kyle lifted his hips to help, then reached for him, but James slid off the bed, taking Kyle's trousers with him. Kyle lay back on the pillows, gazing up at him shyly and biting his bottom lip.

He was now completely bare, spread on his back in the moonlight, and James took a moment to simply look his fill. He could have wished for daylight for this moment, but if he were honest, he probably would have embarrassed himself if he'd gotten that wish.

"So beautiful," he said huskily.

Kyle's pale skin glowed in the silver light. His slender shaft arched beautifully over his smooth, flat belly, rising out of the coarse black thatch at its base. Lean limbs lightly dusted with dark hair lay spread wantonly on the bed as elegant, long-fingered hands reached out to him.

James purposefully avoided those hands and slid down the bed to lie between his thighs, and Kyle spread them wider to accommodate him, his glazed eyes fixed and his swollen lips moist and parted. James held his gaze as he lowered his face, stopping with his open mouth hovering just over Kyle's leaking crown. He expelled a hot breath over the glistening head, smiling as it jumped and twitched over Kyle's belly. Kyle gasped and fisted his hands in the linens.

"Please," Kyle begged.

Needing no more encouragement, James wrapped his fist around Kyle's cock, drawing down slightly on the foreskin, and ran his tongue over the flushed head. As the evidence of Kyle's need exploded over his tongue, he hummed in pleasure and drew him further in, sucking and laving his way down to the base before drawing back up to the crown in one long, slow glide.

Kyle's low moan vibrated through his body, and James felt his lover's thighs clench on either side of him. Running his thumb over Kyle's slit, spreading the beads of moisture that were escaping, he kissed and sucked down the underside, then ran his tongue wetly over Kyle's bollocks, sucking one and then the other into his mouth. Kyle was whimpering in earnest now and bucking against him, but James put his palm flat on his belly to keep him still.

"Patience, sweet," he said, waiting for Kyle to still beneath his hand before taking Kyle back in his mouth and sucking on just the crown. As Kyle stilled beneath him, James let him slide slowly in and all the way to the back of his throat, then swallowed around him in reward. Kyle let out a strangled cry, his chest heaving and his body trembling with the effort not to thrust.

"Good lord," Kyle whimpered.

Feeling his own need throb in response to Kyle's obvious pleasure, James decided perhaps he wasn't going to be capable of slow and easy after all and began to suck in earnest. Drawing his lips tightly around Kyle's shaft, he slid his hands around to cup his buttocks and urge him upward, giving his permission.

It didn't take long before Kyle took his meaning and began to thrust into his mouth, his back arching off the bed. Relaxing his throat and increasing his suction, James let Kyle thrust with abandon. He knew it wouldn't be long by the shaking of Kyle's body and the sweet, soft cries that were coming almost unbroken now. A few more quick thrusts, and Kyle's hand flew to his mouth, stifling his cry as James felt his spend rushing into his mouth. James swallowed all that Kyle gave him and milked his shaft a few more times before relaxing his hands and allowing his lover to collapse back down on the bed, panting.

James licked his lips, savoring his lover's flavor, then climbed up his body, taking Kyle's mouth in a hungry kiss and giving him a taste of himself. Kyle returned the kiss with enthusiasm, wrapping his arms around James's back and pulling his knees up to cradle his hips.

The position sent a fresh pulse of need to his already aching cock, and James nudged Kyle to roll on his side, sliding behind him and pressing his erection against Kyle's firm backside. Kissing and nuzzling Kyle's neck, he cupped his hand behind Kyle's knee and urged it upwards. As he continued to lick and nibble at Kyle's neck and shoulders, he moved his hand to Kyle's mouth, sliding his fingers across moist lips and pressing them inside.

The feeling of his lover sucking and licking at his fingers sent a fresh wave of heat through him, and he was forced to rest his forehead against Kyle's shoulder and just breathe for several moments before he could master himself enough to continue.

He withdrew his hand and slid it down to Kyle's exposed opening, playing lightly around it and feeling Kyle tremble against him. Wetting them again himself, he swirled his thumb around it, then moved to press his middle finger in to the first knuckle. He pumped the finger in and out only that small amount, teasing his lover.

He knew he would have to find oil before they could go much further. Kyle was tight, and he didn't want to hurt him, so for now he would content himself with simply playing... at least until he could be assured his legs would support him long enough to stand and go looking for the vial.

He continued to play and tease, steadying his own breathing and nibbling on his lover's shoulder and neck until he felt Kyle go completely still against him. It was then that James realized the panting and moaning breaths had ceased and Kyle was no longer writhing in his arms.

James stilled his hand as soon as the realization hit and asked, "Kyle, are you all right?"

"Yes," he replied, but James could hear the strain in his voice.

When the rest of his blood finally made it back up to his brain, James understood his mistake.

"Damn!" he swore, removing his hand completely. "Kyle, forgive me. I'm a bloody fool. I know what happened, and I was still too blinded by my own passions to think. Please forgive me."

"No, please don't stop, please!" Kyle turned in his arms, and James could see his eyes glistening in the moonlight. "I want you to, truly!"

James shook his head and pulled further from Kyle's back, appalled with himself, his shaft already softening. "No, you don't have to do this, Kyle. Not for me, I promise you. I know what you went through must have been terrible. I would not be the cause of more pain."

"No, please, I need this, I need you. I know you won't hurt me. I need to feel you, to know the feeling of you inside me, to make me forget... anything that happened before. I know you'll be careful with me. I know it," Kyle said, his words tumbling over each other as he reached to grab James's hip to keep him from pulling away.

James stilled at the anxiety in his words and allowed the young man to pull him close lest he think James was rejecting him completely.

"Kyle," he sighed, running his hand down his lover's cheek. "You're afraid. I can feel it in your body. I can hear it in your voice. I *will* hurt you if you're afraid and can't trust me. I won't do that. I *can't* do that."

"Please, my lord. Please do this for me. I promise you won't hurt me. I promise," Kyle pleaded, and to James's horror tears spilled out of the corners of his eyes.

James closed his eyes. Kyle was obviously getting more upset by the moment, and he didn't want their first time together to end badly, but he wasn't sure what to do. Gathering Kyle into his arms, he simply held on while he tried to think.

He wanted to give Kyle what he asked for, how he wanted it, but he couldn't bear the thought of hurting him when there were so many other ways for them to enjoy each other.

After a while Kyle obviously became impatient with him, because he felt his hand grabbed and placed firmly on his lover's arse. It was more of a command than an invitation, and the move startled him from his thoughts and gave him an idea.

He drew back, brought his hand back up to Kyle's jaw, and lifted his face into moonlight. Looking into his eyes, he said, "If this is truly what you want, then I won't deny you. But it will be on my terms. I believe we may both get what we want if you can trust me and do as I bid. Can you do that?"

"Yes, oh yes, anything," Kyle replied eagerly.

James stared into Kyle's eyes for a moment longer before he nodded and rolled to the edge of the bed.

"First, I would like you to call me by my given name, James. I believe we're long past the need for formality," he said with a wry smile that Kyle returned shyly.

"Second, I believe we need more light. I need to be able to see you," James said as he rose to light the lamp on his night table. He then rooted about the room, finding his vial of oil and two cravats. Smiling at Kyle's confused frown, he returned to sit on the bed, placing the vial of oil on the night table and handing him the cravats.

"Do you trust me?" he asked again, looking deeply into those enchanting green eyes now that they could see one another better.

"Yes… James," Kyle said simply.

He smiled again. His name sounded every bit as sweet coming from Kyle's mouth as he'd imagined it would, and he felt his blood heating again in response.

He leaned in to capture those wonderful lips, keeping the contact teasing and light. He plucked at Kyle's lips over and over with his own, never lingering long enough for the other man to deepen the kiss. He continued to tease Kyle's lips and tongue as he crawled around him, forcing the young man to follow. He leaned back against the headboard, and Kyle leaned into him now that he couldn't get away. He let Kyle deepen the kiss for a few moments before drawing back and placing fingers against his lips.

"Now, I want you to use those to tie my wrists to the bed," James said, pointing to the cravats lying forgotten in Kyle's lap.

Kyle looked startled for a moment; then he swallowed, bit his lip, and pushed up on his knees to comply. James raised his arms to make things easier, and soon Kyle was crawling around him to tie the other wrist.

Having never been on this end of this kind of play, he was surprised to find he enjoyed the delicious thrill of fear that tingled across his skin as he was bound. It heightened his senses such that every brush of Kyle's skin against his was magnified. Even the slightest brush of those nimble fingers on his wrists or of thigh against thigh felt as if he were being stroked somewhere far more intimate. He made a mental note to visit the idea again in future, when he wasn't so distracted with concern for his lover.

After Kyle finished, he sat back on his heels, looking to James for more direction. He made such a pretty picture kneeling on his bed in the lamplight that James couldn't help a proprietary smirk from playing across his lips before he turned to examine his lover's work.

The restraints looked more like bows than knots, but James hid his smile, not wanting to hurt Kyle's feelings. He had undoubtedly tied them loosely because he was afraid to hurt him, but it didn't matter. They would have the desired effect, and that was all James really cared about. He would be able to free himself if absolutely necessary, but Kyle would believe him helpless.

James tugged on them gently, demonstrating his "helpless" state for his lover, and said, "Very good, now kiss me."

Kyle seemed quite willing to comply, leaning in and claiming James's mouth with enthusiasm. He knew the very moment Kyle realized James could no longer do anything to hold him back, because he suddenly cupped James's jaw in surprisingly strong hands, and his kiss became ravenous. James allowed him free rein, simply enjoying the feel of Kyle's lips and tongue on his own and the pressure of Kyle's renewed arousal against his hip.

After several long moments, Kyle broke away, panting, and stared uncertainly into James's eyes, seemingly a little startled at his forwardness and perhaps afraid of criticism. James smiled encouragingly and took a moment to catch his breath, then said, "You may touch me and explore me as you please, however, if I tell you to stop, you will stop. Is that understood?"

Kyle nodded and began running his hands over James's chest and stomach, then looked back into James's eyes, biting his lip. He looked so nervous that James took pity on him again and said, "Would you like me to tell you what to do?"

Kyle blushed and nodded again, smiling shyly. "I don't know what you intend," he said quietly. "I've never done anything like this."

As Weir had always struck him as a selfish and unimaginative man, James wasn't surprised to hear it.

Smiling gently and settling himself more comfortably back on the cushions, he said, "Then it will be my pleasure to instruct you."

He spread his legs further apart, saying, "Come and sit between my knees, facing me." When Kyle obeyed, he added, "Drape your legs over mine and put your feet flat on the bed by my hips." Kyle flushed and spread his lean thighs up and over James's larger ones.

"Lovely," he murmured as his eyes hooded and his cock came fully awake again.

In that position, Kyle lay fully exposed before him, and the sight was breathtaking. In that moment, he was more certain than ever that he had never met a more beautiful man and that even should he live to be a hundred, he probably never would.

Taking a breath and clenching his fists in the restraints, he ordered, "Stroke yourself for me. I want you to imagine it's my hand on you, caressing you, giving you pleasure."

The command came out a little huskier than he had intended, but Kyle seemed to react as much to the sound as the words. His eyes became heavy with desire, and his lips parted as he wrapped long, slender fingers around his shaft and stroked. He seemed tentative and shy at first but soon warmed to the idea of putting on a show for his helpless audience. Spreading his legs a little wider, he licked his lips and locked his eyes with James's.

"Put your fingers in your mouth and suck. Make them good and wet." He continued watching, trying to control his breathing, and as Kyle obeyed, he had to clench his jaw hard to keep from groaning at the sight.

"Pull and pinch your nipples for me with those slick fingers," he managed, and Kyle's head fell back a little and his eyes closed as he complied. James let him continue stroking his cock and playing with his nipples for several moments until Kyle's pace increased.

"Stop." They both needed a moment, or they'd spend before they even touched one another again.

Kyle's eyes flew open, flashing green fire in protest, and his swollen lips fell into a pout. The sight was so endearing that James almost didn't want to continue, but he decided to take pity on them both.

"Grab the vial of oil from the night table, then lie back where you were," he said, nodding to his right.

Kyle clambered over him so fast James nearly burst out laughing, but he held it in for fear of offending his young lover. Kyle settled back between his legs, glass vial in hand, and looked back at James expectantly.

"Pour some into your palm and spread it over your cock." When he did, James had to swallow before he could continue.

"Move lower and cup your bollocks. Coat them in oil; I want to see them shine." James's breath was coming harder now as he watched Kyle flush again and his hand move over himself.

Time to move things along.

"Coat your fingers in more oil. Good. Now pull your bollocks up high and slide your fingers beneath," he breathed. "Higher, show me where you want me. Show me your sweet pink rosebud. I want to see it open for me."

Sweat beaded all over James's body as Kyle groaned and did as he was told, cupping his sac against the base of his shaft in one hand, pulling it taut, then sliding the other beneath.

"Now push inside, make yourself ready for me," he panted. "Stretch yourself with your fingers so I can slide into that tight arse in one smooth, slick stroke." Kyle's crown flushed purple above his fist as the fingers of his other hand explored his entrance, sliding in and out, stretching.

"That's right, sweet, deeper, go deeper," he choked out as he watched the work of art in front of him. James knew when Kyle found his sweet spot because his lover jerked suddenly and another drop of pearly fluid slid down his crown.

"Yes, sweet, that's what I want. That's what I want to do to you. I want to fill you, to slide my cock over that place deep inside you over and over until you spend around me." Kyle was panting now as well, and James decided he couldn't take anymore. He had to have Kyle *now*.

"All right, sweet, come to me, come and kiss me," he commanded breathlessly, and Kyle climbed up his body, sealing their mouths together. The kiss was desperate, Kyle's lips and tongue begging him for more.

Turning his head from the kiss, he whispered in his lover's ear, "Now, sweet, you're ready for me. Spread the oil over my cock and lower yourself onto me. Take me inside you. Go as slow as you need, but do it *now*."

Kyle's eyes were a bit glazed when they met his, but he nodded and moved to obey. James had to grit his teeth, close his eyes, and count to ten as Kyle's hand slid over his shaft, slicking it with oil.

When he felt that hand grip the base of his shaft firmly, his eyes flew open to lock with Kyle's, offering what encouragement he could. Kyle's blush had spread all the way down his neck, and his lower lip was caught between his teeth as he positioned James's crown at his opening and began to lower himself. James would have thrown his head back and moaned at the feel of Kyle's tight heat surrounding him if he didn't want so desperately to watch Kyle slide onto him for the first time, to watch that beautiful face change as he was filled.

At the first twinge of pain on Kyle's face, James mastered himself enough to gasp, "Don't rush, Kyle, we have all night. If it hurts, ease back a little and start again." James hoped for both their sakes that it didn't take much longer. He had reached the limits of his control. He'd already admitted to himself he wasn't a saint, but if things kept up at this pace much longer, he might be a candidate for martyrdom.

Kyle rose up a little at his suggestion, then began rocking his way back down, taking James a little deeper each time. When he was finally seated all the way, Kyle let out a sigh and stilled. James would have offered more advice or encouragement, but he couldn't seem to form the words, and any desire to try was quickly swept away on a tide of pleasure as Kyle began to move on him.

After gripping James's shoulders for support, Kyle started a smooth, slow rhythm that had James's eyes rolling back in his head and his mouth falling open in a moan. Kyle soon joined him, whimpering and grunting with each pump and twist of his hips.

"Yes, Kyle. Oh lord, yes," he panted. "Stroke yourself now, I want to feel you spend with me inside you." He needed Kyle to hurry.

As he watched, Kyle gripped his shaft and pumped into his hand with each forward thrust of his hips. Near blind with need, James used the bindings on his wrists as leverage and lifted his hips to meet each downstroke, and together they set a frenzied pace.

It couldn't last long, not for either of them, and suddenly, Kyle slammed down on him hard, grinding his arse against James's hips, crying out and clenching around him. Warm seed spattered across James's stomach and chest, sending him over the edge. Straining against his bindings, James stifled a shout and arched off the bed, his stomach and thigh muscles burning with the strain as he shot into Kyle's hot channel. He froze trembling in that position until his vision cleared, then lowered both of them back onto the bed.

Kyle fell against his chest, panting, and James dropped his cheek to Kyle's damp hair, shaking and gasping. They stayed like that for only a short time before James's thighs began to cramp.

He kissed the top of Kyle's head and chuckled, saying, "Lovely, you can't keep me like this all night. Will you untie me now?" Kyle looked up with a heartbreakingly sweet, sated, and sleepy smile, then kissed James tenderly while he fumbled with the restraints.

When his wrists were released, James slid his arms around Kyle and pulled him close, shifting enough to give his thigh muscles some relief.

"Beautiful boy," he whispered against Kyle's hair. "Sweet boy." He didn't fully understand the clenching in his chest and the lump in his throat, but he knew at that moment that he didn't want to let Kyle go, not for anything in the world.

When he felt Kyle's body become heavy and languid, he could tell that his lover was almost asleep in his arms. James had to admit he was almost there himself. Too many sleepless nights, combined with what had to be the most intense release he'd ever had, made sleep a foregone conclusion for both of them. He didn't want the tender moment to end, and he knew they had much to talk about, but it would have to wait. They both needed sleep.

He wiped them off with his nightshirt and tossed it on the floor, then settled Kyle against his side and put out the lamp before drawing the linens over them.

"Did you lock the door?" he whispered against Kyle's hair. When he felt Kyle nod and heard a sleepy "mmhhmm," he lay back and closed his eyes.

"Good night, Kyle," he murmured before sleep claimed him.

Chapter Ten

KYLE woke to the pale glow of predawn coming from the windows and the feel of his lover's warm breath against his neck. James's large, muscled body lay curled around him, his arm draped over Kyle's waist, and he had to close his eyes as the rush of emotion he felt caused his chest to swell painfully. He could still hardly believe James had allowed him into his bed... and the things he'd done to him there.... James had been passionate and kind, strong and gentle and more wonderful than Kyle could have imagined.

So different from Victor... even in the beginning.

He shook his head. He didn't want to think about Victor at a time like this, but he had been the only other man Kyle had ever lain with, and he couldn't help the comparison.

There is no comparison.

Never in his life had he felt so cherished and wanted. How a man could be so masterful and commanding yet tender and giving all at the same time Kyle didn't know, but he was nearly overflowing with gratitude for it. He stared at his lover's face for long moments, committing every line and curve to memory. This man embodied everything he could possibly have asked for, and he couldn't bear the thought that their time together would end.

But it must, he thought, clamping his eyes closed on the tears that threatened. *The dream has to end sometime, and it will be easier if it happens now.*

There was no future for them. Lord Warren was a respected peer of the realm, so discreet it seemed that Kyle had never once heard even a hint of a rumor about him. If such a rumor had existed, he felt sure Victor would have known about it. Victor and his friends seemed to thrive on that sort of gossip, and never once had Victor mentioned the viscount's name.

A man like that couldn't afford to keep someone like him around. He couldn't stay at Kentwood. It would be out of the question. James lived alone, had always lived alone, and though the servants seemed quite loyal, Kyle knew a man like James wouldn't risk rumors starting on his own estates.

You're assuming that he'd even want you for more than one night. Just because the man let you sleep in his bed and made you feel lo—how he made you feel, doesn't mean he wants to keep you. You're the one who insisted when he tried to refuse you.

Kyle shook his head, gritted his teeth, and opened his eyes. He was just avoiding the inevitable with his woolgathering. Even if, by some miracle, James actually did want him, there could never be more than a short holiday together.

Perhaps a few short months if he wanted me enough to set me up somewhere.

But that would leave him back in the same situation he had been with Victor, and he couldn't do that again. He couldn't have his life so completely dependent on the whim and regard of another. The fact that he had to go groveling to his aunt was bad enough.

No, no matter how wonderful the night before had been, he knew he had to let go and face the real world again. There was no other choice. He had to leave now. He knew himself well enough to know that if he allowed himself to taste more, to dream of more, it would only tear him to pieces.

He felt so brittle even now, and the passion he had had for Victor was a pale, sickly thing in comparison to what he felt for James. He was certain he wouldn't survive if he allowed himself to acknowledge the depth of his feelings for this man and then lost him.

Easing away from James's sleeping form and getting out of that warm, soft bed was the hardest thing he'd ever done. Looking down at his lover's handsome face, he positively ached with the need to forget everything else and kiss those firm lips again.

Swallowing the desire, he turned and searched out his trousers and shirt, making his way to the antechamber. He dressed as quietly as he could and, after listening at the door for any noises from the hall, stepped out and made his way back to his room.

After washing and dressing himself for his journey, he decided he wouldn't disturb any of the other servants. He would simply go to the stables himself and wait for them to saddle Gwinny. He would saddle her himself if he had to. There was no point in delaying, and if he waited much longer, he'd weaken and lose his resolve.

The sun had barely crested the horizon when he trotted past the gatehouse toward the village. He would inquire at the inn as to the best roads to travel and perhaps have something to eat, though he changed his mind when the thought of food made his stomach turn.

Looking back at the Hall, he couldn't help the pain that tightened his chest. He knew he would be back that evening or the next day. He had to return the horse and say goodbye to everyone, to James, face to face. He owed him, *them*, at least that much. It would be incredibly wrong and ungrateful of him not to, but he couldn't help but feel his heart break a little with each step his horse took.

As he cantered down the road, his saddle reminded him that perhaps his choice of activities the night before could have been better thought out, and he smiled wryly at the thought. Today's ride would be rather unpleasant for certain parts of his anatomy, but he couldn't be sorry. The memories of last night would have to last him for the rest of his life.

JAMES woke to birdsong and soft morning sunlight. He stretched lazily only to have his thighs and wrists twinge and complain. Coming fully awake, the memories of the night before washed over him, and he grinned. Looking about him, he realized he was alone, but the rumpled state of the bed and the faint smell of their coupling assured him he hadn't been dreaming. He looked down at his wrists and chuckled.

Perhaps it would be best for me to dress myself today, or at least don my own shirt. It would give the marks on his wrists a little time to fade before Edwards saw them.

Though part of him dearly missed waking up with Kyle in his arms, he was thankful the lad had had the presence of mind to leave before they were discovered. He'd told Ellis that he would be sleeping late, but he supposed they couldn't be too careful. He'd never had a lover in his home before, and the state of the bed linens was going to be suspicious enough.

And such a lover. Grinning like a fool he leaned back on his pillows.

Kyle, sweet Kyle, beautiful Kyle. How had he gotten so lucky as to have someone so lovely want him enough to come to him in the night, ignoring his every protest?

Rationally, he should never have allowed it. He had been reckless and indiscreet in his own house. But he couldn't help being almost giddy with joy at the night they had shared. He hadn't felt this good in a very long time. There had always been some small part of himself left unfulfilled, an ache of loneliness that had been a part of him for so long he could barely remember being without it. Even the twins, whom he loved almost as his own children, had never been able to touch it.

But now?

He shook his head. He just didn't know. Kyle made him want things he hadn't even considered in over fifteen years: a partner, a helpmeet, someone to share his days and nights with. In a few short days, the young man had made him begin to dream of things he'd never dared before, and he wasn't quite sure what to do about it.

There must be some way.

He decided not to ruin his good humor by dwelling on all of the obstacles to his happiness. He needn't come up with all the answers this very morning. There would be time to figure out what they would do.

He rose to wash and put on his trousers and shirt. After removing what evidence he could of what he had been doing the night before, he rang for Edwards. His valet was prompt as always, and James was dressed for the day in short order.

Descending the main stair, he heard voices from the drawing room and moved to join them, fighting the urge to whistle a tune. On entering the room, he found his niece and nephew chatting over breakfast. They made a lovely scene, Anna in white and pink embroidered muslin and Andrew in a green and brown striped waistcoat and fawn trousers. Heads of nearly identical brown tousled curls turned in his direction, and James couldn't help but smile.

He was disappointed Kyle wasn't there, but the thought that the young man needed to sleep in after his exertions of the night before made him feel inordinately pleased with himself.

"Good morning, Uncle," the twins said in unison, as they had done often as small children, and James's smile widened to a grin.

"Good morning, imps, and how are you this fine day?" he said in return.

Two identical sets of raised eyebrows met his question a moment before Anna answered, "We are quite well, thank you, Uncle. Will you join us?"

"Certainly, my dears, I would be glad to." His grin hadn't faded, and the twins were both looking at him oddly.

"Why, Uncle, I don't think I've seen you this lively in ages. Your trip to the village yesterday must have been quite fruitful," Andrew said with a chuckle.

James decided he needed to sober a little or they would get too curious about his queer mood. "Nothing out of the ordinary, nephew, I assure you, though it was a beautiful day for a ride. I do apologize for disappearing on you yesterday and the day before. I shall endeavor to be a better host from now on."

"Oh, don't be silly, Uncle," Anna replied. "When have we ever demanded that you be a proper host? We're family. We've never stood on ceremony before, and I refuse to allow you to start now. If I have to deal with all the same nonsense Mother makes us deal with in town, I might as well have stayed in London."

"Too true, niece, I am rightly rebuked." He rose and bowed to her with a twinkle in his eyes. "I shall, therefore, withdraw my apology and make myself scarce for another few days. There, will that make you happy enough to stay with me?"

"Oh, Uncle," she said, giggling as Ellis entered the room with his tray of coffee.

"Good morning, my lord," he said, placing the tray on a nearby table and pouring. Handing James the cup, he asked, "Will there be anything else, my lord?"

"No, Ellis. Thank you. This sweet ambrosia is all that I require," he said, grinning at him.

Ellis's own brows shot up, and an answering grin split his face. "May I be so bold as to comment that my lord seems quite refreshed this morning."

James winced a little internally, wondering if Ellis would be smiling so broadly if he knew the reason for his lord's good humor, and chastised himself for being so foolish. Pushing the thoughts away, he said, "I am, thank you, Ellis. And I apologize for yesterday. It was wrong of me to make myself so much the bear that the rest of the staff had to nominate a champion to brave my den."

"My lord need not apologize. We are simply grateful to see your good humor restored. Is Mr. Allen expected to return for dinner, my lord?" Ellis asked as he straightened to leave.

"Return?" he asked, confused.

"Yes, my lord. The stable master informed me he left early this morning. I didn't have the opportunity to speak with him before he left, so I was unable to inquire as to his plans for dinner," Ellis said, his brows now drawing down in concern at James's apparent shock.

James was struck dumb, and his stomach clenched and roiled around the tiny bit of coffee he'd had. He looked to the twins.

"Mr. Allen said he was unsure about when he would return, perhaps not until tomorrow," Andrew answered, looking at Ellis. "He said not to wait dinner. He would see to his own meal before he returned."

"Thank you, sir, my lord," Ellis said, bowing and casting one more concerned look toward James before leaving the room.

When James found his voice again, he croaked, "Tell me."

"I'm terribly sorry, Uncle. We thought he would speak to you before he left. He received the letter from his aunt yesterday. He said she was willing to speak with him and that she had summoned him to visit as soon as he was able. When he asked to borrow a horse, I thought there would be no harm in offering him Gwinny. I suppose you returned too late for him to speak to you and he didn't want to disturb you this morning," Andrew replied, frowning in concern.

"I see," James said, forcing himself to relax. *He's only gone for a few hours, at most a night. His clothes are still here. He'll be back.*

But his good humor had fled with surprising swiftness, and he couldn't seem to bring himself to say anything else.

"Uncle?" Andrew said. "Did I offer something I should not? Perhaps I should have consulted you before I did, but I thought, since Gwinny is mine, that you wouldn't mind. I apologize if I did wrong."

James sighed. He needed to get himself under control.

"No, Andrew. No harm done. I simply didn't know any of it had taken place. You did the right thing. I'm glad Mr. Allen heard from his aunt and that she was willing to see him. That's wonderful news. I'm sure he simply didn't wish to disturb me," he said, forcing a smile. "So, what shall we do today while we wait to hear his news?"

Andrew and Anna seemed to relax at his words and began to chat about prospective walks and a visit to the village. James listened with only half his attention. Kyle had received the letter from his aunt, had even made a plan to see her, and hadn't said one word to him. Granted, he had been gone the whole day, and they'd both been preoccupied during the night....

But why didn't he wake me before he left?

That hurt him more than he wanted to admit. Perhaps Kyle didn't feel as strongly as he did. Perhaps his concerns over how he and Kyle might manage some kind of relationship safely and discreetly were moot.

He realized, then, that he'd been acting like a lovesick fool all morning after only a single night of passion. He needed to talk to Kyle, but that couldn't happen until the young man returned. Until that time, he must remember that he was a grown man, not some mooning schoolboy. He would have to get hold of himself and show dignity and composure as befitted his station.

And for God's sake, show some consideration for your family.

Forcing his face into a more pleasant mien, he joined his niece and nephew in their conversation and tried to put his ill humor behind him. He and Kyle would talk when he returned, and then he would know how to proceed.

KYLE closed the door to the small bedchamber his aunt had given him and leaned his aching head against the door. He had spent hours on horseback, his bum complaining loudly, only to be ushered directly into his aunt's drawing room by a sour-faced butler, without a moment to compose himself.

He had then been subjected to a two-hour long interview, during which his aunt had regaled him with the seemingly unending litany of his failings, read directly from a letter that his father had sent her. She looked and sounded enough like his father that he'd almost felt like he was back home again, though the feeling gave him no comfort.

To his relief, she had then informed him that, despite her brother's instructions to the contrary, she could make up her own mind without his interference and would indeed consider helping him find employment, provided he gave his word that he would strive to improve himself.

He had assured her in as many ways as he could think of that he would do all in his power to prove worthy of her faith and generosity, until she had finally held up her hand to silence him. But when she spoke again, she'd crushed any happiness or relief he might have even begun to feel with one simple demand.

"You were led astray by the licentiousness of men who can afford such behavior, whose money, land, and titles allow them freedoms which yours do not. How you believed that that man, Mr. Weir, would think you so much the friend that he would provide you with a future, I'll never know. You reached above your station and consorted with who knows what kind of rakes and scoundrels. I don't know what you got up to in your time in London, doubtless gambling and drinking and whatever other immoralities young gentlemen of fashion get up to these days. But I tell you now, if you are to receive any of my help, you will give me your promise to cut off all contact between yourself and anyone you met in London."

At his gasp, she continued on without letting him interrupt. "I do realize that you have to express proper gratitude to the Ashton family, as well as Lord Warren, for their aid. As you said in your letter, they were uncommonly generous and kind to you, and you mustn't seem ungrateful or disrespectful, especially not to so illustrious a personage as the viscount. However, that can be as easily done in a letter as in person. There is no need for you to return and be any more of a burden to them than you have already been."

When she paused, Kyle collected himself enough to say, "I'm sorry, Aunt, but I fear I must return at least once to Kentwood Hall. I have to return the horse I borrowed, as well as collect my trunk."

He had a feeling his protests were falling on deaf ears, and the sinking feeling in the pit of his stomach was confirmed when his aunt's eyes narrowed, her lips pinched together, and she said, "Oh no, nephew, that will not be necessary. I will send someone to the Hall to return the horse and collect your things. I believe the sooner you leave behind this little escapade the better. The servant can deliver your letters to the family, and there will be an end on it. The sooner you leave behind the temptations of your betters, the sooner this sordid business will be ended. Truly, nephew, it *is* for the best… and I insist," she said, looking him sternly in the eye.

He would be given no choice, it seemed. Yet again, someone had control of his life, and there was little he could do about it if he wanted a chance at a future.

And perhaps it is for the best, he thought, remembering how hard it had been for him to leave Kentwood that morning.

How much harder would it be a second time, knowing it was forever? And what if James asked him to stay? Even if it were only for a few more days, could he refuse the man? Could he turn down such a temptation for the cold reality of the life his aunt was offering him?

The answer to that was obvious. Kyle didn't think he'd ever be able to say no to anything James wanted. His aunt was right. He needed to be away from such temptations before they became his ruin and before he became the cause of ruin or scandal to his friends.

Straightening his shoulders, he managed to say, "Yes, Aunt. It will be as you say. Would it be possible for me to have a few moments to refresh myself before I set to writing the letters?"

"Yes, of course, my boy. Ring the bell, and I will have Pratt show you to your bedchamber. You may write your letters there if you wish. Pratt will come for you when dinner is ready, after which we will return here and discuss your prospects. I have already sent out inquiries as to positions for you among my friends and acquaintances. We will review the replies I have received thus far."

"Yes, thank you, Aunt," Kyle said as a wave of melancholy washed over him.

Pratt, her sour-faced butler, returned and led him to the promised bedchamber, and now here he stood, leaning against the door, head, body, and heart aching in concert.

He knew he needed to get started on the letters. It would take him a long time to decide what to say, how to thank the people who had been so generous to him, how to convey the depths of his feeling for the lord of Kentwood Hall in a manner that would not prove incriminating should it be found.

He desperately wanted to tell James how much their time together had meant to him, and he felt like he was betraying their friendship by not going back and thanking him in person, but there was no way he could now.

The best he could hope for was that James would be able to hear all that he *couldn't* say in the letter he had to write and forgive him for the shabby manner of their parting.

He stood and walked to the basin and ewer atop the lowboy in his room and wet a flannel to wash away the road dust and sweat as best he could without a change of clothes. When he was finished, he sat down at the small escritoire with a heavy heart and began his letters.

Chapter Eleven

JAMES sat in the light of the single lamp on the desk in his study, a brandy in one hand and the letter in the other. He knew he should put it down and go to bed, but he just couldn't seem to stop himself from reading and rereading every line, trying to make sense of it, trying to understand the meaning behind the words. He just couldn't make himself believe that Kyle was gone for good and that the letter in his hands would be the only goodbye, the only explanation, he would receive.

"My aunt has judged it best that I begin my new position as soon as may be. I therefore regret that I will be unable to return to Kentwood to thank you properly for all your kindnesses. It grieves me more than I can say that I will not know the pleasure of your company, and indeed that of your family, again for some time, though it is some comfort to know that I need not impose on your generosity any further.

I beg you to accept my sincerest apologies for being unable to deliver my thanks in person, but given the nature of my difficulties, I felt sure you would understand the need for discretion and a swift resolution to my current predicament. It would wound me deeply should any association with me cause you or your family injury...."

The letter went on in a similar vein for a few more lines with promises to repay any and all debts he'd incurred, as well as instructions to send his trunk with the servant who had brought the letters, and ended with: *Your friend always, Mr. Kyle Allen.*

There was nothing else, no mention of when he might be able to have the "pleasure" of their company again, no mention of where he would be going or what his new position would be or anything.

James stared at the letter until his eyes began to burn and the lines began to blur. He needed to sleep, to collect himself, and neither of those things would happen if he continued as he was. He'd been in a state of emotional upheaval for almost two days without rest, and if he did not get some sleep soon, he wouldn't be capable of even the semblance of composure.

The letters had arrived that afternoon, one for each of them, in the hands of a man on horseback with Gwinny in tow. He wasn't in any formal livery, and James's heart had lurched at the sight of Gwinny without her rider. Thankfully, the servant had been quick to introduce himself and deliver his messages. When asked, he had assured them that Kyle was well, and Ellis, with his usual efficiency, had had the presence of mind to send the man to the kitchens for some refreshment.

They had all gone back into the Hall to read their letters, and, to maintain appearances, he had had to pretend the letter had little more effect on him than mild disappointment. His niece and nephew had had similar letters to his, it seemed, and had exclaimed at length in disappointment before they had all separated to write their replies to send back with the servant.

His reply had been short, a few lines expressing his disappointment, a few more wishing him well, and assurances he would always be welcome at Kentwood. He hadn't known what else to say.

He had retreated back to his study after the servant had gone, using estate business as his excuse again and leaving it only to join the twins for dinner. It had been a subdued meal. It seemed they were all feeling the loss of their new friend, and he had been unable to dredge up enough of his usual mirth to lift the mood. If the twins noticed, they said nothing about it, and he had left them soon after the meal to retreat again to his study.

Ellis had come to check on him at some point, and the twins had come to bid him good night, but he hadn't been able to manage more than a few grumbled words in response.

Sighing and rubbing at his eyes, he finally folded the letter and put it in his desk, closing the drawer firmly.

Enough, you old fool. This isn't any way for a grown man to behave.

His only excuse for himself was that it had been so very long since he'd allowed himself to think beyond the comfortable confines of his quiet, predictable life, so long since he'd allowed anyone other than family to touch his heart.

In all his years, he'd fallen in love only the once, and any wild fantasies he had ever entertained about Jonathan had been buried under a tide of grief and duty all too soon. He'd spent years trying to live up to his father's name, the title and all the duties and responsibilities that had fallen to him too young. He'd even managed to convince himself that he'd been too busy to think of anything else.

When he'd met the earl, that first season in London after Jonathan's letter, he'd been happy to learn that he could find some small measure of contentment without damaging all that he held dear, and he'd settled quite comfortably into a safe routine.

Safe and unfulfilling, but it had been better than nothing at all.

Until now.

Having Kyle, someone he cared for deeply, someone he enjoyed simply spending time with, at his home had made him see all that he had given up by taking the safe path. It had been easy to ignore all such thoughts and yearnings in the past because they had always been abstract. Now he had seen for himself what life could be like with someone you cared for beside you, had seen how well Kyle fit into his home, his *life*, and that small taste left him aching for more.

Not that it makes any difference now. He didn't even give me the chance to try to make it work, he thought, getting angry.

But perhaps it is for the best. I wouldn't have taken the risk for anyone else, and with that temptation so conveniently removed, I won't do something I might come to regret.

Sighing again, he took the lamp and his brandy and headed for his bedchamber. The linens would be fresh, and any trace of Kyle would be gone. If only his memories were so easily cleared away. He'd have to throw away the cravats and that damn vial of oil. It would be a long time before he would need it again, and he could purchase such things on his next trip to London if he felt the need.

Having searched out the offending items from the places he'd stashed them the day before, he disposed of them and set to drinking himself to sleep.

Tomorrow, he vowed. *Tomorrow I will make my peace with this and put it behind me. I only met the man a week ago. It can't take me much more than that to rid myself of this self-indulgent and pointless obsession. I'm Lord James Warren, Viscount Sudbury, not some untried girl to swoon and give in to vapors. I'm better than this!*

THE sky was gray outside the tiny window near his desk, and though it suited Kyle's mood perfectly, he couldn't help but wish for a bit of sunshine to lift it.

He had been at Baxter and Clarke, solicitors in Bury St. Edmunds, for all of three weeks now, working as their newest clerk, and he hated every moment of it. He knew he was being selfish, spoiled, and ungrateful, but he couldn't help his feelings.

His aunt had secured him the position disappointingly quickly. He'd been brought before the two partners for a brief interview and instructed to return the following day to begin work. His aunt had finalized all the details of his employment contract, paid his first month's rent at a boarding house, and left him there with instructions to appear at her door on Sunday morning, and every Sunday following, to accompany her to church. Beyond that, he was left to his own devices.

He knew no one but his aunt, and she seemed little inclined to waste any time introducing him to her friends and acquaintances. After some thought, he decided her generosity must only extend so far, and she would perhaps not risk embarrassment on his behalf until he'd proven himself worthy of introduction into her society.

He tried to make friends with the other two clerks in the office but received only coldness and suspicion in response to his overtures. He didn't know what he'd done to earn their enmity, and they seemed disinclined to share, so he left them to themselves and worked quietly at his little desk, trying to make as little a stir as possible.

The only one who paid him any attention at all was Mr. Baxter, his new employer, and the attentions he received from that front made him nervous and uncomfortable. The man seemed to feel the need to hover over him, standing so close he was always brushing Kyle's arm or shoulders with his own, so close his foul breath and stale sweat would nearly suffocate Kyle some days.

He couldn't tell for certain, but something in him said the man enjoyed his discomfort, that he actually stood that close on purpose, though Kyle was afraid to find out why. He hated it, but there was nothing he could do. He couldn't risk offending his new employer, and he couldn't leave a job after only three weeks and expect his aunt to secure him another position. He was trapped.

By the end of the first week, he was desperately lonely and had fallen into a sort of gray melancholy. He slept fitfully, tortured with dreams of strong, warm arms and tender yet demanding lips. Sometimes the nightmares of Victor would come and he would wake shaking and sick with no one to comfort him. Afraid, ashamed, and miserable, he would prop a chair against his locked door, huddle under his covers, and cry himself back to sleep.

His only comfort came from reading and rereading the letters he had received from James and the twins, though James's letter had been courteous and kind but nothing more. He knew, of course, that there *couldn't* have been more, but he couldn't help looking for it between the lines.

He'd promised himself he would be strong. He would accept the pain because it was a punishment he had earned with his own stupidity and because he truly had no choice. But the truth was, he didn't feel strong. He felt weak and lonely and afraid, and he desperately wanted his dream, his fairy tale, back again. The memories weren't enough, no matter how many times he told himself they'd have to be, and he wondered desperately how long it would take until the pain became bearable.

THE past three weeks had been hard for James. That first week after receiving Kyle's letter, he had alternated between melancholy, bitter anger, and determined cheer on an almost hourly basis, and despite his valiant efforts to hide it, the twins noticed. Ellis noticed. Even his horse noticed. They'd probably be consigning him to Bedlam by Christmas if he kept up like this.

The Hall, once his sanctuary and place of peace and contentment, had turned into a source of unhappiness. In a few short days, that damned beautiful man had managed to leave his mark in every corner of his home. Every room James spent any time at all in held memories of Kyle, and James felt his absence all the more keenly because of it.

The second week, he finally decided that he couldn't be angry with Kyle. The young man had done what was best for both of them, and just because James had wanted more of him didn't mean Kyle had wanted the same. He was angry mostly at himself, angry that he couldn't control his own passions, angry that he'd let himself come to this state, angry that he'd been so reckless in the first place, but most of all, angry that he couldn't help wanting the impossible anyway. This time, for some unknowable reason, he couldn't simply let his wants disappear beneath the yoke of duty and honor. He couldn't let it go.

"You deserve to be happy if any man e'er did...."

Elias's words rang through his head more than a few times during that time. Kyle had made him happy, and now Kyle was gone and he didn't know if he'd ever see him again.

The anger and want would ebb during the daylight hours. The twins would remind him that there was joy outside of Kyle. That he had a family to protect and to love, who loved him in return. Instead of avoiding them like he had when Kyle was there, he took to spending every waking moment in their company. It worked, mostly, at least until they went to bed, leaving him alone with his thoughts.

By the end of the third week, not long before the twins would be leaving him to rejoin their parents, James was almost feeling like himself again. The pain and anger had faded to a dull throb, and he had hope that, given time, he would regain the sense of quiet contentment he'd had before.

He was a little concerned that the twins' departure would leave him too much time to think and the wounds would reopen, and he even considered returning to London with them to see if Elias was still in town, but the thought left him cold. He didn't think he could do it even if he wanted to, at least not now. There or here, he knew where his thoughts would lie for some time to come, so he might as well face it and get it over with.

This morning, he was preparing some letters for his steward when he was interrupted by a knock on his study door.

"Uncle, may I come in?" Anna called from the hall.

"Of course, Anna. I was just finishing some business and getting ready to come looking for the two of you," he replied as he stood.

Anna opened the door, stepped inside, and closed it behind her. It wasn't until she walked around the chair in front of his desk that he noticed she carried a letter in her hand. She looked nervous and graver than James had ever seen her. Just for a moment, she looked so much older that he almost thought it was his sister standing in front of him.

"What's wrong, my dear?" James asked in concern, shaking off that frightening image.

"I got a letter from Mr. Allen this morning, and I decided I needed to speak to you about something… only I don't know how to begin," she answered, raising her hands in a helpless shrug.

James's stomach clenched at Kyle's name, and his grip tightened on the arms of his chair. He gestured for her to sit as he seated himself and tried to smile reassuringly through numb lips. "Anna, sweetling, you know you can talk to me about anything. I love you with all my heart. There's no need for you to be nervous with me."

"Oh Uncle, I know, and I love you too, I just don't know if it's my place to speak of such things with you… but there is no one else, and I just can't leave things as they are. It's simply not in me to turn away from those I care for, especially when they're hurting." There were tears in the corners of her eyes now, and James couldn't help but stand again and walk around the desk to kneel beside her chair, taking her hand.

"Anna, what do you mean? Who's hurting?" he asked.

"Both of you," she replied quietly, and James felt a tremor of fear run through him.

"Anna...."

"No, Uncle, now that I've started, let me finish. I... I liked Kyle, Mr. Allen, I mean, very much, from the first moment I saw him." She blushed but took a breath and rushed on. "He was so handsome and sweet and gentle, and I couldn't help but like him, but he didn't seem to admire me the way that I admired him. It hurt. I won't say it didn't, but I kept hoping, if we spent more time together, maybe he would come to feel more for me. I watched him, perhaps more than I should have, I admit, but it wasn't me he kept looking at, or Andrew, it was you. I would catch him looking at you all the time, and the *way* he looked at you confused me. But then I would catch you looking at him in the same fashion, and I started to understand, I think."

"Anna, don't. Please just leave it be. Mr. Allen is gone now, to a new life, without any of us. There's no need to talk about this any further," James said as he stood and moved away from his niece. His heart was pounding in his ears and breaking for his niece all at the same time. Dear God, had he really been so obvious?

"No," she said, standing and moving closer to him. "Uncle, you know I respect you and would normally obey you, as is my duty, but this once, please don't make me. You said we could talk about anything, and I really need to talk to you about this. I need to understand."

James didn't say anything. He couldn't. This was not a conversation he should have with his niece, but he'd never truly denied her anything. He didn't want to create a chasm of any kind between them, but he had no earthly idea what to say to her, so he remained silent.

"Uncle? I heard Kyle, Mr. Allen, crying the night we arrived at Kentwood. I woke to a cry and went to check on it when I saw you go into his room. No one else heard him, I'm sure. Andrew is such a sound sleeper, and Mrs. Holt is deaf as a post, but *I* heard it," she said, looking at him so earnestly he wanted to weep.

"The next day you disappeared all day, and then that next morning you were acting so strangely... you were so happy, but when you heard he had left, you looked so shocked... and these past weeks, you've been so different. I've never known you to be this way, Uncle, and I had to suspect it had something to do with Mr. Allen. What's happening, Uncle? Please tell me."

"I don't know what to say to you, Anna. This isn't a proper conversation for us to have," he replied, shaking his head but not looking at her.

She stomped her foot in what appeared to be a fit of pique, and James almost smiled, would have smiled, if his stomach weren't tying itself in knots. His little imp wasn't so grown up yet, after all.

"No. I won't hear of propriety or impropriety when it's just the two of us having a private family conversation. I may still be young, but I'm not an imbecile or a silly little girl, either." She sounded so much like her mother that James felt the almost irresistible urge to duck his head and slink away.

"Uncle, I know there are things that people simply don't talk about. I spend hours and hours in the salons and parlors of London *not* talking about all of them, until my head is almost spinning with everything I *haven't* heard. And because people will never come out and talk about those things, I never really get the chance to understand them, and I *want* to understand. But most of all, I want the people I love to be happy, and when I see that they aren't, it breaks my heart." The last words were said with a tremor that James couldn't ignore. He gathered his niece to his chest and held her close.

"Anna, don't cry. You know I can't take it when you cry. You'll break *my* heart. Please stop. Please? What do you want me to tell you?" he choked out.

"I'm not crying," she said, though her sniffle belied the statement. "I just want to know the truth, Uncle. Is… are you and Mr. Allen… are you… in love?"

James sighed. There was no way out of this without either refusing to answer or lying, and he didn't feel she'd accept either. "No, sweetling, we aren't in love. We only just met. I… care for him very much, and I will not lie to you, I miss him very much now that he is gone. But it takes two people to be *in love*, and as you see, I am here alone…."

"But you've been so miserable. I've seen it, and you looked so happy that one morning. To be flying so high one moment and crashing into the depths of despair the next, surely that's love, Uncle."

"You've been reading too many novels," he said, chuckling, then held up his hands in surrender when she glared up at him. "I have been wallowing in self-pity and misery quite a bit of late, and it has been very selfish of me. I admit that. I do miss him, Anna, and perhaps more. But please don't ask me to speak of things that can't be. If you know all that you're implying, then you know it is not only considered immoral and a mortal sin, but it's also against the law. I've told no one and I will tell no one, and I would beg you to do the same."

"And if he's as miserable as you are, Uncle? What then?" she asked, pulling away and looking into his eyes.

"What do you mean?" he asked, as the knife that seemed to be permanently embedded in his belly did another twist.

"His letter. I received it this morning. I wrote him last week. I didn't want him to think we'd forgotten him so soon, and his other letter seemed so unhappy that I wanted to make sure he was well," she said as a slight blush crept up her cheeks. "He's miserable, Uncle, I can just tell. He talks of his new position and lodgings and nothing else. I don't believe he has any friends. He… he asks about you, and Andrew and me, of course, but mostly about you. He misses you, Uncle. I know he does. It's just silly for both of you to be unhappy and apart when you should be happy here together."

"It's not that simple, Anna, and you know it. Most, if not all, of England would disagree with you on that score. He has to live his own life, and I have to live mine. I can't just keep him here. People would talk. There would be a scandal. And even if there weren't, I can't make him stay here with me if he doesn't wish to."

"He does wish to. You're both just being silly," she said, sniffing.

It was time to take control of this conversation and act like the grown man he was supposed to be. "No, Anna, we're both being *safe*. The safety and honor of my family and the people I care about are more important to me than anything else. It is a hard lesson to learn, my dear, but there are some things in this world that cannot be changed. The hardest lesson of all is learning to accept that and finding what happiness you can. Perhaps someday things will be different, but they aren't now. I love you. I love your brother, your mother, and your father. That will always be enough for me. It has to be."

If only I could convince my own traitorous heart of that, life would be a lot less painful for me right now.

She looked very much like she wanted to argue, but she held her tongue, and tears welled in her eyes. He gathered her close and held her tight for a few more moments before stepping back and offering her his handkerchief.

"Now, my dear, let's have done with all this nonsense. I am happy enough, and I'm sure Mr. Allen just needs time to adjust to his new life. You'll see, by and by. I am sure his next letter to you will be more cheerful."

At least I dearly hope so.

"All right, Uncle," she sighed. "Perhaps you are right and I'm letting my feelings and my naïveté cloud my judgment. I will leave it for now."

James was a little suspicious of her sudden capitulation, but he decided to let it go for both their sakes. He wasn't sure he could continue this conversation without breaking down himself.

"Good. Then if you don't mind, I have a few more things to get settled before I join you and your brother?"

"Yes, Uncle. We will be ready when you are."

As she made her way to the door, James decided he really needed to say more.

"Anna. As to what you have guessed about me… and Mr. Allen, I would beg you not to speak of it with anyone, including and most especially your brother and your mother and father." He hated to ask her to keep secrets, but he also couldn't bear to lose the love of his family, especially not now.

"I understand, Uncle. You have my word that I will not breathe so much as a whisper of it to anyone, though Andrew has already guessed," she replied.

"He has? Was I that obvious?" he said. *Bloody hell!*

"Not *obvious*, but we aren't blind, Uncle, especially not to the people we love. We've never seen you so discomposed in our entire lives, and we were worried. We talked about it for many hours before some things started to make sense, things we'd always wondered about, like why you hadn't taken a wife or even a mistress…." She giggled. "Oh, don't look so shocked, Uncle. Gossip is the stock and trade of every parlor in London, and if you listen well enough you can learn all sorts of things your mother would wish you didn't."

She was blushing now, despite the mischievous and somewhat smug gleam in her eye. "Well, anyway, Andrew and I haven't talked so much in ages, though I would have been happier about *that* if we weren't so concerned for you. We both hate to see you unhappy, and we realized that perhaps you had been at least a little unhappy for a very long time, especially when we saw how happy you were that morning before you realized he was gone. If Mr. Allen is the reason for that, then we are grateful to him. And if being without him is what has left you so unhappy now, well…." She shrugged and fell silent.

"Is that how Andrew feels as well?" he couldn't help asking. He remembered his nephew's words from only a few days before, but that didn't mean that such acceptance and understanding would be the same for "uncle" as it was for "friend."

"You'll have to ask *him* that, Uncle, though I believe so. He loves you as I do, and we've never been a family to allow others to make up our minds for us. You might perhaps want to give him a little time to get used to the idea before you talk to him. He seemed a bit shaken last night, but I don't think you need worry. As for Mother and Father, well, I will keep my word and say nothing of it. I don't know what they would say, but I'd like to think they'd want you to be happy, as we do."

"Thank you, Anna. I'm quite overwhelmed, and I hardly know what to say. I don't know what I have done to earn such a wonderful niece, but I am so very grateful to have you." He was on the verge of tears again, and that simply would not do. It was bad enough to be having such a conversation with his nineteen-year-old niece, but he absolutely refused to bawl like a baby in front of her.

"Oh, stop now, you'll make me cry again," she said, waving her hands at him and making him chuckle. "Finish your letters and come on that ride with us."

"Yes, I'll be there soon," he said as she turned and left. The door had barely closed before he'd collapsed in his chair and put his head in his hands. When he raised it again, he noticed his niece had left Kyle's letter on his desk, and he couldn't help but pick it up and begin to read.

It was as Anna had said. The tone of the letter was so unlike the bright, playful young man he remembered that it broke his heart... but what could he do? Everything he had told his niece was true. He couldn't just scoop Kyle up on his horse and ride off with him.

What has happened to me?

His entire world had been turned upside down in the space of a few days, and nothing would ever be the same again. He wasn't even sure he knew his own mind anymore.

He was still pondering the letter when there was another knock on the door. "Come," he said.

"My lord, an express was just delivered for you," Ellis said, standing in the doorway, holding an envelope.

"Thank you, Ellis," he replied, taking the letter. His heart sped as he recognized Harrow's seal. Breaking it with shaking hands, he opened the letter and leaned back into his chair to read it, leaving Ellis to stand in the door waiting for him.

The letter was short and to the point, for which James was grateful. But what it held sent a chill of fear through him.

My dear friend,

I apologize for not sending word sooner regarding the matter we discussed some weeks ago, but my inquiries yielded very little until this very morning. The news may be all over London within a day or so, but I felt I should send word as quickly as possible, as the young man we spoke of may be in some danger. I will be brief now, and we may share details at a later time.

The man, W, whom we discussed, is apparently in some serious financial difficulties at present. It seems his appearance of affluence was only that. He is rumored to have mortgaged what properties he had to the hilt and borrowed more based on his connections and prospects. He is also rumored to have involved some of those connections in his dealings with promises of substantial return. His partner, a man named Wells, is said to be telling all to the authorities in hopes of receiving clemency.

Whatever dealings he had have gone sour and are rumored to have been less than legal in some instances. His creditors and friends are all on the hunt for him. There are rumors he is fled to Europe with moneys that are not his own.

I would not have sent this message so urgently if I had not heard other rumors this very morning about the man that had never even been whispered about prior to this scandal. I have heard from one of his friends that there was a scandal some years ago involving a young man in Dublin. They were together for some time. Then the young man vanished mysteriously, and W returned to England without him. My source informs me that W is an extremely possessive man, and the fate of that boy always gave him cause for concern.

I wish I had more than vague rumors to give you, old friend, but I have not. I only wish to warn you that, from all I've been told, W may not walk away from your friend so easily as you would like. Look after your friend and warn him that should W wish to cause trouble, it will most likely be now or never.

Write to me as soon as you can so I will not worry.

The letter was signed with a single sprawling "H," a remnant of their more intimate days together, when the letters they had exchanged didn't bear his seal or any other identifying markers, but the private joke between them failed to make him smile this time.

Kyle could be in danger.

His heart lurched at the thought. Part of him said that it was unlikely Weir would bother traveling all the way to Suffolk when he was being pursued by so many. But another part of him realized that Kyle was indeed worth such effort. If *he* was willing to consider turning his life upside down for the man, it shouldn't surprise him that Weir might be willing to travel a little out of his way for a chance at him.

After a few minutes of quiet, Ellis said worriedly, "My lord?" and James realized he'd left the man standing there while he'd been buried in his thoughts.

"I'm sorry, Ellis. There's no reply. Please see that the man has what he needs and let him be on his way. I must get to the stables at once," he said. He stood and made his way toward the door, and Ellis stepped back to make way for him.

"Of course, my lord. I hope it is nothing serious." Ellis looked deeply troubled, and James took a moment to clasp the man on the shoulder in gratitude. He was indeed lucky to have such people around him, and he hadn't had the decency to show it of late.

"I hope so too, Ellis. Will you tell the twins I had to go out and I won't be back before dark? I will send word if I don't return tomorrow. Tell them I have to go to Bury St. Edmunds on urgent business," he said, releasing Ellis's shoulder and turning to go.

"Certainly, my lord," Ellis replied as James made his way down the hall and out the front doors. Before he'd made it down the steps to the courtyard, he heard Ellis say behind him, "Good luck, my lord."

When James looked up, startled, he barely caught a glimpse of Ellis's smile before he closed the doors to the house. Wondering only for a moment at his enigmatic behavior, he shook his head and strode quickly toward the stables, his mind fully focused on Kyle.

There's probably no need for such a fuss, he reassured himself. *But it can't hurt to warn the lad and make sure he's all right... just this once.*

He hadn't managed to convince his gut of that by the time he took to the road, and Percy, sensitive to his body more than his wishes, took it at a gallop. He reined himself and the horse in before too long. They had nearly fifteen miles to go, and Percy would kill himself trying to keep that pace.

Chapter
Twelve

KYLE had just finished his last letter for one of Mr. Baxter's clients when the man himself leaned over his shoulder to check his work.

"Excellent, Allen," he said leaning close as he always did. Kyle was shaking so much from lack of food and sleep that he'd barely been able to write at all, but it seemed he'd managed well enough.

I'm so tired, was all that he could think at the moment. He didn't even care that the horrible man had put his hand on his shoulder, so close to his neck that his fingers brushed Kyle's throat through his cravat.

Baxter leaned closer to him, and when Kyle didn't resist, he put his other hand on Kyle's left shoulder, mirroring the first. "Since you are doing so well with us, Mr. Allen, perhaps we should discuss an increase in your wages," the man whispered in his ear.

That suggestion, and the bile rising in his throat, managed to rouse him out of his stupor enough that he could pull away from the man, stand, and take a few shaking steps around the desk. "Thank you, Mr. Baxter, but I believe it's too soon for such marked favoritism. Surely the other clerks would take it amiss if I received an increase when they have seniority," he managed weakly.

"Don't be silly, Allen. If the other clerks possessed your skills and attributes, then of course they would receive special regard. As they do not, it falls to you," the man gritted out as he walked around the desk toward Kyle, a distinctly predatory gleam in his eye. "And, of course, there's no need for them to know of it, either," he whispered, holding Kyle's stare and chuckling as Kyle backed a few more steps.

He was saved from any further discussion when Mr. Clarke came out of his office and moved toward them. "Still here, Allen? That's what I like to see, a man who has enough pride in his work to stay until it's done. Mr. Baxter and I have a few more things to discuss this evening, but you may go home now. We don't want you to wear yourself out too soon. In fact, you are looking a little unwell. You should most definitely go home and rest."

Taking his words like a gift from above, Kyle picked up his hat and all but ran from the offices, not even looking in Baxter's direction. He threw a "Thank you, sir" on his way out the door and heard a chuckle from Mr. Clarke. Baxter said nothing, and Kyle was glad for that. He never wanted to hear the man's voice again if he could help it.

What am I going to do? I need this position! He felt sick and shaky and just wanted to get back to his rooms and crawl under his bedclothes and cry.

I know I have to pay for my mistakes, but I thought I had paid enough by now. Damn it all to hell! I'm doing everything I'm supposed to be doing, and I'm still being punished. Why?

He railed inside at God, everyone, and no one in particular. He was so caught up in his misery that he didn't even notice a shadow break away from the alley he had passed and begin trailing him down the street.

By the time he reached the boarding house, he was so exhausted he could barely put one foot in front of the other. His head was spinning, and he just couldn't think any more. He *had* to sleep.

He didn't remember climbing the stairs, but he must have, because before he knew it, he found himself in front of his door. Pulling the key from his pocket, he unlocked the door and all but fell inside. He was just throwing the bolt on the door when someone knocked. Thinking it must be Mrs. Trumble, the widow who owned the house, he pulled back on the bolt and opened the door.

"Hello, pretty," Weir said with a smirk on his lips, then he pushed his way inside the room, knocking Kyle off balance. He fell to the floor, landing on his rump as all the air left his lungs.

Oh God, no more, please, no more! his mind screamed even as he struggled to catch his breath.

Weir threw the bolt on the door, then dropped to one knee in front of Kyle, slapping his palm over Kyle's mouth and saying, "Not a word, you little whore. Not one word. You'll do as you're told or I'll have to punish you, is that understood?"

He stood then, dragging Kyle up by his arm and propelling him toward the bed. "You've led me a merry little chase, little one. I have to be honest. I didn't know you had it in you. It took much longer than I expected to find you. Of course, I had other, more important things on my mind," Victor said as he calmly walked toward Kyle, removing his gloves and placing them on the small table where Kyle ate his meals.

"You have a great deal to make up for, my little whore," he continued as he looked Kyle over appraisingly. "I was going to simply have you pack your things and accompany me back to the inn. But now that I see you, I think you need a little lesson in obedience first. I think your time with the Ashtons may have given you too high an opinion of yourself, and I can't have you causing trouble, now can I?"

Kyle was shaking in earnest now. Victor looked so cold and smug that Kyle wondered how he could have ever been attracted to the man. *Why didn't I see how truly ugly he was before now?*

"Victor please, don't do this," Kyle begged. "If I owe you for all that you gave me, I'll find the money to pay you back, I swear."

Victor laughed, if something so chilling could be called such. "Money? Oh no, little one, such things are beneath us, don't you think?" Victor stood over him now and slid his hand over Kyle's cheek. When Kyle flinched, Victor clasped his chin in a painful grip and leaned in close, hissing, "You are mine. I *own* you. You gave yourself to me the moment you left Shropshire with me, and I keep what's mine until *I* decide I'm done with it."

Victor released his chin and walked back to the small table, sitting down in one of the two plain wooden chairs. As he sat, Kyle noticed the knife hilt protruding from the top of his boot. "Now, take off your clothes and come here," he instructed.

Kyle tried to swallow around the knot of fear in his throat and began untying his cravat slowly, hoping his muddled brain would come up with some way to help him. His hands shook so much that he wouldn't have been able to do it quickly even if he'd wanted to.

"Kyle." The warning in Victor's voice went straight to his already weakened knees. "I would not recommend trying my patience right now. At this moment, I'm willing to consider forgiving you with only a small show of obedience on your part. If you continue to try my temper in this manner, it will be a *very* long time before you earn that honor."

Kyle quickly removed his cravat and jacket before hurrying to unbutton his waistcoat. He rushed through the rest of his clothes in a panic, and his heart was racing so fast in his chest he feared he might faint.

"Better," Victor said. "Now, come here."

Kyle walked on wooden legs toward Victor.

"You haven't been eating, little one," Victor said with a feigned concern that made him want to retch. "We'll have to fatten you back up again lest you fade away to dust before I've had my fill of you. Go wash yourself. I want you clean before I even think of touching you."

Victor waved his hand to the small dresser that held his basin and ewer, and Kyle moved to stand in front of it. With a shaking hand, he grasped the handle and froze. But it wasn't panic that held him still, not this time, not ever again.

NO! No, I won't do this. I don't care what he does to me. I won't simply lie down and submit to him again! If he wants anything from me, he's going to have to take it. I've already given myself to the only man in the world who means anything to me. Victor can't have me.

"*You're braver than you know.*" James's words suddenly drifted through his mind, and he sobbed at the memory of the tenderness the man had shown him.

"Now, now, little one, no need to cry. If you simply do as I say from now on, I will find it in my heart to forgive you. I assure you. No one will ever care for you as I will, you'll see. You belong to me, and I take care of what's mine," Victor said, coming up behind him and resting his hands on Kyle's shoulders.

The touch reminded him of Mr. Baxter's advances, and a black rage welled up inside him so strong it left him nearly blind. Without even seeing what he was doing, he swung the ewer around and felt it shatter against something hard. Victor crumpled to the floor with a thud as Kyle stumbled back against the wall. For several long moments, he stood in shock, staring at the man lying on his floor, blood dripping from his head. Then his legs finally gave out and he slid to the floor, drawing his knees to his chest and wrapping his arms around them.

BY THE time James and Percy trotted into Bury St. Edmunds, the sun was nearing the horizon, and he was beginning to feel a little foolish. What on earth would he say to Kyle when he saw him? "Sorry to bother you, but I heard a vague rumor that perhaps your ex-lover might be a murderer, is now desperate, and may come looking for you before he flees to the continent?"

James shook his head. Perhaps he had been a little silly to ride all this way when he might have simply sent a messenger to deliver the warning. And perhaps his desire to see the young man again had overridden any common sense he had.

Will I ever be able to be rational when it comes to Kyle?

He rode through the streets of the town until he saw the inn he used when visiting in this part of the county. Handing his mount to the stable boy, he went in to ask the innkeeper to board his horse and for directions to the boarding house named in Kyle's letter to Anna.

He decided not to take the innkeeper up on his offer of a bath and a room to refresh himself in. Though he was still feeling a little silly, he couldn't help being pushed by that same sense of urgency that had brought him this far, and he set off across the town to Kyle's rooms without further delay.

He found the house soon enough, and his knock was answered by a plump woman with graying brown hair dressed in black with a frilly white apron.

She looked a bit distracted, but James plowed on with as much dignity as he could muster in his present travel-stained state. "Good evening, Mrs. Trumble. I am Lord Warren, Viscount Sudbury, and I wish to pay a call on Mr. Kyle Allen, if he is receiving," he said, handing her his card.

She looked startled for a moment before she blushed and bobbed a curtsy. "Of course, my lord, I was just going to go check on the lad meself. He seemed a mite ill last I saw him, and I heard a loud noise come from his room just a moment ago. I feared he might have hurt hisself."

James's stomach lurched at her words, and he made quick to offer, "Please, madam, may I go and check on him for you? He is a dear friend, and I am here out of concern for his welfare."

"Oh, certainly, my lord. Please come in. He's the last door on the right," she said, pointing up the stairs.

James ran up the stairs two at a time, his anxiety increasing to the point where he didn't care how unseemly his actions were. He rushed down the hall and knocked on the door she indicated. "Kyle! Mr. Allen, are you there?"

When he didn't hear anything, he pounded on the door again and tried the handle. The knob turned, but the door was bolted from the inside. He was set to knock again when he heard a muffled sob from beyond the door and panicked. Not bothering to knock again, he simply slammed himself against the door until the bolt gave way and let him into the room.

The sight that met him when he entered sent him into a maelstrom of anger and fear. Kyle was naked, curled around himself and leaning against the wall, staring at Weir's bleeding body. Shards of broken pottery were scattered about the floor, and the handle of the shattered pitcher was still gripped in Kyle's hand.

He stood there stupidly, staring at Kyle, for he didn't even know how long. It took the sound of heavy footsteps on the stairs and Mrs. Trumble's voice calling to him to break him out of his shock. Rushing to the bed, he grabbed the counterpane and carried it over to Kyle.

Wrapping him in it tightly, he drew the unresisting young man toward the door and sat him in one of the small wooden chairs by the table. Making sure he was fully covered so the woman couldn't see his state of undress, James moved to the door and stood by it, blocking her view of the rest of the room.

Taking a calming breath, he pulled on every bit of dignity and pride he had before addressing the woman as she came down the hall.

"Everything is well, Mrs. Trumble. I apologize for the door, but when Mr. Allen wouldn't answer, I feared he was seriously ill. He is unwell, as you see, but not at death's door as I feared." He forced a chuckle and prayed it sounded better than it felt. "I was perhaps a bit too hasty, and I will of course pay for the damage to the door."

The woman was flushed and out of breath as she said, "I was as concerned as you, my lord, I assure you. Mr. Allen, are you well? Do you need me to send for the doctor?"

James prayed Kyle would be able to pull himself together enough to answer her. The last thing they needed was for a doctor to come before he could do something about Weir.

He was relieved on more than one count when Kyle managed to say, "No, Mrs. Trumble. I am well enough. I don't need you to send for anyone. I will recover soon enough. I am only tired, that is all."

"I will see to him, Mrs. Trumble. You need not fear for him. He will be well taken care of, I assure you," James said, hoping the woman understood it as the dismissal it was.

"Oh, of course, my lord, I'm sure he is in excellent hands. I just worry about these young men on their own sometimes. They don't take care of themselves without a wife or a mother to do it for them, and he hasn't eaten more'n a sparrow in all the time he's been here," she said, aiming a motherly frown of disapproval at Kyle. "Please let me know as soon as you are better, Mr. Allen, and if there's anythin' else I can do for you." She bobbed another curtsy toward James and turned back down the hall.

James closed the door and crossed to kneel next to Kyle. "Are you hurt, Kyle? Did he hurt you?"

Tears showed at the corners of his eyes and fell as Kyle shook his head. "No, no, he didn't touch me." He felt the knot of fear unclench inside him at Kyle's answer and wrapped his arms around him, pulling him close.

"Thank God," James said, sliding a hand up to cradle Kyle's head and closing his eyes on his own tears of relief.

They stayed that way for several moments before a strangled moan from the man on the floor drew James's attention. Up until that moment, he hadn't known whether the man was alive or dead, and he frankly hadn't cared. But now that he knew the man was alive, he had to make a plan quickly before he raised a fuss.

He didn't want to let Kyle go, particularly after the way the young man jerked in his arms at the sound of Weir's moan, but he didn't have much choice. Settling Kyle back in the seat, he cupped that beautiful face in his palms and said, "Do you still trust me, Kyle?"

Kyle's eyes stayed locked with his as he nodded.

"Good. If you are well enough, then I want you to get dressed and help me get *that* downstairs," he continued, pointing to Weir. "Then I want you to leave us and wait for me at the inn," he said.

When it looked like Kyle would argue with him, he leaned forward and captured his mouth in a tender kiss. Kyle opened for him immediately, and the kiss became deeper and longer than he had intended. Pulling away, James had to catch his breath… and his wits.

"Trust me, Kyle. Do this for me, please?"

Kyle bit his lower lip and nodded, though he didn't look happy about it. James smiled. "Go on now, get started while I look after *that*," he said, nodding again to the moaning body on the floor.

By the time Kyle was fully dressed, James had gotten Weir's hands tied behind his back and had propped him against the wall. The man was moaning louder now, so James took Weir's cravat and gagged him with it. He also took a rag and wiped up any blood that had dripped to the floor, stuffing the soiled cloth in Weir's waistcoat for want of a better place to hide it.

After he finished, James looked up to find Kyle staring at the two of them. His gaze was still a little unfocused, and he looked quite pale.

James worried that the shock might be too much for him.

He stood and walked to Kyle, gathered him into his arms, and pressed his cheek to those soft black curls. Drawing back so he could look Kyle in the eyes, he asked, "Are you sure you can do this? I'll find another way if you say so. You've been through so much, there's no shame in it."

"No, I can do it," Kyle answered, though his voice was barely more than a whisper. "He, he has a knife... in his boot."

"Thank you, Kyle," James said, retrieving it. "Let's be quick about it, then. Go make sure no one's about," he ordered.

He would have preferred to wait for a later hour, but he really didn't think keeping Kyle in a room with Weir for hours, waiting for the dead of night, would be good for him. He wanted to get rid of Weir and get to reassuring both of them that Kyle was truly safe and unharmed as soon as possible.

The sun had dropped below the horizon as they made their way down the stairs. They propped Weir against the side of the building, and at James's instruction, Kyle went back inside to find Mrs. Trumble. James told him to inform her that he would be leaving for a few days to rest and regain his strength and to apologize for "dropping" his ewer in his weakened state, as someone would surely find the mess when they cleaned his room.

That done, he sent Kyle on his way with a hug and a kiss on the forehead, promising he would meet him at the inn soon. As Kyle disappeared in the darkness, James went in search of a cart for hire as well as the home of Mr. Alfred Watts, the chief magistrate.

With a little money and some small explanation, he and the carter got Weir bundled into the trap and set off to find the magistrate. He instructed the boy to stay with their prisoner while he climbed the step to the door and rang the bell.

After apologizing for the late call and handing his card to the butler, he was ushered into a parlor to wait for Mr. Watts. He'd met the man at several house parties in the county. Though Watts was a bit serious for James's tastes, he was an intelligent enough man.

Watts, small, round, and balding, came puffing into the room only a few moments later.

"My Lord Warren, this *is* unexpected, but welcome, welcome. Please sit," he said, indicating the padded chairs to their right.

"Thank you, Watts. I apologize for the hour but I have a rather urgent case for you," James replied.

"Oh dear, of course, my lord, how may I be of service?" His round cheeks were flushed red, and his eyes widened in excitement.

"The hour is late, and I'm sure I've taken you from your supper, so I will try to be brief. I arrived in town just this afternoon to pay a call on a friend of my nephew's, only to come across a known fugitive from justice in your midst," he said smoothly.

This first part, at least, was true. He didn't want to lie to the man, but he wouldn't be able to leave Kyle out of the matter if he didn't, so he sucked in a breath and continued. "A Mr. Victor Weir, recently of London. I was informed only this morning by the Earl of Harrow, a good friend, that he is sought on charges of fraud and larceny against several prominent families but disappeared before he could be arrested."

James's mention of the Earl had the desired effect, as the man's eyes widened even further and his back straightened. James now had no doubt the man would take him at his word and not question his tale any further, not that he would have dared question a viscount, either, but it couldn't hurt to throw a little more weight behind it.

"When I confronted the man, he lashed out at me in a most unseemly fashion, and I was forced to subdue him," he continued. "I, of course, came straight to you, and I fear I must apologize for my most disreputable appearance, but I believed the matter could not wait for me to repair the damages done by my journey and my altercation with the scoundrel."

"The man's name is Weir, you say?" Watts asked, and James saw recognition in his eyes. For a moment, he feared this might be one of Weir's many friends, but his fears were eased when the man continued, "My brother has invested with a Mr. Weir. There's talk of fraud? Thievery?"

"Yes, Mr. Watts. I believe there is. He's in front of your house at this moment. I fear I had to bind him lest the man try to escape again," James said, smiling to himself. If this brother turned out to be someone Weir had swindled, Watts would be more than willing to take Weir off his hands. "I would of course have preferred to leave his capture to you, but I feared, being the scoundrel he is, the man might get away before a proper party could be raised."

"Oh, of course, my lord. Please don't apologize. You have done our little town a great service by not allowing such a man to remain free among us. Who knows what he might have done, had you waited?" Watts stood as he spoke, and James rose to his feet as well. "Now I suppose I must see to this scoundrel myself."

They made their way back out the main hall and through the doors to the street. Weir was more awake now, sitting up and glaring daggers at him.

"Oh my, you did have to subdue him, didn't you?" Watts said, putting a hand to his chest in surprise.

"I fear it was necessary. I would not remove the gag unless you are quite prepared for the most deplorable language," James replied with a smirk only Weir could see.

"I suppose we should call for the doctor to have a look at that head, though," Watts said worriedly.

"That would be a good idea, though I would not recommend removing his bindings unless you have more men about you. The man is quite strong and may commit violence in an attempt to escape," James replied, enjoying himself now.

Watts sent word to the tavern, and a couple of very large men who looked to James to be farmers returned with the servant and carried Weir off toward the back of the house.

"I thank you again, my lord, for your help in apprehending this man," Watts said when the men disappeared around the corner. "My constables and I will take things from here. I will send word to my brother and the authorities in London so I may have a full accounting of the man's crimes. I'm sure we will have no trouble holding him until the proper authorities come to claim him. If my brother is indeed a victim of this man, I feel sure he will come himself to see that he's brought to justice. Will my lord be staying in the area, should I need any more information?" Watts asked.

Now James had to think fast. He needed to get Kyle somewhere private, but Kentwood was too far for them to journey tonight. Luckily, before the man could become suspicious, an idea occurred to him that just might be perfect.

"I had originally planned to stay at the inn, sir, but I fear all the excitement has been a bit much for me. I believe I will seek out more peaceful accommodations at a friend's lodge nearby. Ethan Truitt is an old and dear friend. He is currently in London, I believe, but has offered me the use of his lodge at any time should I wish it," James replied.

Truitt had actually only said he was "welcome any time," and though James knew this wasn't exactly what he'd meant, he hoped the man wouldn't mind him sneaking into the lodge while he was away. He and Kyle needed time alone together, without prying ears or eyes, and he knew for a fact Truitt had yet to find a caretaker for his lodge. "I will be returning to Kentwood Hall tomorrow morning and will of course be 'at home' should you need anything further from me."

"Thank you, my lord, you are most generous. I will send word of any developments."

James smiled and returned the man's bow with a nod. "Thank you, Watts. I will look forward to your news. Good evening, sir."

"Good evening, my lord." The man turned and puffed quickly back into his house, presumably to write his letters, and James hurried back to the inn.

He found Kyle at the back of the inn's common room, holding a pint of ale with both hands as if it were a lifeline. When he caught sight of James, he jumped to his feet and quickly made his way over to him.

"My lord, I—" Kyle began before James interrupted him.

"No, Kyle, not here. Come with me," he said, turning and heading toward the stables. He had them bring Percy out, and he and Kyle walked to the edge of town. Once far enough away from curious eyes, he mounted, drew Kyle up behind him, and continued on the road north.

Truitt's lodge was set back a bit from the road but only a few short miles out of town. The moon was near full, as it had been the last time they were together, so it was not difficult to spot it and find a way inside. After getting Percy settled in the small stable behind the lodge, James made his way into the kitchen, where Kyle stood waiting for him.

"I suppose we would have been more comfortable at the inn," he said, "but I thought you might want peace and quiet more than comfort."

Now that the crisis was over, he wasn't sure how to proceed. Kyle had said nothing since they'd left the inn, and James's doubts were beginning to surface.

"Thank you, my lord," Kyle began before turning his back on James and hunching his shoulders. "I didn't thank you yet for rescuing me *again*. I apologize."

"Nonsense, Kyle, you didn't appear to need any rescuing. I merely helped clean things up a bit, that's all," he said, taking the last few steps to stand behind Kyle.

He reached out a hand to touch but drew it back again. He wasn't sure if that was what Kyle needed or even wanted. His chest ached with the need to comfort and reassure him, but now that they were alone together, his uncertainties were returning full force.

Kyle made the decision for him by turning and burying his face in James's shoulder. James's arms came up instinctively to hug his lover fiercely, and the ache in his chest eased. Had he really thought he could find any kind of peace and contentment without Kyle? One touch and he knew that he'd been fooling himself.

"I missed you, Kyle," he murmured, pressing his lips to that lovely hair.

"Oh God, I missed you too, my lord," he replied, and James pulled Kyle more tightly against him.

They stood like that in silence a while longer before James said, "Kyle, we have much to talk about, but it's been a very long day for both of us. I think we need to rest first."

"Will you stay with me?" Kyle said into his chest.

"Of course. Come. Let's see if we can find us a place to sleep."

James stepped away from him and clasped his hand, drawing him further into the house as he sought the guest room where he'd stayed in the past. The lodge had been closed up for months, and the furniture was draped in cloths that reflected the moonlight, making it easier to navigate the unfamiliar rooms. The guest room was as stuffy as the rest of the house, so James let go of Kyle's hand long enough to open the drapes and windows, airing the place out.

The late summer evenings were still warm enough to be comfortable, but the slightly cooler air was fresh and clean and felt wonderful against his heated skin. He found bed linens in the chest at the foot of the bed. They'd been packed away with lavender and other herbs, and the crisp, fresh scent wafted through the room as he draped them over the mattress. He'd never made a bed in his life, so he didn't even try to accomplish the task. He simply spread the linens across the mattress, making a nest, and hoped that would be sufficient.

He then began removing his clothes, happy to be out of the soiled garments that now clung to him from the heat of the day. Kyle helped him off with his boots and set about removing his own garments. When they were both naked, they slid into the pile of linens, and Kyle climbed halfway on top of him, resting his head on James's shoulder.

He wasn't surprised when Kyle's breathing slowed almost the instant his head touched his shoulder. He'd looked worn almost to death *hours* earlier, and James didn't know how he'd managed to keep going as long as he had.

Though he was tired as well, it took James a while longer before he could surrender to sleep. The long ride and all the worry had drained his body but not quieted his mind. It felt so good to be lying there with Kyle sleeping in his arms, part of him didn't *want* to miss any of it by sleeping, even if his whirling thoughts would allow it.

He had to chuckle at himself after a while. For someone who considered himself a man of action more than thought, he'd been doing a lot of thinking of late. The young man in his arms had stirred up a veritable hornet's nest within him, and, not being used to the sensation, he'd been at a loss as to how to deal with it.

But that night, with a pleasantly cool breeze coming from the window and the man he loved lying safe and sound in his arms, a sense of peace flooded him that he hadn't known since before the death of his parents. The feeling gave him a clarity of thought he'd been unable to achieve up until that very moment.

Yes, he was in love with Kyle, there was no doubting it. Now all he had to do was determine where to go from there. His thoughts slowed and began to take on shape and order for the first time in weeks.

The crux of the problem, he finally decided, was that he'd always followed the same path to achieve his goals: he determined what it was he wanted, he developed a plan of action to achieve it, and he implemented that plan until he was successful.

In the current situation, "what he wanted" was something he couldn't have, not without risking nearly everything else. It was a risk he couldn't bring himself to take, the one time in his life that his name and title could not give him what he wanted, but it was a dream his heart had been unwilling to let go. And therein lay the dilemma that had been tearing him apart.

Anna's words to him from that morning chose that moment to echo in his mind. *"It's just silly for both of you to be unhappy and apart when you should be happy here together."* And he realized she was right. It *was* silly.

He was an intelligent, educated man, for God's sake. He should be able to find some way to have Kyle in his life. Even if they were only to meet once or twice in a year, it would be better than not having him at all. Bury St. Edmunds was not so far away. He could visit easily enough. He would have to find a more private place for Kyle to live, of course, but it could be done. It wasn't truly ideal, but it was a place to start, at the very least.

Feeling better by the moment, now that he had decided on a goal and could move forward with making a plan, he pulled the linens a little tighter around them both and finally allowed sleep to claim him.

Chapter
Thirteen

KYLE woke to warm arms and soft linens tangled about him. Bright sunlight and birdsong streamed through the open windows, and he thought he'd never seen a more beautiful day. He would have liked to stay just where he was forever, but he desperately needed to relieve himself and had delayed it as long as he possibly could.

He slid out of James's embrace, trying his best not to wake the man and, after a quick search, found the chamber pot in the bedside table. He decided for modesty's sake to take it into another room to take care of necessities. Once he'd finished, he scurried quickly back to their shared bedroom and slid back under the warm covers. Though too early still to hold the chill of autumn, the air was cool on his naked body, and James's warmth a relief.

He settled back next to James as quietly as he could, not wanting to disturb him, and propped himself on his elbow so he could gaze at the man to his heart's content. He was every bit as handsome as Kyle remembered, but he couldn't help but notice faint shadows beneath his wonderful eyes. He wondered if perhaps their parting had been as hard on his lord as it had been on himself.

"I missed you, Kyle." He remembered those words from the night before with thrill of pleasure.

He missed me and he came for me. Kyle was giddy with the thought that such a wonderful man could care enough for him to come and find him. He still didn't know why James had come when he did, as they hadn't spoken of it, but at the moment he didn't care. He was safe and warm in the arms of the man he loved, and it would have to be enough. He wouldn't spoil it yet with thoughts of Victor and annoying practicalities.

Continuing his examination, he noticed that James had let his hair grow in the time they had been apart. It tumbled in thick brown waves across his forehead. He liked the longer length. It begged to be played with, and as Kyle leaned in to do just that, he found those beloved warm brown eyes regarding him and crinkling in the corners with a smile.

"Good morning, my lord," he murmured past the heat of his body's reaction to that smile.

"Good morning, Kyle," James said, as his smile deepened and those wonderful eyes darkened. "I think we already established that you would call me James from now on, didn't we?" James chuckled, then leaned forward, stopping mere inches from his mouth, and whispered, "I want to hear you say my name."

That warm breath ghosting over his lips combined with the husky whisper caused Kyle's heart to race and a shiver to run the length of his body.

"James." It was more of a whisper than the seductive purr he had wanted, but James's reaction proved he was not disappointed.

Kyle's eyes widened as James rolled on top of him, pressing him into the mattress before claiming his lips in a passionate kiss. His lips parted under James's onslaught, allowing his lover to plunder his mouth for long moments, luxuriating in the possessiveness of it.

James broke away first, trailing hot kisses down his throat, then he pulled back and looked deeply into his eyes. "Are you sure, Kyle? After all that happened yesterday, if you need time, if you want to rest...."

"No, don't stop. I don't want to talk about it now. I don't want to think about any of it right now. Please. I need... I just need you. Here. Now," he said, desperately trying to make James understand what he needed.

James looked at him only a moment longer before smiling that warm and wicked smile that made Kyle's belly flip and leaning back down to capture his lips.

Kyle was torn between wanting to submit, allowing himself to simply melt into that kiss, and wanting to dig his hands into those broad shoulders and return the kiss with equal ferocity. He ended by doing a little of both, allowing his body to relax and mold itself to that warm, powerful chest while plunging his tongue into James's hot mouth, dueling with his tongue and nipping at his lips.

Oh God, yes. This was what he needed. This man and no other. All the pain and misery of the last few weeks faded to nothing under the tenderness and passion of that kiss. He was safe there, and cherished. This man was home, and he knew he'd never truly be happy anywhere else.

James pressed him back into the pillows and gentled their kiss, taking control of the encounter and forcing Kyle to slow down.

His lover then moved to lie alongside him and stroked those broad strong hands over his body in long, lazy caresses. When Kyle opened his eyes, he found James's awed and proprietary gaze fixed on him.

"You are so lovely, Kyle. I think I could simply lie here and drink in the sight of you for hours," he said in that deep bass that Kyle could feel through every inch of his body.

James's hands then lit upon his nipples, teasing and tugging until Kyle let out a whimper. In response, James's fingers pinched harder, making him gasp at the sudden sting.

"So much for simply enjoying the view," he heard James comment with a somewhat husky chuckle. "You'll make a liar of me if you keep making such pretty sounds."

Kyle had almost pulled his wits together enough to make a reply when he felt James's hair brush his chin and warm, wet lips latch onto one of his stinging nipples. James gently soothed the hurt away with his tongue, then moved to do the same to the other before Kyle felt him pull back and blow cool air over each of them.

By now, Kyle was near to bursting with need. His fine, handsome lord might be able to wait all afternoon, but he certainly could not. For three weeks, he'd dreamt of being in James's arms again, and though he was enjoying the teasing torment, he needed more. He needed those hands and that mouth on the aching flesh pulsing against his belly, and he needed so much to be claimed again, to be taken by his lord and possessed fully, to be shown whom he belonged to.

He felt a little ashamed at that need, particularly after his relationship with Victor and his promises to himself, but deep down he knew that James could never be like Victor. That belonging to this man wouldn't mean shame and humiliation but being cherished and treasured. That he could allow himself to be claimed without losing himself to it.

Looking into the eyes of the man he loved, he said, "Please, James, please take me again."

The gorgeous man beside him groaned and closed his eyes for a moment before saying, "Not this time, sweet. We have nothing to ease the way, and I would not hurt you."

Kyle felt his face fall, and he knew he was pouting in a most infantile fashion, but he couldn't help showing his disappointment. He felt more than heard James growl and capture his lower lip between bared teeth. "Don't pout, Kyle. Though it's utterly charming, there's no call for it. There are more ways for us to please one another than that. I won't leave you wanting, you have my word."

"I don't doubt you, James," he replied, loving the way his lover's name felt on his lips. "I only want to feel you inside me again, filling me, making me yours."

Victor had taken him almost dry more than once, and it had hurt, but he was more than willing to take the pain if it meant he could be with James, if only his lover would accept that.

"Oh, Kyle, you *are* mine. All mine," James told him as he leaned forward for another deep kiss, and Kyle felt his cock gripped firmly in one of those big hands.

As a broad thumb stroked over his slick crown, Kyle realized there was a way he could get what he wanted, if only he could overcome his embarrassment and convince his lover of it. He'd had a difficult enough time not blushing with his earlier declarations.

Too embarrassed to say his thoughts aloud, Kyle decided to show his lover what he wanted. As James slowly caressed his aching shaft, Kyle took both his hands and captured James's hand between them. Looking deeply into James's eyes, he began thrusting into the cocoon created by their three hands clasped together in a fast but steady rhythm.

He watched James's surprise fade to the same bemused look Kyle had seen on his face before, when he'd been bold with his desires. Even in so short a time, Kyle knew that, though James liked to hold the reins, he would indulge his lover in most anything he wanted.

As Kyle continued to thrust himself to climax, he never took his eyes from James's, watching as those warm brown depths turned nearly black with desire.

"Yes, beautiful boy. Show me," James said, and that was all it took to push Kyle into bliss. He couldn't maintain eye contact in that moment. His back bowed and his head slammed back onto the mattress, and he arched his throat and cried out as his spend shot into their clasped hands.

"So beautiful," he heard his lover murmur as he kissed and licked a line down Kyle's neck, dipping his tongue into the hollow at the base of his throat.

Kyle took a moment to come back to himself, but when he felt James attempt to disentangle their hands around his softening cock, Kyle tightened his grip, not letting him go. One of his lover's dark brows arched in question when Kyle met his gaze again, and Kyle smiled shyly as he worked up the courage to pursue the next part of his idea. Cupping James's hand in both of his, he reached down and slid them over his lover's straining cock, coating it in his spend.

James's startled gaze soon turned to one of understanding, and that devilish smile spread over his lips, easing Kyle's fears that his act might somehow offend his lover. "Clever boy," James said with a chuckle. "You certainly have a way of getting what you want from me, despite my protests. Not that I'm complaining, mind you. But I have a feeling I may have to use a firmer hand with you in the future, lest I spoil you too much."

Before Kyle could absorb the meaning implied by those words,

James slid his hands under Kyle's knees and drew them up to his chest. He then slid his fingers through the slick fluid that had escaped their hands and fallen on Kyle's belly, thoroughly coating them in it before reaching down to Kyle's entrance. Kyle lay back and moaned as he felt James's finger slide inside him, gently stroking several times before another finger joined the first.

The fingers moved in him, stretching him, opening him, slowly sliding over that wonderful place inside him, and he was lost in the sensation. Without the urgency of his own need distracting him, Kyle could simply give himself over to the pleasure of his lover's gentle ministrations. James was so tender with him, exactly as he'd imagined he would be, that Kyle became almost drunk with the sensual pleasure of it.

When James removed his fingers and rose up between his thighs, Kyle followed him with sleepy eyes. But the drowsy pleasure didn't last long. He soon felt himself hardening again when his lover lowered himself into the cradle of Kyle's hips and slid his thick cock alongside Kyle's own. He watched with growing passion as James moved his cock through the last of the spend coating his cock and belly, grasping both their shafts in his large hand and pumping them together. When he was fully hard again and his hips were jerking against that hand, James released his hold and drew one of Kyle's legs over his shoulder.

Kyle watched as James grasped his glistening shaft and shifted downward. He met Kyle's eyes again, and in the bright light of day, he could see the passion and desire in his lover's eyes as he felt the slick crown circle his entrance several times before being nudged forward. "Open for me, sweet. Breathe out and take me in." James's choked whisper drifted up to him, and Kyle relaxed and did as he was bid.

Kyle felt himself slowly being filled as James worked himself gently inside. *Yes!* This was what he wanted, what he needed. The last time they were together had been wonderful, but having James fully in command this time, taking charge of him, was all that he'd dreamed of and more.

His other leg was drawn up on the opposite shoulder as his lover bent forward to take his mouth, and the feeling of being completely surrounded, filled, enveloped in the man he loved drew a moan from so deep within him it seemed born from his soul. James must have felt some of the depth of the emotion in that sound, because his own moan rumbled through both their bodies, adding to Kyle's already indescribable pleasure.

He reached out to capture James's head in his hands and hold him close, and James responded by deepening the kiss and quickening his thrusts into Kyle's body. He pulled back only enough for both of them to gasp for breath and pressed his forehead to Kyle's. James then lifted Kyle further up with strong hands digging into his hips, and the new angle slid James's fat cock over that glorious spot inside him with every thrust. Soon Kyle was lost to anything but that feeling and the need to meet each thrust with equal force.

He drew his hands away from James's head and braced his palms flat against the head of the bed, arching his neck as the pleasure in him built and the blood pounded in his ears. He didn't even know what the sounds that were coming out of his mouth were, but they seemed to inflame his lover, who began pounding him even harder, saying, "Yes, Kyle, sing for me. Let me hear you."

He felt James's big hand engulf his cock then, and his bollocks drew up tight against his body. He gave in to the pressure almost immediately, cried out, and spent, riding the waves of pleasure as his vision faded out. The clenching of his body must have been too much for his lover, because moments later he heard James shout, felt his hard fingers dig into his hips and his full weight slam against his arse, straining against him as if he wanted to go even deeper.

When Kyle's vision cleared and he'd relaxed his body onto the mattress, James leaned in and pressed their foreheads together again. They lay like that, panting, for several long moments before James chuckled, tenderly kissed his lips, and said, "What you do to me...."

He received another heart-wrenchingly sweet kiss before James moved off him and lay back on the mattress, drawing Kyle partially on top of him. Kyle closed his eyes and rested his head on that broad chest as the sweet peace that he felt whenever he was in James's arms stole over him. Though he wanted to savor the moment for as long as he could, the trials of the past weeks caught up with him again, and he was asleep in moments.

JAMES held Kyle's sleeping body in drowsy contentment until the summer heat became too much for him. He slid out from under his lover as carefully as he could, hoping he wouldn't wake. In the light of day, it was even more apparent that Kyle had not been eating or sleeping well since the last time they were together, and he wanted him to get as much rest as he could.

He gathered his clothes from the floor and slipped down to the kitchen and out the back door. He drew water from the well and rooted around until he found a flannel to wash with. He experienced a queer sort of pleasure and pride in fending for himself, though he supposed that was rather silly of him. He was fairly certain the novelty would wear off quickly enough.

A quick search of the kitchen revealed that there was no food to be had. The staff had been very thorough in closing up the lodge, so he and Kyle would have to return to the inn before their bellies could be filled. They would have to have their talk on empty stomachs, it seemed.

Brushing off his clothes as best he could, James realized they were in a frightful state, but there was little he could do about it. He would have to send Kyle into town alone to make arrangements for the food, as he really shouldn't be seen in such a state. While he wasn't a vain man, he did have a reputation to uphold, and he would draw the wrong kind of attention dressed as he was.

He washed his shirt and hoped the September sun would dry it quickly, then donned his trousers and boots and went to see to Percy, watering him and brushing some of the dust from his coat. Playing the part of a groom was also a novelty, though his father had made sure he was taught proper care of his mount from an early age.

At least Percy will look respectable, he thought as he allowed Percy to graze in the field next to the lodge.

His shirt was still damp but he decided that it would have to do as he couldn't continue to roam around half-clothed. To give Kyle a little longer to rest, he took a short walk around the lodge, enjoying the air and letting his protesting muscles relax with the exercise. The air was fresh and the sun a comforting warmth on his shoulders now that he was out of the house. He felt truly happy, despite lingering doubts as to their future together.

After another hour had passed, he decided he had given Kyle as much time as he could and returned to the lodge. He didn't want to wake him yet, but they really needed to make a start. There was much to do and talk of, and truth be told, he couldn't wait any longer to hear Kyle's answers to the questions he wished to ask.

As he entered the room, he was struck again by how lovely Kyle was. His lean body was stretched out on the bed, linens tangled about his legs, and his black curls were tumbled over his forehead. James knew he would never grow tired of that sight. In sleep, with his thick eyelashes fanned across his cheek, he looked even younger than he did awake, and the rush of desire he felt at the sight made James feel a little like a despoiler of innocents until he remembered the ferocity of Kyle's responses the night before and let the feeling go with a chuckle. If Kyle was being despoiled, it was because he wanted to be.

Grinning, James sat on the edge of the bed and leaned in to wake his lover with a kiss. He drew back to find those green eyes gazing warmly at him and a shy smile playing about those soft lips.

"Good afternoon, my sweet," James said as warmth bloomed in his chest at that smile.

"Good afternoon. Have I slept too long?" Kyle replied with a yawn.

"No. In truth, you need more than you've had. I would love to keep you in bed all day"—he paused a moment to waggle his eyebrows and watch the blush creep over Kyle's cheeks before sighing dramatically and continuing—"but alas, I fear we have much to discuss, and we need to find something to fill your belly before a strong breeze carries you away from me." They both laughed as Kyle's stomach chose that moment to make its wishes known.

"I see what you mean. I fear I have not eaten well of late," Kyle replied.

"You should take better care of yourself, Kyle," he said, sobering. "But as I am here now, I will do it for you, at least today. We shall make a start soon, and I will find food for us both, but first there is much I would say to you and much I would ask, if you'll allow it."

Kyle's smile faded to a worried frown as James took a breath and took both of Kyle's hands in his before starting the speech he'd been preparing all morning. "Forgive me, but I am no great speaker, Kyle. I can only speak from my heart and hope it proves enough. So much has happened in so short a time I can hardly credit it. We've barely spent more than a few days in each other's company, and yet I feel so strong an attachment to you that it frightens me. In short, I believe I have fallen in love with you, Kyle. I think I fell the moment I saw you walk through the doors of my Hall."

He watched as Kyle's eye widened and his mouth opened in apparent shock. Squeezing Kyle's hands more tightly, he pressed on. "The days you were in my home were the happiest and most torturous days of my life. I spent a good deal of time at war with myself because of you. I knew I wanted to have you there with me, forever if I could, but I could not reconcile that wish with the demands of my honor and my family, so I said and did nothing."

He pulled Kyle's hands to his lips, kissed each one, and held them there as he continued. "But you were brave enough for both of us the night you came to me. You were so sweet, so passionate. I knew I was lost, and I cannot tell you my pain when I heard you had gone." He paused and took another breath, letting Kyle absorb what he was saying and watching his reactions.

"After receiving your letter, I convinced myself that your leaving was for the best, that what I wanted was impossible and you would be happier here. But now, I think perhaps I was wrong. If I am, please tell me, for I am more than willing to face any difficulty to have you in my life, Kyle, in any way that I can, if that is what you want."

Kyle wasn't looking at him now, he was staring at the linens covering his lap, and tears were sliding down his face.

"Kyle? Won't you speak to me? Tell me what you're feeling?" he said over the lump of fear in his throat. Perhaps he had misunderstood.

He watched with trepidation as Kyle breathed deeply and withdrew his hands from James's grasp. "Oh, James, I don't deserve you. I'm so ashamed of myself it hurts. Of course I feel the same. How could I not? But you don't know all that happened. You don't know… and if you did, I fear you wouldn't want me."

An image of Kyle crouched naked on the floor crying next to Weir's body flashed in his mind, and his stomach twisted. "Oh, Kyle, I didn't even think, forgive me. Yesterday, did he… did Weir hurt you?" James's stomach roiled, and his rage returned.

"No, no, nothing like that. I hit him before he could hurt me again. I'm ashamed because of before, because I let him do those things to me." Kyle looked up with anguished eyes. "I never tried to stop him, not once. I let him make decisions for me, let him argue with my father for me, let him dress me, tell me what to do, all of it. I never fought him. Even that night, the night he… hurt me. I didn't fight. I didn't do anything but… let him. What kind of man does that make me? How could you possibly love someone who is such a coward?"

"Kyle, you are *not* a coward," he said, reaching forward and cupping Kyle's chin in both hands. "You stood up for yourself yesterday. You thrashed the villain soundly. That is not the act of a coward. As for before, you are young, Kyle. That is the only crime you could possibly be accused of, and it's a small one, at that. Weir took advantage of your innocence. You trusted him, and he betrayed that trust. That is not weakness or cowardice. It takes a great deal of courage to trust as you did."

Kyle still wouldn't look at him, so James tried another tack. "You remember what I told you before, in London and at Kentwood? That if you could not trust your own judgment, that you should trust that your friends would not choose so poorly? Trust in me, Kyle. Trust that I have the discernment to know a good man when I see one. I would not fall in love with a coward, my sweet."

Kyle looked up then. There were still tears in his eyes, but James read hope there as well. James smiled and leaned forward to claim Kyle's lips before pulling back and resting their foreheads together.

"Tell me you can trust me enough to prove to you that I am right. Give me that chance." He looked into Kyle's eyes until the young man nodded, then leaned back. "I know it will take time, Kyle. All I ask is that you give us both that time. There are still many things that we will have to overcome, but as long as we both want this, I believe we may find a way."

"I want that very much," Kyle replied.

"Good. Now, today we need only decide where you would like to go. Weir will no longer trouble you. I have seen to that."

At Kyle's shocked look, James chuckled. "Never fear. Much as I would have liked to, I did no harm to the man. I only delivered him to those he has harmed. He is this moment on his way to London to answer charges of fraud and larceny. And though he has many friends, I believe few of them will come to his aid in this. You may return to your life in Bury St Edmunds without fear, if that is your wish. Is that what you want?"

"No, I don't want that. I don't really have much of a life there. My position, I fear, may be already lost," Kyle said. "As I am not at my desk this morning and have sent no word, my new employers may have already decided to terminate my contract. If that is the case, I fear my aunt will have no more to do with me. I don't wish to sound ungrateful to her, but she made it clear that her generosity would extend no further than it had already gone."

"I'm sure your employer would understand if we explained that you were unwell, Kyle. I hardly think they would sack you for missing one day due to illness," he tried to reassure Kyle.

"Well, that may be true, but…." Kyle lowered his head and paled a little, making James worry. "I would rather not go back there, if it's all the same. I… I didn't like it there, and Mr. Baxter is not a nice man. He, well, he makes me uncomfortable."

James's hands tightened around Kyle's, and he asked, "What is it he did that made you uncomfortable, Kyle?"

When Kyle wouldn't look at him, James's stomach knotted and he reached for the lad's chin to raise it, forcing Kyle to meet his eyes. Kyle looked pained, bright spots of color showed on his cheeks, and his mouth twisted in a grimace as he replied, "He touches me all the time, and yesterday he offered to raise my wages if I went with him to his office to 'discuss' the matter. I left the office as soon as I could after Mr. Clarke came in and distracted him. I don't want to go back there."

"Nor shall you. If that's how it is, there's no way I will allow you to go back there," James said, almost growling the response. The thought of someone with his hands on Kyle set his temper simmering. "We can still visit your aunt, if you wish, and try to explain things to her."

"No, it would not help to see her. She ordered me not to see any of you again, believing that my spending time with people above my station led me down paths of temptation that I could not afford. She won't be softened by a visit from you, I think," Kyle said, shaking his head. Then he smirked, and some of the humor James had seen far too rarely showed in his eyes as he said, "And perhaps she's right, though I don't believe she knew what kind of temptation you represented."

James smiled at Kyle's attempt at humor and said, "Well, I suppose that means you're all mine then, doesn't it?"

Kyle sobered and looked questioningly into his eyes as he whispered, "Yes, only yours... if you'll have me."

James pulled Kyle into his lap, kissed him soundly, and said, "Of course I'll have you." They stayed like that for several moments, fussing and cooing over one another, until the touches became heated and they were both breathing heavily.

"Enough for now," James panted, pulling back. "We'll have plenty of time for that later. Right now we need to head to town and gather your belongings. After we procure some food from the inn, we'll hire a horse for you and ride for Kentwood. I'll send a servant for your trunk, and we can figure out what to do next after we've both had time to rest and think on the matter some more. You *should* at least write to your aunt. Perhaps in time she'll forgive you and accept your decision. I would not wish for you to lose all connection to your family, Kyle."

Kyle sighed against his chest and said, "I suppose you're right. I will write to her as soon as we arrive at the Hall. I can at least promise to pay her back for the expenses she incurred securing me that position, even if I hated it." Kyle tipped his head up and captured James's lips again before whispering, "Can we go home now?"

He couldn't help the little leap of his heart at Kyle's use of the word "home." Though he didn't know how they would manage it, he dearly wanted for him to be able to call Kentwood that for the rest of his days.

Chapter
Fourteen

A SHORT time later, they were cleaned and dressed as well as they could be, and they left the lodge and headed back to town. They collected Kyle's things, purchased food for their journey, and hired the horse without incident. James remained a short distance off, mounted on Percy, as Kyle made the necessary arrangements, hoping no one would notice the sad state of his clothes. Using James's name, it took Kyle no time at all to find a horse, and shortly thereafter, they were on their way home.

They set a slow pace, as Kyle was a little sore, and James couldn't help a wicked grin every time his lover grimaced, knowing he was the man responsible. Even so, it took less than three hours to reach the gates of Kentwood, and by the time they reached the courtyard, Anna, Andrew, and Ellis were waiting for them on the steps to the house.

As they approached the group together, he began to feel nervous over the reception they would receive, though Anna dispelled the feeling as soon as they dismounted.

"Uncle, Mr. Allen, welcome back! We can't wait to hear your news," she said with her usual cheerfulness, and he was relieved to see her looking concerned but happy to see them.

The grooms had come running at the sound of hooves on the drive, and soon Percy and Kyle's hired horse were led away to be cleaned and pampered.

As they approached the steps, Andrew extended his hand to Kyle and said, "Yes. Welcome back, Allen. We were… concerned for you."

James could not read anything from his nephew's tone or his expression, but Anna had asked him to give Andrew time only yesterday morning, and he consoled himself that one day probably did not constitute enough time for his nephew to get used to the idea of him and Kyle together.

"Well? Come on into the house. We want to hear all about your adventures," Anna said, breaking into his thoughts.

"Yes, my dear. You'll hear all about it *after* I've had a chance to bathe and Allen has had a chance to rest," he replied. At her disappointed pout, he promised to be down as soon as he was fit to be seen, and she sighed in resignation, turned, and shooed her brother before her, heading for the drawing room.

"Welcome back, Mr. Allen," Ellis said after the twins had gone inside, then he turned to James with an enigmatic smile and said, "I hope all is now as it should be, my lord?"

James raised an eyebrow at the smile but replied simply, "Yes, Ellis, thank you, all is now well. Will you have baths drawn for both of us and send Edwards to me? Mr. Allen has been unwell and will rest in his room this afternoon, so would you please send up a tray in case he becomes hungry?"

"Very good, my lord," Ellis replied with a bow.

Kyle looked like he would protest, but James cut him off. "You need your rest, Allen. It's been a long three weeks, and we'll have plenty of time to talk later." He gave Kyle a pleading look, and the young man surrendered.

"Yes, my lord, thank you. I *am* a little tired," he said.

They both headed up the main staircase while Ellis went to see to his master's wishes. They were alone in the hall when they reached Kyle's door, so James took the opportunity to pin his lover against it and kiss him soundly. He broke away after footsteps sounded on the servant's stairs, and he bid Kyle good afternoon with a twinkle in his eye and a smirk that promised more to come later.

After Edwards got him settled in his bath, James sent him to check on Kyle. When his valet returned, he was informed that Kyle had fallen asleep in his bath, confirming his earlier suspicions that his lover had been hiding the extent of his fatigue. Edwards assured him that Kyle was no longer in danger of drowning and was, even now, tucked into his bed for the afternoon.

When James finished his own bath without falling asleep, Edwards helped him dress for dinner, and he descended the stairs with a strange mixture of joy and unease twisting around in his stomach. When he reached the drawing room, he found both his niece and his nephew pretending to read books, evidenced by the fact that Andrew's was upside down and Anna dropped hers the second he appeared in the doorway.

"So? Tell, tell!" Anna said impatiently.

"My dear, didn't your governess teach you patience?" James teased.

"I believe the subject of my education is one we've already covered, Uncle, though Mrs. Holt is in the kitchens if you would like to ask her," she harrumphed.

"No, no need for that," he said, chuckling. "All right, my little imp, I won't tease you any further. I'll tell my tale if you pour me some of that lovely tea."

She rushed from her seat to comply and settled on the couch next to him as he sipped.

"I apologize for leaving you so suddenly yesterday. After our talk that morning, I received word from an old friend in London that Mr. Weir was on the run from the law and his creditors and that Mr. Allen might be in danger from him." He paused at their shocked expressions and sipped his tea before resuming his narrative.

"When I arrived at the boarding house where Mr. Allen was staying, I found Weir on the ground with a broken head and Allen nearby in shock." The twins didn't need to know Kyle had been unclothed at the time; the story appeared to be distressing enough for them.

"Oh, Uncle, how horrid! Was Mr. Allen injured?" Anna exclaimed with wide, concerned eyes.

"No, he was unhurt. He bested the blackguard with nary a scratch," he answered proudly. "I decided that it would be best if Allen weren't involved in a scandal, so I took Weir myself to the chief magistrate and turned him over. He shouldn't be back to bother any of us again."

"Oh, that's good news. Who would have ever guessed we'd have such high adventure in our quiet little lives," Anna said with a flush in her cheeks that worried him.

"Hardly high adventure, my dear. And criminals aren't as romantic as they seem in novels, Anna. Allen could have been truly injured by that man, and several families have lost their fortunes to his treachery," he felt compelled to mention.

"I know, Uncle, but you have to admit it was exciting," she murmured in a somewhat chastened tone, though he wasn't sure he could believe it.

"Will Mr. Allen be staying here now, Uncle?" Andrew asked, changing the topic and drawing his attention.

"Yes, Andrew, at least for the time being. He needs time to rest and recuperate, and the position his aunt found for him was not ideal; he won't be going back there," he answered, watching his nephew closely for any hint as to what he was feeling.

"Oh, that's wonderful news. I'm so glad. He didn't seem at all happy there," Anna said before dropping her voice to a whisper and grabbing his hand. "I'm happy for both of you, Uncle."

"Thank you, Anna," he murmured back, kissing her hand before glancing at Andrew.

His nephew looked like he was about to say something when Ellis arrived to call them to dinner. Andrew rose and followed him out without another word, and James was left wondering what he had intended to say.

At dinner, he went into greater detail about their adventure, leaving out the best parts, of course. Anna sat and listened with rapt attention, joking with him and asking questions, while Andrew remained markedly silent and pensive. Kyle did not come down to dinner, and though he worried, James decided it was better not to disturb him.

After dinner, Anna played for them while he and Andrew sipped their port. They played a few rounds of Whist with Mrs. Holt before she and Anna retired early, leaving him and Andrew alone. In the uncomfortable silence that followed, he suggested they retire to the library for billiards, and Andrew readily agreed.

During their second game, and not inconsequentially, their third glass of port, Andrew set his stick down and cleared his throat. Part of James hoped that he and his nephew were now going to clear the air between them, while the other part hoped that they weren't.

He feared what his nephew might think, and he didn't want to risk losing his nephew's respect, but Pandora's box had already been opened, and there was no going back to the way things were. He needed to know where his nephew stood, even if the answer tore his heart out, but he wanted the young man to come to it in his own time, so he waited as the silence stretched between them.

"Uncle, I've been thinking a great deal over the last two days," Andrew started, then sighed. "Damn, but this is uncomfortable."

James had to chuckle at that, and Andrew joined him with a rueful grin. As he watched, his nephew took a deep breath and started again.

"It isn't any of my business, really, this thing between you and Allen. It isn't anyone's business but yours, in truth. Mother and Father taught us that if you aren't hurting anyone, you should be able to think however you choose. They were discussing the Church at the time, but I think the same rule applies. I won't say that this wasn't a shock, but I suppose I will get over it in time."

Andrew paused, picked up his port, and finished the glass in one gulp, then cleared his throat again and looked James in the eye. "You are still one of the finest men I know, Uncle. I love you and because I love you I want you to be happy." The last was said in a rush of words, as if he were embarrassed to say them.

"And I am blessed with having some of the finest men *I* know within my own family," James said over the lump in his throat. He held out his hand to his nephew to shake like men, though in truth he dearly wanted to hug the young man like he did when he was a boy. "Thank you, nephew. I can't say how much those words mean to me."

Andrew shook his hand, still looking a little embarrassed, then picked up his stick to continue their game. They played a while longer in silence, allowing themselves to settle after their emotionally charged conversation, and James decided it was probably time for him to say good night and check on Kyle. When he set his stick down, however, Andrew had another surprise for him.

"Before you go, Uncle, there is something else I've been thinking on these past two days that I would like to speak with you about, if I may," he said with a speculative gleam in his eyes.

"Of course, nephew," he replied, unsure if his heart could take any more conversations with his family.

Andrew picked up his glass and refilled it halfway, leaned against the wall nearest him, and swirled the contents of his cup. Watching the liquid in his glass and purposefully *not* looking at James, he said, "I believe I've decided that I should perhaps expend a little more effort with regards to my inheritance. To that end, I believe it would benefit me greatly to be more involved in the workings of the estate here at Kentwood, to learn at your knee, as it were."

James watched with a bemused smile, and his nephew stood away from the wall and began to pace the room, gesticulating as if he were on a stage. "As mother is always saying, it's high time I stopped wasting myself in aimless frivolity and learned more about the duties and responsibilities of my birthright."

Here he paused and looked back at James from under his eyelashes, a mischievous smile playing about his lips. "When the time comes, hopefully in the *far*-distant future, I will, of course, want my own man to help me run the place. Jackson, your steward, is, I'm sure, a very fine and capable man, but he *is* getting on in years and will want to retire before too long. I think it might be best if we found a man whom we both can agree on to be his successor, someone of good breeding who is loyal and trustworthy. Such a man is a rare find indeed these days. Perhaps we should even look for someone my own age so that we may learn this business together."

When James's smile widened, as he began to catch Andrew's

meaning, Andrew continued, "Now, I know that it's said to be bad business to employ your friends, but I think the risk is well worth the reward in this case. I couldn't oversee all of my friend's training, as I will be back at Cambridge, and I must visit my father's estates as well, but I'm sure you could serve as well in my place. And, as my friend, he will of course be invited to join us on family trips and holidays should he choose."

At that, James couldn't help but chuckle. He was tempted to say his nephew was being rather high-handed, but as it was all to his benefit, he decided to hold his tongue.

Andrew tried to give him an arch look, but the quirk of his lips ruined the effect. Clearing his throat, he said, "As I was saying, he may travel some with me and the family, so I see no need to find a permanent place for him in the neighborhood just yet. I dare say we could find room for my friend in the Hall, at least for the foreseeable future. And after Jackson retires, well, the steward's house may come empty, but I see no need to rush the man and his wife out of it if they do not wish to go. Don't you agree?"

"Certainly, nephew. There should be no reason to force Jackson out before he's ready," James replied, playing along.

"I will of course pay his salary from my own allowance until such time as he takes up official duties on the estate. Perhaps Jackson himself could provide some input as to what salary his deputy should receive."

Then Andrew waved his hand dismissively and said, "But these are all matters that can be ironed out over time, I think. My friend has obviously been a little ill of late and needs time to rest and get his strength back. It would be ungenerous of me to put him to work before he is fully recovered, if indeed he chooses to accept the position I am offering at all. Perhaps you could mention it, Uncle, the next time you speak to him, and we can discuss it and decide upon the details when I am home for Christmas?"

James couldn't help but walk over to his nephew and clap him on the shoulder. "I think that is an excellent idea, nephew. Your sister is right. You have quite the head for schemes and strategy… when you choose to use it," he said, then he chuckled at Andrew's slightly affronted frown.

"Thank you, Uncle… I think," Andrew replied.

"Well, if we are done with your revelations for today, I believe I am ready to go to bed. It's been a long day," he said as Andrew nodded his agreement.

They headed up the stairs together, but when they reached Kyle's door, Andrew left him, calling, "Good night, Uncle" over his shoulder.

He was just about to knock when he saw Ellis coming down the hall.

"Will you be needing anything else tonight, my lord?" Ellis said.

"No, thank you, Ellis. I believe I have all that I require," he replied.

"Very good, my lord. I have taken the liberty of informing the staff not to disturb you or your guests tomorrow morning unless rung for. I hope that meets with your approval?" Ellis said, then he smiled innocently at James's raised brow.

"And, if I may be so bold," he continued, "I would like to say how very good it is to see your good spirits returned, my lord. I have been very concerned for you."

"Ellis, I…" James started, then stopped as he realized Ellis had nodded toward Kyle's door when he'd said "good spirits."

As James continued to stare at his butler and friend, trying to discern if there were deeper meanings to his words, Ellis raised his own brows, but his face otherwise remained blank.

"If that is all, my lord?" Ellis prompted.

"Yes, thank you, Ellis, that will be all," he replied, and he watched as the older man headed toward the stairs with a strange smile on his face.

Before his butler made it halfway down the stairs, James called after him, "And Ellis? I am glad my good spirits have returned as well, thank you for your concern."

Ellis's smile widened, and he bowed before turning back to the stairs to finish his duties for the night.

James turned back to Kyle's door with a bemused smile but barely raised his hand to knock before the door opened.

"Is he gone?" a somewhat rumpled Kyle asked, blinking in the light of the lamp he carried.

"Yes. How are you feeling, Kyle? We missed you at dinner," James replied quietly, stepping into the room.

"I *am* sorry. I seem to have slept the day away. I felt as if I hadn't slept in months, but I am feeling much recovered now," Kyle said.

He looked so adorable in his rumpled shirt with his black curls scattered at odd angles about his head that James couldn't help but set his lamp down and pull his lover against him for a deep, slow, and sensual kiss.

Kyle melted against him almost immediately and opened his mouth to suck James's tongue inside. He stayed there a while, exploring Kyle's mouth languidly, running his tongue over every inch before pulling back to suck on that plump lower lip. When he pulled away completely, Kyle whimpered in protest, and James had to chuckle.

"Patience. We shouldn't go much further here. I fear the walls are a little too thin and my niece and nephew are too close," he said, willing his pulse to slow long enough for him to plan a few practical precautions. "My rooms are further away, and the bedchamber is much better insulated. Come."

He opened the door, checking the hall for servants, then grabbed the lamp with one hand and Kyle with the other. He led his lover down the hall, taking a moment to lock Kyle's door with the skeleton key only he and Ellis had copies of. That way, should any servant happen to have missed Ellis's instructions, it would simply appear as if Kyle had locked himself within his chamber.

They entered his rooms, and James turned to lock his own door behind him. When he turned around, he found that Kyle had already removed his nightshirt and was walking backward toward the bedchamber with a teasing smile on his face. All thoughts of taking a moment to discuss Andrew's plan flew from his head at the sight of Kyle naked and taunting him. With a devilish grin of his own, he stalked his lover to the bed, planted his hand in the center of Kyle's chest, and gave him a good shove.

With a rather endearing squeak, Kyle fell back onto the bed, and after removing his own jacket and cravat, James crawled on top of him, pinning his lover's arms above his head. He crouched down, his knees straddling Kyle's hips, and leaned in for another deep kiss. He could feel Kyle's arousal pressing against his belly as he claimed his lover's lips and took a moment to rub the smooth wool of his trousers along Kyle's naked flesh.

Kyle moaned in his mouth and arched against him, seeking more contact, but James decided to be a tease and arch away from him. Now that he finally had his love back in his bed, he wanted to draw out the sweet torment as long as possible.

While their tongues waltzed, sliding warm and wet against each other, James pushed Kyle's wrists together and held them pinned to the bed with his left hand alone. He slid the knuckles of his right down Kyle's naked chest, grazing his nipples and exploring the contours of his muscles before flattening his palm against Kyle's belly beneath his erection. Using both hands to keep Kyle pinned to the mattress, he drew his mouth down his lover's neck, nipping and sucking as he went. Kyle's body quivered beneath his lips, and with every nip of his teeth, he could feel the smooth silk of Kyle's shaft move over his knuckles as it jerked above his belly.

He feasted on his lover's neck for long moments, simply enjoying the sensual delight that was Kyle's body. Before Kyle, he never would have considered himself to be such a hedonist, but it seemed his love was making him discover more and more facets of himself that he'd never known existed.

"Please!" Kyle's strained whisper and writhing body sent a pulse of heat through him, making his own cock jerk within his trousers. The minx knew too well already how to manipulate him. It was time to get some of his own back.

"Not this time, sweet," he admonished as he moved away and stood next to the foot of the bed, leaning against the poster. "Move up to the head of the bed and lie back on the pillows," he commanded.

Kyle's pout at his abandonment heated to something far sultrier at

James's command, and he quickly moved up the bed. When Kyle was settled and James was sure he had his lover's attention, he began unbuttoning his waistcoat, slowly sliding his fingers down from button to button. He slid it from his shoulders just as slowly and folded it neatly before draping it over the chair near his windows.

Keeping his gaze locked on those gorgeous emerald eyes, he removed his braces and unbuttoned his trousers. He couldn't help a flattered smirk at the intensity with which Kyle's gaze followed his hands and decided to put a little extra effort in his show. He pulled his shirt over his head and tossed it over the chair, then slid his hands inside his trousers and drew out his cock, displaying it in front of him and giving it a few good strokes. He grabbed it at the base and drew his bollocks into his other hand, rolling them in his palm, making sure Kyle could see every inch of him on display.

When Kyle's eyes widened and he licked his lips, James had to bite back a groan. He decided to change tactics there and then and removed the rest of his clothing much more quickly, climbing back onto the bed. When Kyle rose to meet him, he shook his head and pushed him back into the pillows, holding him there with hands on his shoulders.

"Stay there," he commanded, and then he straddled Kyle's hips again.

Rising up on his knees, he grabbed the bedframe above Kyle's head with one hand and positioned his cock in front of his lover's face with the other, gripping it and running the head lightly over those gorgeous lips, smearing them with the pearly fluid already leaking from the tip. Kyle's eager mouth opened at once and descended on him as his hand wrapped around the base of James's shaft. James couldn't hold back the groan this time, and within moments, he was rocking into that wet haven.

He watched avidly as Kyle's pale cheeks hollowed as he sucked, and he felt Kyle's other hand reach round and squeeze his buttock, the move tugging at his hole with every thrust of his hips into Kyle's mouth. It took every ounce of control he had not to thrust himself to completion between those lips, but he wanted this to last, and he wanted to be buried deep in Kyle's sweet arse when he spent.

After a few more moments of glorious bliss, he gritted his teeth and tugged on his lover's hair to get his attention, then pulled himself out of Kyle's mouth and hands. Before Kyle could protest, James slid down his body and kissed him deeply, tasting some of himself mingled with the flavor that was uniquely Kyle's. He savored the flavor, sweeping his lover's mouth for long moments before pulling away and growling, "Stay here."

He climbed off the bed and went to rummage through his toilet, hoping to find something he could use in place of the oil he had disposed of after Kyle left. He was relieved to discover a jar of knitbone unguent hiding amongst the numerous bottles and tins of creams, tinctures, and powders his sister and niece insisted on gifting him with every Christmas. With no other options visible, it seemed he would make do with that. Happily, he grabbed the jar and returned to the bed, setting it on the mattress close to his lover's body.

Kyle's hungry eyes followed his every move, and he couldn't help but smirk as he slid back onto the bed. It did wonderful things to a man's pride to have someone so bright and beautiful look at you as if you were all he needed in the world.

"Roll over. On your hands and knees," he commanded. Kyle bit his lip as he obeyed the gruff words and looked back at James over his shoulder. James moved next to him, sliding his hands between Kyle's shoulder blades and pressing down. "Elbows on the bed," he ordered.

Kyle's eyes widened a little, and he flushed but he did what he was told. The position forced his arse higher in the air and exposed all to James's ravenous eyes. Moving behind his lover, James nudged Kyle's thighs apart, exposing him even further. He heard Kyle whimper and suddenly thought perhaps he'd pushed too far too soon.

"Are you all right with this, Kyle?" he asked, concerned.

"Yes, oh yes, don't stop," Kyle panted, and James realized with relief that the sound he'd made and the quivering of his body were from desire, not fear.

"Good, sweet boy. You have only to tell me if I do something you don't want. I will stop whenever you need. You have only to say the word. Do you understand?" he asked as he slid his palms over Kyle's back.

"Yes," Kyle groaned as James's tongue followed his hands down the length of his spine.

He kissed the dip just above his lover's arse before spreading him wide and trailing his tongue down that valley. When he reached Kyle's entrance, he trailed his tongue in lazy circles about it, wetting it liberally before pressing the tip home.

"Oh *God*!" Kyle moaned, gasping, forcing James to use his grip on the man's arse to keep him still as his body bucked.

He pulled back only long enough to wet his thumb, then went back to tormenting his lover, swirling his hole with it and his tongue, then pushing both inside. When Kyle bucked against him again, James used his other hand to give the boy a stinging smack on the arse, eliciting a startled yelp.

"I said before that I might have to use a firmer hand with you. Now be still," he growled, then he chuckled to soften the rebuke. He smoothed his hand gently over the red mark he'd left, soothing the sting, before sliding it down to fondle Kyle's bollocks and resuming his torment of his entrance.

He continued to lick and suck at that divine opening in between tonguing his bollocks and the sensitive expanse between. James couldn't help but smile at the fact that, though Kyle was mewling and shaking with need, he remained still as he was commanded.

"*Please!*" Kyle begged again, and James decided it was time to end the torment for both of them. The ache in his body had become nearly overwhelming.

He fumbled for the jar of unguent with shaking hands and coated his fingers in it. The crisp scents of beeswax and herbs filled his nostrils as he smoothed it lovingly over his lover's entrance before sliding his middle finger inside. Kyle's body was so open and welcoming that he slid another finger inside almost immediately thereafter. Curling both fingers forward, he rubbed gently across Kyle's sweet spot and heard him choke out a muffled curse into the mattress.

He couldn't help but chuckle. He loved it when he broke Kyle down enough for him to use profanity. Proper decorum was a necessity in society, but behind closed doors, he found it incredibly arousing to have that sweet mouth become coarse and vulgar. One day he would have to explore it further, see how obscene he could make his lover become, but not tonight. Tonight his need was too great.

Taking another dollop of the cream, he spread it quickly over his throbbing erection and grabbed it firmly at the base, pinching enough to keep himself from spending the moment he entered his love. He placed the blunt head at Kyle's opening and took a moment to breathe and simply enjoy the feel of his lover's heat just barely kissing the tip of his cock.

"Oh God, please, please, please!" Kyle begged as his entrance quivered against James's crown, begging him to enter.

He couldn't have refused that invitation even if he'd wanted to, and he slid his shaft inside in one long, fluid stroke, burying himself to the hilt. Kyle let out a long, low moan and fisted the bed linens, pushing back against him as his channel gripped him tightly.

He couldn't stop a moan of his own as he leaned over Kyle's back and whispered against his neck, "You are heaven on Earth for me, sweet. Your body is an altar I could worship at for the rest of my days."

He surprised himself with his eloquence at a time like that. He didn't think he had any words like that in him, but it appeared Kyle would never cease to surprise him, even with himself.

But all such serious thoughts flew from his head the moment Kyle began to wriggle against him. The profound and the profane would have to wait until he had satisfied the needs of his flesh and claimed what was his.

He lifted up and grabbed his lover's hips, setting a slow, steady rhythm, pumping into Kyle and pulling his hips against him with every thrust. He wanted it to last this time, to draw it out as long as he possibly could, but Kyle was having none of it. Arching up and grabbing the head of the bed, he slammed his arse onto James's cock with ever-increasing ferocity, and James was lost.

Apparently his lover had had enough of being submissive, and just as before, the change in him inflamed James beyond measure. He grabbed Kyle's shoulder in one hand and his hip in the other and set to pounding that sweet arse with all the passion he possessed, the slap of their bodies echoing off the walls and ceilings of his rooms.

One of Kyle's hands dropped between his legs, and his arm jerked furiously, soft cries and pants issuing from his mouth. When Kyle froze suddenly, dropped face first onto the mattress, and cried out into the pillows, James bit back his own yell and thrust hard once more, collapsing over his back and wrapping his arms around him, holding him tight.

They lay there for several minutes as their panting breaths and racing hearts slowed; then he slid slowly out of Kyle's body and collapsed next to him. Kyle rolled onto his side, facing James, and they simply gazed adoringly at one another for several breaths before James raised his hand to cup Kyle's cheek and leaned forward to brush a gentle kiss across his lips.

"I love you, James," Kyle whispered, his eyes suspiciously bright in the lamplight.

"I love you, Kyle," he murmured in response, pulling his lover more tightly against him and simply holding him there, putting as much emotion as he could into that embrace. Kyle was his now, and he was never going to let him go again, not for anything.

Tomorrow they would talk of Andrew's schemes and figure out how best to make this work. There were still obstacles they would have to overcome....

But tomorrow. He would worry about all of that tomorrow.

Tomorrow... was his last, happy thought before he drifted off to sleep.

ROWAN MCALLISTER quit her day job in 2007 and moved to her dream home in the woods of Virginia to follow her muses and explore her creative side full time. She's a firm believer in practical romanticism, requires a strong cup of coffee every morning to be even remotely human, and has a healthy obsession with romance and fantasy fiction, small (and not so small) furry creatures, and anything to do with working with her hands. She can be found most days either hunched over her sewing machine or hunched over her laptop. Though she has spent a lifetime making up stories in her head when whatever task she was occupied with failed to keep her full attention, she only recently discovered the challenge and reward to be found in committing those stories to paper. Now that she has, there's no going back.

Historical Romance from DREAMSPINNER PRESS

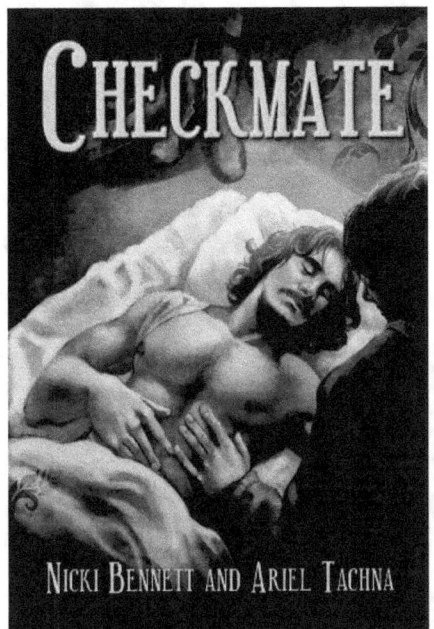

http://www.dreamspinnerpress.com

Historical Romance from DREAMSPINNER PRESS

http://www.dreamspinnerpress.com

For more of the
best M/M romance,
visit

Dreamspinner Press

www.dreamspinnerpress.com

www.ingramcontent.com/pod-product-compliance
Lightning Source LLC
Chambersburg PA
CBHW070005260626
47159CB00005B/1684